KIRSTY BRIGHT

THE
TITANIUM
TRILOGY

REAP

FOR THE GREATER GOOD

REAP
The Titanium Trilogy: Book 3
By Kirsty Bright

Copyright © Kirsty Bright 2023
ISBN: 978-1-7399978-4-7
Published through Untuned Publishings LTD

First Edition: June 2023

All rights reserved. No part of this book may be used or reproduced in any manner whatsoever without written permission from the author, except in the case of brief quotations embodied in critical articles or reviews.

This book is a work of fiction. Names, characters, businesses, organisations, places, events and incidents either are the product of the author's imagination or are used fictitiously. Any resemblance to actual persons, living or dead, events, or locales is entirely coincidental.

Book and Cover design by Untuned Publishings LTD

For information contact:
kirstybrightauthor@gmail.com
Or visit
www.kirstybrightauthor.wixsite.com/welcome

For the hopers and the dreamers.
Your cottage by the sea is coming.

PROLOGUE

PRESENT DAY

HIM

Gretta is dead.

I should know. I killed her.

PART ONE

3 DAYS AGO

CHAPTER ONE

ARES

It was four months since I last felt human. More important thoughts often occupied my mind, such as running The Farm and the war against the vampires, but my animal alter-ego always stirred beneath the surface. That's okay, though. So long as I kept my cool, I had no reason to worry. I had no reason to fear the mutant taking over my body and refusing to give it back. It wouldn't happen just so long as I remained calm—tasking, now that the future of humankind lay solely on my shoulders.

It was three months since I'd killed my brother and mother in one move. The memory of pushing the titanium dagger into Mom's chest, Marshall's hands firmly set over mine in encouragement, haunted my nightmares whenever I eventually found sleep. My family's red eyes lingered every time I welcomed darkness, and Marshall's last words were a horrifying reminder: *I don't have time to rest.*

REAP

I had to train, lead, and prepare for war.

Two months ago, we'd located Gretta—Queen of the Day Walkers—and every other Day Walker to exist. I figured that Gretta resulted from Mother's failed attempt to cure vampirism, although nobody remembered seeing Gretta on The Farm—not even my uncle, Dr. White. There were no files, no footage, and seemingly no memory of the Day Walker other than the day she broke free of her prison and killed my father and hundreds of humans in her escape. And now she was building an army of vampires. As we were expecting her return, we assembled our own army.

One month ago, we launched a training program for young hybrids, Titanium and Veno. Both hybrids trained together. I would never have believed it possible in Phase Two. Thankfully, those trialing days were over. Dickward now followed me, as he had Marshall.

Venos were obedient creatures. Scary, unpredictable, and deadly? Absolutely. But the Alpha relied solely on my orders, and therefore Lora's—my Alpha. We were a team. One unit. A sole entity.

Sometimes, I swore I could sense her heartbeat just as she could mine.

Things had been different since Dr. White injected me with Alpha hormones. I'd slowly lost my connection with the Titanium pack thanks to my inner animal. I was no longer Alpha to them, but Lora and I still shared a spiritual connection.

I could mind jump to her whenever we touched, and she could reply without using her hybrid powers. It was unusual. Beyond explanation. It made me question if I wasn't completely powerless after all. Perhaps I could evolve like the others despite being a Gen. 3. There was still hope.

I spent every morning in the training rooms—in the custom-built machines that told the Gen. 2 hybrids exactly what they needed to think of in order to evolve. These were machines I designed and engineered with a little help from the farmers, and yet they worked for everybody except me.

Still, I tried my luck.

The training rooms were always my first stop after breakfast, and today was no exception. I jumped into the identifier, setting the program for half an hour, and then placed the mask over my face.

I'd rebuilt the machines from the incubators that once filled the room, and like the incubators—vertical machines standing at ten feet tall and made of glass and steel—the identifier was full of thick slime which suspended me within the container and allowed me to move whilst under simulation.

I lowered myself into the sticky goo, breathing through the glass mask as its solid frame weighed me down. The lid closed, and the program began.

The simulation took me to a semi-conscious state—

impossible to remember—and I rose to unscrew the lid once I came back around, climbed out, and found my results waiting for me on the attached device.

Error—Genome Not Recognized.

Every day, I wished for a real answer. I adjusted the identifier, updating its programs, but nothing ever worked. Dr. White still refused to tell me why my mother made me different from the other hybrids, and part of me hated him for it. I tried to bury that part of myself—the feelings so intense that I could barely stand to look at my uncle some days. If only he told me the truth, I could have evolved—to use the power within me. I could have trained alongside my pack instead of watching from the Observatorium. I could have been part of the war.

Although, I never wanted to fight.

I would much rather have stayed safe, buried within the solid white bunkers of -3, but what kind of leader would that make me? What kind of person hides while their friends fight their battles? I was that boy once, but not anymore.

I washed off in the rinse zone, my clothing acting like skin, and aggressively towel-dried my hair as I wound through the corridors to the council meeting, unable to shake the error screen from my mind. Weeks upon weeks of the same message, labeling me as different. Wrong. A fault in the system.

The doors to the Observatorium opened with force, my mind elsewhere, and I hoped the council members saw it as eagerness. I threw the towel to the sofa and took my place at the table.

Unlike Marshall and my father, I leaned on my peers for advice. I'd seen the damage it could do to run The Farm alone, what the pressure could do to a human mind, and I didn't want to follow in the footsteps of my family before me. In fact, I would have done anything to prevent it.

So, we created the council, made up of leaders from different sectors of The Farm. Lora sat at my side, always, and the rest of our pack had a place at the table. Dr. White voiced the opinions of the scientists. Tim stood in for the farmers. Wilson earned a place as he was stationed within the Observatorium, overseeing data and technological issues, and Dickward—or Steven, rather—represented the Venos.

"Good morning, all," I greeted them as I sank into my seat, collecting the papers I'd left behind late last night. The bodies around the table fell silent, but I could sense the anticipation in the air. It would be a monumental day. "I hope you're prepared for today's arrivals?"

Tye grunted in response and Jayleigh snickered, replying, "Prepared doesn't begin to cover it. Are you sure this is the right move, Ares?"

I looked at Lora for help. She barely seemed to follow the

conversation. Her eyes focused on a faint coffee stain on the table, but she quickly jumped to my aid when she noticed the silence and my pleading expression.

"The Sanctuary will reinforce the numbers we lost when the vampires attacked last year," she said. "They're agreeing to train alongside the farmers so that they'll be prepared to fight in battle. I know it might ruffle some feathers, but we're on the same side of the war. The Sanctuary are our allies."

"Safety in numbers. They'll be here by nightfall," I said, directing it at Jayleigh. "There's no turning them around now. They've already survived a day and a night outside their boundaries. Asking them to turn back is too dangerous." I searched for Wilson then, to confirm my statement. Wilson waved his tablet in the air, and although I couldn't see the live footage from the drone which aided The Sanctuary, I understood his gesture as an act of reassurance. They were still on track. "I trust everybody knows where they're stationed from the plan Jayleigh put together last week?"

Hail glanced at me in question, but Jayleigh saw it coming, leaning across the space between them to whisper his role into his ear. Hail nodded, a foolish smile spreading over his face.

"Any updates on Gretta?" Lora asked, changing the subject to one that always made my stomach churn with nerves. I inhaled, looking at the screens on the wall as I waited for an answer.

Gretta had been keeping a low profile since we discovered her nest of Day Walkers sneaking into a town just east of The Farm several weeks ago. I wondered if it was part of her plan, to stay in hiding—to regroup and rebuild the numbers lost since I'd killed Mom, and therefore Mom's entire bloodline—or if they were rethinking. My mother was supposed to turn the Titanium pack into vampires like them. We weren't yet sure why, but we followed Gretta with the drones in hopes it would give us insight into her plans.

So far, no luck.

"One satellite is down," Wilson said to Lora, pointing towards the blacked-out screens on the wall. "The one covering the south exit of the nest."

Bad news. If Gretta used that exit, we wouldn't know until it was too late. "How fast can we fix it?" I questioned.

"The satellite is outside The Farm's gates, maybe a mile or two away. I'll be able to fix it soon enough if you're able to spare a Titanium to protect me?"

"Diego and Tye are manoeuverable," Jayleigh said.

Wilson gave his thanks as Diego volunteered himself.

"Oh, and take the wolves, too," I said. "It'll do them some good to get outside the fence for a while."

And I worried that Chipper would try to steal Solace back.

Wilson nodded as Dr. White noted a few worries the scientists had about medical supplies running out since our numbers were growing. Tim barely spoke a word for the entire meeting, much like Dickward—who'd spent his time glaring at me.

"If there are no more questions, we'll regroup again at 09:00 tomorrow?" I brought the meeting to a close and kissed Lora on the cheek, promising to catch up with her when I could.

It turned out that there were too many distractions leading up to the arrival of The Sanctuary: campsite issues, dining problems, Solace refusing to listen to Diego's command once they were outside the gates. Aggravating, but manageable. The next moment I was able to catch up with Lora was much later that day as The Sanctuary arrived.

I rushed to get there in time, sweat building on my forehead despite the late winter temperatures, and my gaze locked onto Lora's perfect silhouette as she stood atop the Gate Tower and overlooked the incoming crowd. I climbed the ladder, needing to be beside her. A full day without seeing her smile was a lifetime.

She kissed me upon arrival, and instantly the stress of the day faded away. Everything was okay so long as we were together. I gripped Lora's hand as the human army marched up the road towards the Gate Tower we stood atop.

"You good?" Lora asked as the wind attempted to push us from the podium, her hair flowing around her face. I brushed a few strands behind her ear with my spare hand.

"I'm fine. It's just all happening so fast. I can't believe they're here."

Time had escaped me with all the new routines, procedures, research and developments. And not to mention the returning memories of my life before the metamorphosis. Three months had passed in no time at all. We'd been planning this for weeks, yet it still felt too soon. The hairs on the back of my neck stood with unease.

"Are you sure we've got enough food for the farmers, the hybrids, and the sanitary?" Hail said from the ladder. His head poked through the floor of the Gate Tower as he climbed to meet us.

"The Sanctuary, Dumbass," Jayleigh corrected, giving us an amused smile as Hail made room for her on the podium.

Hail rolled his eyes. "That's what I said, *Dumbass*." He mimicked Jayleigh's tone and turned out towards the road, a frown shadowing his eyes as he witnessed the number of humans rounding the corner towards us.

Chipper led The Sanctuary towards The Farm, now free of the vampire compulsion which had ruled their minds for too long. One of my first jobs as leader of The Farm had been to make peace with the people of The Sanctuary.

They had been just as much a pawn of the vampires' games as we were, so it was crucial for them to join us.

Jayleigh lifted the gates as the humans approached, and I

followed Lora to the ground to welcome our new guests and put our latest technology to the test.

"Chipper." Lora held a hand in his direction as he approached. "A pleasure to see you again."

"The pleasure is all mine." He brought her spare hand to his mouth and placed a kiss there, his toothless smile making an appearance as she retracted.

"Rather you than me," I said so that only she could hear.

Lora coughed back her laugh, giving me a warning glance. *"Behave,"* she said, returning the words through the brush of our hands.

"Chipper." I shook his hand in one swift motion. "We're so glad that you decided to join us." I motioned towards the gates and Tye, who lingered on the other side. "Welcome to The Farm."

We led them one by one, scanning their eyes as they entered.

"We've advanced our technology in recent months. We're now able to detect any human under vampire compulsion," I said as Chipper's results flashed green. Clear. Free to control his own mind. "It's a simple matter of pupil dilation, but I won't bore you with the technicalities."

I might have found an interest in the engineering, but that didn't mean everyone else shared my enthusiasm.

Tye scanned the eyes of the people, the machine flashing

green for each.

Once everybody was clear, we led them towards camp. Of course, we'd sectioned off a separate field for the human visitors, not wanting any discomfort or rivalry between The Sanctuary and the hybrids.

The last thing we needed was a civil war…

CHAPTER TWO

LORA

Ares' time was running out.

I'd been working closely with Dr. White to keep Ares' shadows at bay. We knew he was struggling more than he'd ever admit, more than he likely realized, and our results proved that no matter what we tried, there was no way to stop the inner animal from taking over.

But I wasn't ready to give up.

There had to be a solution.

Ares always talked about loopholes. I just had to be smart enough to find one. And I tried—the gods know I tried—but I was tired.

So bloody tired.

My body worked overtime with hundreds of Titanium hybrids now under my wing. Maintaining the Alpha bond was demanding, and my energy was the only known way to keep

Ares' humanity intact...

Benji had said the light of my aura banished Ares' shadows, and it turned out that my touch was enough to keep Ares in control of his inner animal, but he drained me of my energy with every kiss, brush of our skin, and touch of our fingers. He didn't know it, and I planned to keep it that way. He couldn't find out that he was using me as a battery to power his humanity—to fight off his animal alter-ego—until we found another solution.

And we needed one, pronto.

Between sharing my energy with Ares and my connection with the other hybrids, there wasn't enough to go around. But I had an army to oversee. Hundreds of hybrids relied upon my leadership, and they'd die without the Alpha bond.

It was an endless game of tug-of-war and I was the rope.

So that's where Dr. White stepped in. We'd been working on a replica of sorts—energy like my own to balance the darkness inside Ares. We already knew that his aura could steal power from mine, and he could use it to keep the animal at bay. So what if we could recreate the energy? To provide an antidote for his alter-ego. Not a permanent fix for Ares' situation, but certainly a good place to start.

I swayed a little as we stood in the camp we'd built for The Sanctuary. I needed to sleep. The lack of energy was taking its toll.

REAP

"Why don't we show them the improved program?" Ares asked, placing a hand firmly against my lower back. Steadying. Had he noticed my fatigue?

"The program, of course!" I tried to hide my exhaustion with enthusiasm as I turned towards Chipper's group. "I'd love to introduce you to the hybrids."

The humans shared a look, turning to watch the scurrying bodies of The Sanctuary as farmers helped them settle into their tents.

"Your people will be safe here," Ares assured them. "You're part of The Farm now. We're all on the same team."

"The hybrids are exceptional," I said. "We no longer follow Joseph and Marshall's training regime and the results are more promising than we could have dreamed."

Chipper nodded slowly.

Watching his skepticism, I figured there might have been honesty in his promise to take down The Farm all those weeks ago. It was obvious he didn't agree with the old training program—like most of us.

Would he find it difficult to accept that our new leader would deviate from past methods?

"Since waking the hybrids last month," I said, trying to fill Chipper and his companions with confidence, "only two Venos have died. An allergic reaction caused one death, while the other was a heart failure. Both were unrelated to the training program."

Chipper chewed his bottom lip as he considered, eyes scowling. "And how many hybrids are there, exactly?"

"Eight-hundred-and-twenty-six," Ares said.

"Seven-hundred-and-three Titaniums, one-hundred-and-twenty-three Venos," I finished.

Chipper whistled through his rotting teeth. He was old, considering the life expectancy of a civilian beyond the fence. But the Sanctuary had been under the vampires' control for years, providing a ready supply of human blood whenever needed—until I killed the Night Walkers in control of that area, at least.

I tried not to wince at the memory of turning them to ash and playing right into Samantha's evil Day Walker plans. I'd killed Benji's pack in that explosion, too.

Why the older Titanium pack had teamed up with the Night Walkers still baffled me. Traitors.

"The training isn't based on anger or confusion, as the old program had been," I said. "We understand that the most effective way to train is through knowledge, so we've first been teaching the young hybrids about the world, the vampires, and the apocalypse. They practice skills to help them outside the fence. The deadly challenges are no more. We don't force them to mutate, but encourage it in a safe and controlled environment within Phase Two. Combat training is still essential, but we never wage the hybrids against each other." I shivered at the memory of my past, and the Alpha Arena. "And Phase Three is for evolved Titaniums. Would you like to see the training facilities? The Sanctuary are welcome to use the equipment."

Ares' thumb rubbed small circles into my back as Chipper considered. It worked wonders at releasing the tension building there.

"I'm intrigued by your facilities." Chipper nodded, a few of his comrades joining in with approval.

"I'm sure you've already seen it through our drones, have you not?" Ares laughed, referring to The Sanctuary's camera-hacking abilities.

I held the breath in my lungs. Was it too soon to be making jokes like that? We barely knew Chipper, and I doubted he'd understand Ares' risky sense of humor. Thankfully, the humans joined in with Ares' laughter, and I let the air out in a nervous sigh.

"Don't worry, Ares," Chipper said. "We have been directing all of our spying efforts on the vampires since you informed us of your leadership over The Farm."

"We're glad to hear it." I steered them through a gate and down the hill towards the hybrids' camp. We thought it important to give the humans the higher ground as their numbers were smaller, and their defense? A human would never stand a chance against a hybrid unless they had a taser.

The only humans with tasers were the farmers. There was no chance we'd allow The Sanctuary that kind of power soon, so the least we could do was offer them a view over the hybrids in false comfort.

We approached a group of Omegas, pulled from their hibernation much sooner than we'd have preferred. There were questions about what we should do with the teens, too young for battle. They trained among the rest so they'd be war ready by the time they reached the age of sixteen, but it still felt wrong to me—that the youngest would live like this for four years. Waiting for the day they'd be able to leave The Farm and fight back. It was better than being outside the fence, though. At least they were safe.

"Lora." They nodded their heads in respect as I passed. Some stared, unblinking.

The Alpha bond was still holding strong enough, it seemed.

I gave the largest smile I could. "How's it going, guys? Yiri, did you tie a fisherman's knot like I showed you yesterday? It will come in useful when setting traps and hunting."

Yiri, taller and seemingly wiser than her male comrades, didn't reply—her twelve-year-old eyes were wide as I spoke. She nodded slowly.

"That's great. Can you show me later?" I asked. Once again, she responded with nods, but no words. "And how about you boys? How did you get on?"

REAP

The small group of mixed Titanium and Veno males grumbled in defeat.

"You'll get there," I said, offering a pat on the shoulder or a squeeze of the arm. "Keep up the good work." I gestured to the farmer in control of the tent, giving a small wave in appreciation, then turned back to Ares as he explained.

"The farmers work with the same hybrids each day, building familiarity and trust. There are three farmers per group, and we train each in a specific set of skills, teaching the hybrids how to adapt to their new abilities without losing control."

"And what if they do?" one of Chipper's friends asked. "What if the hybrids lose control?"

Ares removed the tablet from his arm, presenting it to the gathering. "Farmers have tasers for the hybrids within their group. They're able to send the hybrids to sleep if there are any issues, and I can monitor them all from here. As you can see," he pointed to the top right corner of his screen, "there have been no incidents for three weeks."

"Well," Chipper scoffed, "it seems you've got everything under control."

I shared a look with Ares, knowing that things were far from in control, but glad that it at least appeared that way from the outside.

"After you," Ares said and gestured further down the hill, urging The Sanctuary leaders further into the hybrid compounds.

Titanium eyes met us as we walked, but the Venos among the group didn't stop to watch. The rattling of their breath slowed as they focused on us in their peripheral. It was the only sign our presence bothered them.

"Good afternoon." I smiled as I passed each Titanium, meeting their gray eyes, and reaching for the spiritual branch which connected us and rooted us to the ground. It was difficult to navigate the Alpha bond now that I was no longer in charge of eight hybrids, but seven-hundred. Getting to know each Titanium personally made it easier to narrow down and focus on one of them, and I still had a long way to go. There were so many names to remember and so many faces. It was important that I spent as much time with them as I could.

We approached the lake, passed over the stoned bridge and stopped near the Titanium barn.

"This is where you can find a senior Titanium hybrid, such as myself, Lora, Jayleigh, Hail, Diego, or Tye, during the night hours if you ever need us," Ares said as he pointed towards our home. "Although, I admit we rarely stick to a routine schedule. Our sleeping pattern is nonexistent at this point."

"The true sign of a good leader." Chipper dropped his guard just a little. I hadn't expected him to act so tense. After all, he'd played us.

Did he think we were out to get revenge?

Or was it the change in location? The Sanctuary wasn't a place, but a community. They'd picked up and moved for the first time in history, so Chipper had every right to be nervous.

We watched the hybrids cross the lake, no weighted belts in their jackets as I'd once worn, but still swimming multiple lengths to the island and back, building stamina.

I focused on the female who led the group, Serina, and studied her data on my tablet. Her statistics were impressive for a girl of sixteen. I'd met her two weeks ago in target practice, throwing knifes with such precision that she'd give Jayleigh fair competition. She was ready to proceed to a re-imagined Phase Two; to learn combat skills and mutate for the first time. I alerted the farmer in charge of her group via my tablet, whilst Ares made small talk with the humans.

And I choked.

The air turned to smoke, poisoning my lungs. My heart stammered with an all too familiar feeling, and my body burned from the inside; blistering, scarring.

No…

I stumbled, and Ares rushed to catch me, registering the look on my face with troubled eyes.

This couldn't be happening. It had all been going so well.

"The hybrids?" Ares questioned though his touch on my arm, as though sensing what was going on inside.

"Four of them," I replied and gasped. The pain was intense,

and the more painful the break, the longer it had been since they'd passed; the weaker the hybrids had been. *"Omegas."*

My body trembled as I struggled not to scream, the tears stinging my eyes. I couldn't alarm our guests.

"Is everything okay?" Chipper asked as he watched me shatter into a million pieces.

"Just the exhaustion," Ares reassured him, wrapping a powerful arm around my waist for me to lean on. I'd never felt so thankful.

The pain had never been this destructive.

But this was the first time I'd ever lost four hybrids at once.

CHAPTER THREE

ARES

I sensed Lora's pain before seeing it in her eyes. My body reacted automatically, rushing to her side to ease the suffering, but there was nothing I could do to help. I was a comfort, but not a cure.

There was still much to learn about the Alpha bond and the spiritual tie between Lora and the Titanium hybrids, and I'd realized that it was better explained through magic than science.

The work that Dr. White and the other farmers did below ground was extraordinary; I appreciated it now that I was one of them and no longer a hybrid put through the system. The metamorphosis was a balance of skill, energy, patience, and real-life *magic*—and magic was a mystery. Losing four hybrids at once would likely have larger consequences on Lora's body.

I reassured Chipper and his posy that everything was okay despite how fragile Lora felt in my arms. Abnormal. She might have collapsed if I let her go. I hugged her tighter, aching for her safety but feeling helpless.

"We're needed below ground." I tried to hide the worry from my voice as I addressed the group. "Look around and find your feet. We'll catch up with you later."

It was not a question, but an order.

Chipper didn't seem to realize. "I'd love to see the hidden world if you'd allow us to come with you?"

I clenched my jaw, avoiding all eye contact with the human in fear that my anger might show itself in a flash of glowing blue eyes. Mutating into my animal state wasn't a subtle change —my Gen. 3 genetics made sure of that—and thanks to the growing alter-ego, I could easily let my humanity slip and never return, but I wouldn't allow it at this moment. Chipper wasn't worth it.

Keep it together.

I took a breath and held it, releasing it only as I glanced down at Lora's tearful eyes.

My Alpha was in too much pain already.

"This is a private matter, I'm afraid." I finally looked back to Chipper, my words sharp. "Family business. I hope you understand."

Chipper recoiled, his head jerking backwards. Rejection must have been new to him. Being the leader of The Sanctuary meant he didn't often hear the word *no*.

REAP

"I will gladly show you the underground levels tomorrow once you've settled in."

"Oh… Well—"

Lora's grip loosened. I needed to get her to Dr. White *now*. "Cross the bridge near the silo, then veer right. The path will lead you towards your camp. Take your time, there's no rush," I called back to him as I led Lora to the lift that would lower us to -3.

I didn't glance back, but I knew the group still stared as we walked away.

"Lora?" My heart raced, but I focused closely enough on our connection to sense Lora's heart rate overtaking mine. "Tell me what I can do. How—"

"I'm okay." Lora's voice wobbled, weak, mouse like, as we loaded into the lift and the doors closed behind us. "But, four of them, Ares… four hybrids are gone."

Her eyes followed the lump in my throat as I forced myself to swallow. "How…" My words died, and we both stared at the well-polished metal floor, presumably thinking the same thing.

Neither of us spoke as the lift came to a halt at level -3. Lora could stand without my support now, but her arm clung to mine as we walked towards the Observatorium where Dr. White had adopted a secondary desk.

I swiped my tablet in front of the scanner and pushed the doors open. My uncle's gaze landed upon us as we entered.

"Ares? Lora?" he said. "I thought you'd be—Oh Lora, you look as though you've seen a ghost." His voice carried across the room as he descended the ramp from the balcony. "Dear Lord… take a seat, Lora."

I steadied her into a nearby chair. My ears rung with a high-pitched squeal, like tuning in to the electricity which ran through the walls of the underground bunker. I barely heard my uncle's questions to the farmers around us as he asked them to draw up her data and search The Farm for the dead hybrids via the cloaked drones.

Lora's skin was a warm shade of gray, her eyes hollow and hands shaking.

We'd lost Titanium hybrids before, but I'd never seen her react like this.

I felt nauseous.

I cupped my hands around hers and crouched beside her.

"Omegas, four of them," I recited Lora's information to my uncle whilst Lora closed her eyes and relaxed into the chair.

"Any idea of their identity?" Dr. White asked. Lora shook her head *no*. "That's quite alright. I'll search the system."

My eyes remained on Lora, a flower in need of water. "Can I get you anything?" I asked her.

She shook her head once more.

I kissed the back of her hands one by one.

From the corner of my eye, Dr. White scanned the

database for red lights. He filtered the search for the deceased, but no records showed, and scrolled through the Titanium Omegas, yet they were all lit in green. He ran several more searches and flicked through the entire seven-hundred Titaniums.

All green.

"I don't understand," he said, pinching his nose beneath his glasses. "We have no record of the hybrids."

Lora's eyebrows twitched ever so slightly.

My stomach churned.

I squeezed her hands and then reluctantly dropped them, and joined my uncle at the computer, glancing over my shoulder every few seconds to check on Lora.

"Any luck on locating their bodies?" I asked the tech team, watching the screens as several drones were in motion, scouting The Farm, passing over Jayleigh as she trained a group of Phase Twos in combat, and Hail aided the people of The Sanctuary as they settled into their camp. Tye and Tim chatted in the center of the hybrids' camp.

I connected to Tim's tablet. "Tim, we have a code red. I repeat, we have a code red."

Tim glanced around the camp, his nose flaring. Tye's eyes landed on Tim's tablet. He squinted in disapproval, most likely because I'd chosen to contact the farmer instead of him.

"I'm going to enforce a lockdown until we find them. Can

you reassure The Sanctuary that this is a procedural drill and nothing to worry about?"

"Yes, Sir," Tim's reply was stern as ever. I had a hunch that he still didn't like me—hated that I was his superior even more. I smiled in response.

Winding him up would never get old.

It would have been easier to contact Hail as he was already in that area, and Tim would realize it as soon as he reached the human camp. Tye was now alone.

My smile grew for a moment, imagining Tye call me *Nerd*, and then I turned again to check on Lora, whose eyes were open. She gave a reassuring nod.

"No sign of them, Sir," Mika said from the tech zone of the Observatorium. "We've scanned the camp twice over."

I shared a look with my uncle, our concern growing by the second. "How's that possible? We've no record of them and no bodies?" I asked him before turning back to Mika. "Scan further afield. Check the entire farm."

"Run a thermal scan," Dr. White contributed as Tim reached The Sanctuary camp on the screens, and I signaled the lockdown.

All hybrids returned to their tents in a swarm of well-composed bodies, maneuvering between each other in a calm and controlled manner. The group in the lake swam to shore and jogged towards camp. Everybody was in position within five minutes. Council members were the only ones free to walk The Farm, and now Chipper's group, who lingered by the lake.

"Strange," I thought out loud, "how everything has been fine until this point, but the day The Sanctuary joins us, four Titaniums die with no trace of them ever being here. Curious, don't you think, Doc?"

"It is strange," Dr. White said. "But I'm sure it's entirely coincidental. And we'll find the bodies."

I pursed my lips. Checked back on Lora.

Dr. White's gaze followed mine, then he looked at the computer.

"How many Titanium records were there this morning?" he asked.

Lora and I replied at the same time. "Seven-hundred-and-three."

Dr. White's face paled. "Well, there are only six-hundred-and-ninety-nine now. So either you've both got your numbers wrong, or somebody has deleted their files from the system."

CHAPTER FOUR

LORA

"What do you mean, deleted?" I stood, my legs shaking beneath me. As time passed, I became more aware that everything about these hybrids dying was wrong.

Why?

There was no theory that made sense.

My body withdrew as I swayed. Staying in my evolved state for a day required less energy than what I was currently experiencing.

The rift in the bond usually resealed after ten minutes, so why did I still feel its amputations like open wounds? Where were their bodies? How had they died? Why couldn't we find them?

"Their records no longer exist. It's as though they were never here," White said.

Ares rushed towards me as I stepped in their direction. I

stopped myself from saying I was okay, that I could walk without his help, because it was a lie. I needed him. "Thank you," I whispered as he led me to the computer.

"Of course." He pulled another chair forwards and steadily lowered me into it. "How were the records deleted? Who has that kind of authority?"

The files on the screen meant nothing to me. I studied them, not understanding much, but hoping that a fresh pair of eyes might help.

"Us, Tim, Wilson… and everybody else is dead," White's words lingering.

Ares' scanned the room. "Where is Wilson? When was the last time anyone saw him?"

White rested a hand on his nephew's shoulder and gave a small squeeze. "It wasn't Wilson. He left this morning to fix the satellite with Diego. He can't have deleted the files. Besides, what reason would he have? He's happy on The Farm. He has no motive."

"That we know of." Ares seemed to consider this for a while, his eyebrows falling lower over his eyes as more time passed. "Okay, so if not Wilson, who? Why would anyone do this?"

"The only other option is that somebody has found a way into our system." White spoke carefully. He was as concerned as I was that Ares could become angry like Marshall when exposed to information that didn't please him. "They've hacked us."

Luckily, Ares didn't react like his brother. Other than a slight movement of his jaw and a twitch of his nostrils, there was no reaction.

I rested a hand on his sleeve, strategically placed so that our skin wouldn't touch.

Ares' expression softened. "The Sanctuary were in our security footage for years. Do they have access to our records, too?"

"I don't think it's fair to point the finger without evidence," White said, "but it is a possibility."

"It takes balls to do that," I muttered. "To accept our protection, join our people and agree to fight our wars, and then pick us off from the inside as soon as they step foot within our boundaries. I can't see their reasoning. They're no longer under vampire compulsion."

The pain eased, my heart slowly resealing itself, but the scars of the lost hybrids remained, never forgotten.

Only, this was the first I'd ever lost a pack member and not known who.

I should have spent more time with the hybrids and made more effort to get to know them.

That had to be my top priority over the following weeks.

We watched the screens as the drones lapped around The Farm. The steady cameras showed the hybrid camp under lockdown, everybody tucked within their tents whilst Tye searched the ground by foot, tracking for any sign of the fallen.

The human camp continued to unpack their limited belongings—whatever they could carry—blissfully unaware of the tension building up within the Observatorium.

"The thermal cameras aren't picking them up." Mika interrupted the collective silence. "And there's no sign of them outside the hybrid permitted zones, either."

White pushed his glasses further up his nose. Ares rubbed a hand across his jaw.

I sunk lower into my seat.

"We need to identify the hybrids," Ares said to White. "Contact each farmer. See who's missing from their tents and track them on the cameras throughout the day. If they're Omegas, as Lora suggests, they might have died several hours before she felt a rupture in the Alpha bond. This will be the fastest way to identify and locate them."

White nodded.

"And, Doc." He pulled White back by his arm. "It'll be worth locating Wilson, just in case. It's best to cross him off the suspect list sooner rather than later."

Dr. White slowly retracted his arm. "Yes. I believe so," he agreed.

We remained still as White communicated with the farmers, neither of us speaking.

"I don't trust Chipper," I said finally. It still didn't sit well that he was strolling around The Farm whilst everybody else was on lockdown. He had free rein.

"Me either," Ares said. "This is stress we don't need."

If I'd had more energy, I would have fixed him with an icy stare and asked him what he meant by his words. These hybrids *died*. They're lost to the world, their bodies still out there, left to decay.

Ares' lack of sensitivity appalled me.

Where was the kind-hearted boy who woke on The Farm? He'd once been so delicate, so fragile. Of course, the past few months had given us all thick skin, but Ares had transformed from a raindrop to a tidal wave in the matter of weeks.

But I couldn't blame him. It was the inner animal breaking through, tearing down his humanity one shred at a time.

I'd first noticed it the day Marshall, and so many others, died. His mother had him pinned into her arms, her Day Walker teeth so dangerously close to his neck, but he hardly blinked at the sight of Katie by my side. No sorrow for the friend-turned-Day Walker.

Again, he didn't react to seeing her body turn gray after I'd killed her. He barely noticed as we lowered her into the ground.

I thought it was everything else. Too much to process all at once. His mom, Marshall, killing them both…

But even in the busy weeks that followed, he seemed

unfazed by the mention of Katie's name and the fact she didn't return to The Farm with us. I could have it wrong, but I'd assumed they were friends. Farmers rarely talked to hybrids, but Ares and Katie always chatted in line when they shouldn't have.

Maybe I was overthinking their relationship.

My jealousy was probably misplaced. Not that I'd been *that* jealous. She was human, and at least thirty, but even when he'd struggled to talk to me, he'd always found words around her.

As though he sensed my internal battle, Ares took my hand in his and curled his fingers around my own. "We'll find them," he promised, offering a warm smile.

I watched his thumb brush over mine in small circles. Our skin was touching, and for the first time in a while, he wasn't absorbing my energy.

Maybe I had no more energy left to give.

CHAPTER FIVE

HAIL

Tim's nostrils flared as he pushed humans out of his way. "What are you doing?" he asked.

"Helping," I replied. "As I was told to."

"There's a code red. Didn't you hear the bell? Look at your tablet. It's flashing. Everyone is to get inside. It's just a drill, but The Sanctuary needs to follow our rules, too."

My tablet *was* flashing, but I had no clue what the different colors meant.

"Bro, chill. It's all under control. The tents are up and the humans are happy—"

"Don't you ever," Tim got close, pointing a finger at me, "call me Bro. We might now, somehow, hold the same level of authority, but I'm still your elder. It wouldn't hurt to show a little respect."

"Damn." I looked down my nose at him. Tim was nearly as

tall as me, but I was taller. "You're scaring the kids." I nodded towards a group of people standing near us. "Tell me what you want me to do and I'll do it."

My words made him happy enough, and he stepped back, offering a half-hearted smile and a small wave to the people. He took a breath before turning to face me. "We need to get The Sanctuary into their tents."

"Say no more." I bowed to my elder and walked away, keeping the smile from my face until there was enough distance between us.

"…been spending too much time with Ares…" I heard Tim say under his breath.

"Hey there, little dudes." I crouched next to the kids who'd been watching and offered high-fives all round. "Ready to see your new home?" I asked.

Their yeses were excited, but the kids' parents weren't. The adults were worried.

"Where is Chipper? He's been gone for almost an hour," a short brunette with upside-down eyebrows asked. I had to fight not to tilt my head.

"I—um. Who's Chipper? I'm sure he's about here somewhere—"

Tim interrupted as the woman's mouth dropped. "Hail, you know what? I'll take it from here. Why don't you head to the hybrid camp and help Tye?"

"But you said—"

"I've changed my mind." Tim's nose widened. "Just go."

I nodded and offered the kids more high-fives, "Later, little Bros."

"Get the people to their tents… don't get the people to their tents, make your mind up…" I said to myself as I left the human camp on the hill.

As I walked, I realized I didn't know what was going on. Tim said everyone needed to get inside, but why? What *was* a code red?

The Farm was empty.

I'd never seen it this quiet.

A small shiver crawled all over my skin. Even though it was deserted, I felt eyes on me.

It's the dead people. They're back for me.

But Ares had said I was safe inside the gates. The Farm had better security now. Still, I didn't feel safe.

I walked faster along the track to the hybrid camp.

My head spun at a snapping twig in the woods to my left. I stopped walking, squinting as I focused on the trees.

Nothing.

Your mind is playing tricks again, Bro.

I hadn't been right since returning to The Farm. Now and then, I saw something that wasn't there or heard a voice that nobody else could. The doctor said there was so much vampire venom in my blood at one point that this was likely a side effect. It left me questioning what was real and what was a dream even now, all these months later.

But it was slowly getting better, I was told.

The doctor helped. I met him once per week but never talked to him about what I saw or heard, only how often I questioned myself. And I definitely questioned myself now.

I continued walking.

The tents were small from this distance, like the stones underneath my feet; I couldn't imagine so many hybrids hiding in each one.

I counted them as I walked.

One… Two… Three… It's not real… *Four…*

And then I heard it again.

I spun on the gravel, kicking up dirt as I looked into the trees.

Red eyes. Red eyes. Red eyes.

I froze in place, like the dead person in the woods had already bitten me.

It's not real… It's not real…

We stared at each other.

I couldn't look away.

All I needed to do was blink—the visions always vanished when I blinked—but I was totally stumped and my eyes were in tears at the sight before me.

The vampire isn't real…

Had she already taken over my mind?

Was it too late?

I waited for the red and blue smoke to swarm around me.

"Boo!" Jayleigh pounced at me from behind and I startled, flinging my arms out in defense. "What-cha looking at?"

"Bro, don't creep up on me like that!" I blinked at her. I blinked back at the red eyes; the woods were empty. "There… oh. It doesn't matter." My hands trembled as I pointed. "I thought I saw something again."

Jayleigh's gaze followed my gesture towards the trees and she smiled before looping her arm through mine and leading me away. "It's okay, vision boy. What did Dr. White say that one time, when Mad Marshall and Ares tried to kill each other? Something about deserving a moment of madness?"

I shrugged, having no memory of it.

"I think you deserve a moment of madness more than anyone." She nudged me with her elbow.

"Thanks, I think."

Between looking at her and the woods, I noticed Jayleigh's eyebrows tilt with concern. "Did you take your tablets this morning?" she asked.

I nodded again. "All five of them." But… I had no memory of that either. Forgetting to take them would at least explain the red eyes in the woods.

"And… you're okay?" Her voice softened as we closed the distance to the hybrid camp.

"I still hear her singing sometimes." I didn't need to say her name for Jayleigh to know I was talking about Donnah.

"And what about…"

I shot her a look. I wouldn't talk about *that*.

Ever.

I didn't know why I'd even told her.

I'd imagined a lot over the past months and I knew it could easily have been a dream, or a vision, or whatever, but it disturbed me. Still, I liked that Jayleigh knew—even if it wasn't real. It was comforting. I didn't enjoy having secrets. They ate away at me.

This one more than others.

"You didn't tell anyone, did you?" I asked, slowing my pace as we reached the hybrid camp.

"My lips are sealed." Jayleigh drew her fingers across her mouth and threw away the imaginary key. "Your secrets are safe with me."

"And you won't tell Ares or Lora?"

She smiled at me. "I won't tell anyone."

And I believed her.

It was a relief because, of all the people I wanted to find out, Ares and Lora were the last. If they did, and it was just a vision? I could tear them apart.

But if it was real?

Well, then we were all in danger—really, really big danger.

CHAPTER SIX

ARES

I led Lora back to the barn, where she collapsed onto the bed and fell asleep within minutes. I'd never seen her so physically exhausted. Never had she appeared weak to me, but she did now as I watched the dust float above her head, illuminated by the sun's rays which crept through the gaps in the barn's infrastructure.

It was peaceful here; one reason we remained in the barn instead of moving to the Guesthouse—where the council members stayed—or the bunks on level -2 and -3, which most farmers called home.

We'd switched things around, Lora and I now sharing a stall. Tye was on the furthest end of the barn, whilst Hail and Jayleigh occupied separate stalls opposite ours. Diego housed the one opposite Jayleigh's. It wasn't a coincidence; I figured.

Lora's breathing fell into a steady rhythm, her chest rising and falling in time. As beautiful as ever. I placed a small kiss on her forehead, moved a silver lock from her face, and left her to nap.

I excused myself from the barn and closed the door, stopping to glance over the lake.

The lake where my father had died.

The lake I'd almost drowned in.

Sometimes the prettiest things were the most deadly. They had a way of luring you in, romancing you, gaining your trust, and then sweeping the world from under your feet when you least expected it.

Lora had done the same to me once. I looked back over my shoulder, thankful that we'd now fallen into a consistent pattern —an understanding.

Lora would always be a lake, but I was a river; an ever changing gully of water, easily influenced by the surrounding environment. I knew peace, and I knew how to meander through life, but I also knew how to take. I could erode, I could push people without their permission.

I could.

But I didn't.

I wouldn't.

I needed to remain trustworthy, my head screwed on, and my heart in the right place.

I walked in the same direction I always seemed to drift

whenever I found time alone, towards the Guesthouse. The Sanctuary were stationed nearby, so I made a mental note to stop and show my face once I was done.

The old farm building was three stories tall and made of dirt colored stone, with wooden windows—paint flaking and peeling—and a green cottage door.

I let myself inside.

Farmers occupied every bedroom except for the primary suite. That was Marshall's room, and my parents' beforehand—so Dr. White told me.

Most council members were busy throughout the day, so the house was empty. Still, I crept through the kitchen and hallways, and avoided the creaky floorboards as I climbed the stairs. I felt out of place here, like I didn't belong to a house.

I was an animal. The barn was my home.

I was trespassing within these solid walls, unable to feel the breeze.

My hand fumbled through my pocket for the key to Marshall's room, briefly grazing over my mother's photograph and the necklace I'd taken from her body before we'd buried her. I'd always intended to return the photo to Dr. White, but something kept me from doing so.

It was selfish to keep it. It wasn't of sentimental value, as I still struggled to understand my feelings towards my mother. My only recent memories were those of her as a Day Walker, but sometimes I'd get flashes of a life I no longer remembered. When anxious, or angry, or nervous, and my animal alter-ego inched over the line which separated our two individual identities, I became overwhelmed by the memories: planting trees in the Biome with Mom, finger painting with Dr. White and Uncle Flynn, spying on the strange older boy in the classroom whom I'd nicknamed Floppy.

If only I'd known then that he was my brother.

Maybe some part of me always had. I'd always bothered him as a child, even when he told me to get lost. To him, I was another helpless refugee, destined for a life under the microscope.

To me, he was a boy much older than the rest, observant and skilled. Of course, I'd made it my infant life's mission to learn more about him.

But I never had.

Even when I discovered he was my brother and he'd left The Farm with us to find Hail, I'd always been too skeptical of him—a result of the trauma he inflicted. Justified. But I wished now that I'd had more time to get to know him—the person he was before he died.

All I had now was his room.

The key turned stiffly in the lock and I let myself in. It always surprised me how tidy the room remained, which was crazy as I was the only one with access to it, the sole key left in the box with a collection of postcards which Marshall named Protocol Six.

He loved the theatrics, the drama.

And he also liked to keep things in order.

The room was on the larger side; the bed taking center stage, facing the windows with views of the lake. Marshall had pulled a bedspread of red linen tightly across the mattress, not a single crease in sight, four pillows standing upright and a smaller cushion chopped in the middle.

I struggled to imagine him delicately making his bed.

The same Marshall who'd shot a boy right in front of my eyes.

The same Marshall to paint landscapes at the desk in the corner; neatly organized with brushes, and blank card forever waiting to be used, and acrylics in yellows and blues and greens. I added the red to his collection when I'd returned from Hail's rescue mission.

And then there was a small stack of finished artwork, landscapes carelessly piled on top of each other as though he'd disregarded them as soon as they'd dried. They were postcards of his own creation; images of The Farm that the world would never see.

The same Marshall who'd forced Hail and Beckle into a death-match.

The same Marshall who'd saved my humanity.

My brother was a man I would never truly understand, and that idea upset me just as much as losing him.

I tried to ignore the pain in my chest, unsure if I should mourn a man who'd once stabbed me. Was I right to grieve the heartless monster who'd caused as much death and destruction whilst leading The Farm as a vampire outside the gates? Probably not, so I kept my visits to Marshall's room a secret.

But I was sure I had a right to mourn my brother.

They were two separate people in my mind now, as though he was a hybrid—a human and an animal alter-ego: my brother and Mad Marshall.

And I'd killed both versions of him.

My right hand slid down my shirt, as though I could so easily wipe away the blood I'd spilled and the ghost of Marshall's fingers guiding mine over the dagger. But, even as my hand wrapped itself in the black fabric, the memory remained.

I bypassed the wardrobe at the far end, full of gray uniform and rain jackets—no hats, as we'd buried his only cap with him—and targeted the punching bag in the corner.

I'd never considered hitting it before, but I did today. I was no stranger to this boxing activity after using punching bags in training, but it was odd that he'd have one in his bedroom.

With a solid blow from my fist, the bag swung back and forth, and I felt a small ripple of pain creep up my arm. I watched as the bag steadied itself, like the pendulum of a clock.

REAP

Time was ticking.

I should go.

Hiding out in Marshall's room was a sad way to pass time. I was avoiding my responsibilities, cocooned in a room taken from history and belonging to a man that no longer existed.

The Farm needed me. The world needed me. As I clicked my stiff fingers and turned back to the door, I wondered how often my brother had thought the same.

My hand ached from that one small punch. It had been too long since I'd done any proper training. I sighed, lingering, and my eyes tugged my attention towards something over the dresser.

My body stilled.

Ice crept over my skin, and I slowly turned back.

That wasn't there last time.

I squinted at the chain hanging from the mirror, an unusually shaped pendant weighing the necklace down. Even from this distance I recognized it immediately. Mother's necklace.

Only, I still had it in my pocket… my fingers brushed over it, pulling it out.

I dangled both necklaces in front of me. The pendants spun around as my mind tried to make sense of it, both intricately designed and with a soft, metallic feel, but with slight differences in their shapes. One necklace carried by my mother, the other belonging to somebody else; the same somebody who'd left it here for me to find.

They had a key to Marshall's room, and they wanted me to know.

But why the secrecy?

This person, whoever they were, wanted to play games, but after everything I'd gone through, I hadn't the time or energy.

My playing days were over.

CHAPTER SEVEN

ARES

I received a call from Dr. White after an hour of answering Chipper's questions. I'd been helping The Sanctuary set up when I spotted their leader and his disciples across the camp, but the intended five-minute chat turned into an interview, six of them firing questions in my direction. So when my tablet lit up, I looked at the sky in a silent *thank you* and I used it as my opportunity to leave.

The Farm was still on lockdown as the missing hybrids were yet to be identified and their bodies were still missing, so the path back towards the silo was empty until I spotted two figures lingering at the entrance of the hybrid camp.

A smile tugged at the corners of my mouth as though it

had been fighting for an excuse to break free. "God, am I glad to see you guys," I said as I approached.

"What's going on, Bro?" Hail jerked his head in the direction of the camp behind him.

"Is everything okay? You look frazzled," Jayleigh said.

I wondered if my dishevelment was visible to everyone or just those closest to me.

"Walk with me." I nodded in the silo's direction. "I'll tell you on the way."

Hail and Jayleigh shared a momentary look which I couldn't quite place, but it was gone in the blink of an eye, and they fell into line beside me.

"Where's Lora?" Jayleigh turned around as though expecting to find her following behind.

I explained this afternoon's events, the two of them listening with wide, flittering eyes.

"And there's still no sign of them?" Jayleigh asked. "I know it would be difficult for Titaniums to track their scent, with Lora still tired, but maybe we should try the Venos? They're some of the best hunters we have. Or the wolves when they return from their rounds?"

"I thought the same, but we'd need a belonging from each hybrid for that, and we don't even know the hybrids' identities yet." Although I hoped that's why Dr. White had beckoned me.

"How can they just disappear?" Hail asked, and I wasn't

sure if it was to himself or a genuine question.

"We're still trying to work it out," I said. "I was hoping you two could spot something we've missed. Fresh eyes and all that."

"What eyes?" Hail's face twitched.

I smiled as I loaded into the lift and pressed the button for level -3. "Oh, it doesn't matter."

"We'll do our best to help in any way we can," Jayleigh said, "but I won't lie, all that computer stuff in the Observatorium confuses the hell out of me. Give me a dagger and a vampire any day; just don't ask me about technology."

"You take on the action, and I'll be the guy in the chair," I said. We'd watched enough of the old movies stocked in the abandoned entertainment rooms of the infirmary to understand the common roles often used in films. "We make the perfect team."

Jayleigh approved with a quirk of her eyebrows as she drank from her flask.

"And where do I fit into this team, Bro?" Hail's face remained serious.

I considered and smiled. "You're the leggy blonde damsel in distress."

Jayleigh spurted water from her nose, spraying it over me in a shower of laughter. I wiped my face as the lift doors opened, and Hail muttered, "Not cool, Dude." He ducked out.

We followed, both of us eyeing his abnormally long legs. Jayleigh whispered, "Perfect," and offered me a fist bump after wiping her nose on her sleeve.

We reached the Observatorium a few minutes later, and I sensed the shift in atmosphere as soon as we entered the room. Dr. White stood to greet us in the doorway and led us up the ramp to the balcony.

"Ares, Hail, Jayleigh," he welcomed us individually. "I'm glad you're here." Concern creased his forehead as he whisked around his desk and flicked through the folders on his monitor.

"Is everything okay? Any update on the dead hybrids?" My heart beat a little faster; the anticipation hung in the air. My words lingered, and I shared a look with my friends, wondering what the silence meant.

The anxiety ate at me.

The animal inside woke, bringing several flashes of childhood memories. I inhaled—held the breath to steady my heart.

My fingers fiddled with the two necklaces in my pocket, fumbling over the pendants and twisting them about each other.

"We successfully identified the hybrids," Dr. White said finally. I released my breath and hoped the news would settle me, but it didn't.

"Who were they?" I asked. My uncle's nervous tone revealed that there was more to the story. "Have you found their bodies?"

"They were Kyla, Orah, Geeno, and Fleur. All Omegas between the ages of twelve and fourteen. They were last seen after lunch, returning to their tent to wait for the farmers in charge of their group."

"So what happened?" My voice rose in volume as my panic heightened. Several heads turned in our direction from the lower level of the Observatorium. "Were they missing when the farmers got to the tent? Why didn't the farmers report them missing?"

My fingers clawed faster at the necklaces in my pocket, tangling the chains into a tight knot.

Dr. White hesitated as he pointed towards the screens. "We have footage of the farmers leaving, walking from the hybrid camp, and settling on a fallen tree near the lake, where they remained for an hour before splitting up and heading in different directions."

My mind spun with possibilities. What happened in that tent? What did they see?

The whole scenario screamed trauma to me.

"We need to talk to the farmers," I said. I needed context and insight, and I wanted to see the footage of them leaving the tent.

"We already have, Ares. They don't remember a thing." Dr. White's voice held a certain level of caution, and we looked at each other, thinking the same, but not wanting to voice our conclusions.

My ears rang.

"What about the tent? Surely the hybrids' bodies will be there?" Jayleigh interrupted.

Dr. White swallowed. "Here."

He pointed to the monitor, opening the file he'd brought up on his computer when we arrived. It was a replay of the footage from camera 192, recorded at 13:16, and sure enough, it revealed four hybrids entering the tent.

The frame was still for a while, and Dr. White skipped the video forward. At 13:30, three farmers stepped out of the tent, their faces expressionless and unreadable.

"Do we have footage of the farmers entering the tent? What time did the farmers get there? They must have been waiting for the hybrids, but why? Where are the farmers now?" I asked my uncle. The questions spilled from me in an uncontainable rush as I leaned closer to the monitor.

"Breathe, Ares," Dr. White reminded.

I complied, but I said, "I'll breathe when we sort this out."

"Very well. We're holding the farmers in the interrogation rooms." He nodded towards the screens in the far corner.

"Good." It was the first time we'd used the rooms that once contained Gretta. "Keep them there."

Jayleigh looked at me in confusion.

REAP

I tried to shake the idea from my head, but I couldn't deny the facts. "It looks to me like the farmers planned this. Claiming that they remember nothing makes the whole situation more suspicious."

"You think three farmers could take down four hybrids?" Jayleigh's orange eyebrows rose in shock.

"I think three humans armed with tasers could take down four kids who don't yet know how to use their abilities to their advantage, yeah."

My tablet didn't show that we had used any tasers today, but maybe they'd found a way around it. Maybe they'd found a loophole.

"Why would the farmers do this? What reason do they have to attack innocent hybrids?" Jayleigh braced her hands on the back of the empty desk chair we crowded around.

I shook my head, scowling at the screens on the wall. My fingers still turned the necklaces in my pocket.

How coincidental that somebody left a necklace for me to find the same day that the hybrids died and The Sanctuary arrived.

"Maybe it's not about the hybrids," I said. "Maybe they're trying to send us a message."

"What do you mean? If the farmers are upset about something, they'll happily report it to Tim," Jayleigh said.

"You think they're planning something?" Dr. White

focused on me, studying. "An uprising?"

I rested my head in my hands, reminding myself to breathe... *breathe... breathe.*

If only Lora was there.

"I don't know what to think," I said.

"But what about the hybrids?" Hail still watched the screen, oblivious to our conversation. He pointed at the timestamp: 13:35.

"There's nothing else to show." Dr. White clicked the video into fast-forward once more. "Based on the footage, the farmers never entered the tent, and the hybrids never left. But we've checked the camp since and the bodies are no longer there."

I stared at the screen, my mind a mess.

"So, what?" Jayleigh folded her arms across her chest and leaned to one side. "They just vanished?"

"Like... magic?" Hail added.

"Either that," Dr. White suggested, lowering his voice to a volume only we could hear, "or somebody within this room has tampered with the recording."

"You think they're working together, killing the hybrids and destroying the evidence?" I asked.

"I think nothing, Ares," my uncle replied. "I know for certain. Somebody looped the footage and they're covering their tracks."

CHAPTER EIGHT

LORA

I awoke as everybody else retired to bed, staring at that old knot of wood on the beam above my head.

Ares passed the stall, only to backtrack as soon as he realized I was awake. The shadows of his aura seemed controlled, yet still too visible for my liking.

"Lora!" He rushed in to greet me. Solace trailed behind him and folded herself on the floor next to the bed. "Did we wake you? I'm sorry if we were too loud."

I shook my head. "No. You didn't." I squinted at the round window above the doors, the moon lighting the barn in pale blue. "Did I sleep all afternoon?"

"Yes. We didn't want to wake you after everything that

happened." Ares sat at the foot of the bed and rubbed my knee through the blanket. I tried not to laugh at how much it tickled. "How are you feeling?"

"Better, thanks."

"Can I get you anything? You skipped dinner. I could—"

"Ares." I rested my hand on his and he calmed in a matter of seconds. "Stop worrying. I'm okay."

His gaze was so intense that I felt a small shiver run through my body.

I'd never get enough of those gray eyes and the way they pierced straight to my soul, exposing every secret I'd kept and healing every wound on my skin.

"What's the latest on the hybrids?" I asked, focusing on my latest scars and the healed Alpha bond, relieved to find everything again felt normal. I felt recharged. Holding Ares' hand like this barely affected me at all.

"We've not had much progress. I'll give you the details in the morning."

My stomach churned. I wanted news that the hybrids' bodies were found and identified, and their deaths had been painless and accidental.

Ares provided me with none of these details as he prepared for bed and climbed in next to me. A cold draft momentarily coated my skin as he lifted the cover, but Ares' body heat vanquished it, his arm sliding beneath my neck as I turned in to face him, and his other hand resting on my waist. Our noses were touching. His lips were so close.

I expected him to kiss me, as was the usual routine, but instead, he surprised me by saying, "Do you want to get out of here?"

I stared in confusion, not replying straight away.

The Farm? The bed?

"Come on." He was out of the covers just as quickly as he'd climbed underneath them, pulling on his rain jacket and shoes. He ordered Solace to stay put as I followed his lead with nerves in my stomach. Ares wasn't the spontaneous type. Sneaking out in the night wasn't something we'd ever done together before.

I could cross the barn without making much of a sound. I knew how wide the door could open before making a noise, but Ares pulled it too far and it screeched on its rail, echoing through the barn.

My body cringed at the sound.

The pack would certainly know what we were up to now. I'd try to convince them I was hungry and Ares wanted to update me on the missing hybrids, and it wasn't at all how it looked. I wasn't sure exactly what we were doing, but my skin tingled with excitement as I closed the door behind us.

Ares led me to the silo, loaded me into the lift, and pressed the button for -1.

I didn't ask questions, enjoying the element of surprise for what may have been the first time in my life, and I watched the shadows of his aura dance through the confined metal box as I gripped the sea glass in my pocket. I'd refused to part with it since Ares found it on the sand. The doors dinged open, and I followed him through the common room and down the tunnel to the rock pools. I was finally gaining an understanding of where his head was at.

"Stay here," he said as he opened the door.

"Is that an order?" I cocked an eyebrow, enjoying the recognition in his eyes.

He gave me a playful scowl, a kiss on the forehead, and then disappeared through the door, his head popping back into view just a moment later to add, "Do you want it to be an order?"

My heart squeezed, and I smiled so wide that my jaw ached. "Go on, Ares. Do whatever you need to do."

"Yes, Alpha." He saluted me before closing the door. I heard him walk away and then pressed my ear to the wood separating us, trying to match his sounds to actions.

Several minutes passed, and I heard nothing.

I expected anything and everything, and when he returned, I absent-mindedly gripped my thumbs between my fingers—my skin cold, and nerves floating around my stomach.

Maybe I should have eaten something.

REAP

The door reopened, and I stared at the sight before me. Ares was soaked, his brown hair slicked back against his head, and water dripped from his hands as he reached for me.

"Ares, you could have gone for a swim without my supervision, you know?" I frowned even though the smile was yet to drop from my face.

"You're so funny," his tone was sarcastic—we both knew that comedy wasn't my forte—but he laughed at my attempted humor despite it all.

He intertwined our fingers and led me into the torch lit room. The familiar warm and steamy air hit me in a rush, but music played quietly in the distance, soaking into my senses.

"Oh, Ares. It's beautiful," I whispered as I took in the new improvements. He had added blue lights to the pools, bathing the room in a soft, hazy turquoise glow.

"Spare lights from damaged drones," he said. "I found them in storage on level -2. I control them via my tablet, turning them on and off. But that's not the best bit."

He guided me further into the room and then turned away, removing his clothes.

I blinked at him. This certainly wasn't usual behavior for him, often too shy to strip when the pack was around.

Did he have lights on his underwear, too?

He didn't. I chose not to voice my disappointment as he turned back to help me out of my own clothes, slowly unzipping my jacket and sliding it from each arm. My top was next to go, my boots, and then my cargos.

All the while, those hypnotic gray eyes remained on mine.

I felt exposed. Was this how he often felt removing his clothes around others? I'd never experienced it before. I'd never cared what others thought of my body. Maybe that was the animal within me.

Now, I felt more human than I ever had. I wondered what he had planned as he crouched to lift one foot from my cargos, and then the other, and he kissed each ankle as he removed my socks. It was an unusual place to be kissed; his soft lips felt foreign to the skin of my legs, but I enjoyed it.

His aura settled at our contact, but the darkness lingered in his granite eyes.

We were in nothing but our underwear as he stood, holding my body against his, and my breath hitched as he tucked loose hair behind my ear; a quick, fleeting touch I only wished would linger. I wouldn't mind if this night lingered, frozen in time.

"Follow me," he said, turned, and stepped into the water, holding his hand out for mine.

Another order.

I could get used to it.

I complied with no reservation while Ares smiled to himself, as though laughing at his own joke. My hand grasped his as I lowered myself into the pools, steam clouding my face, and my body relaxed into the warm water like a familiar hug.

Ares swam forwards and I followed suit, crossing the rock pools towards the larger waterfall at the far side of the cave. My body felt lighter within the water. I still ached from the break in the Alpha bond. Despite still feeling overwhelmed, swimming with Ares calmed me and took my mind off the events of the day.

He lingered in the pool; the water falling from a great height in the rock wall beside us. The sound swaddled us in this moment like a bubble. His gaze fixed on me, and I couldn't work out his expression, or what we were doing, or why we were here. But I didn't want to be anywhere else.

"Do you trust me?" Ares asked, his usual playfulness edged in grit.

Something in the back of my mind suggested I shouldn't. He was acting unusual, but I liked it.

"Yes," I said without another thought and he smiled as though I'd just sold him my soul. Although, in a way, he'd already been stealing my soul for the past three months.

His arm wrapped around my waist, reeling me through the water towards to him. "Hold your breath," Ares instructed, and I did. He smirked as he dragged me down into the misty blue depths.

CHAPTER NINE

LORA

My mind swirled with a thousand worries as Ares dragged me to the pools' bed. I had to fight not to swat his arm from my waist; to break free of his grasp. Having somebody else in control of my body was foreign to me. Not even my inner animal could control me.

So now, to put all my faith in somebody else was daunting.

It's Ares. He wouldn't do anything to hurt you.

My only rebellion against his actions was a small squeal, which released bubbles through my nose as we sank deeper and deeper.

With the pool lit up, the amusement was clear on Ares' face as he steadied us, let me go, and pointed to something in the rocks.

My gaze followed.

More lights revealed a small underwater tunnel which Ares swam towards, motioning with his hand to follow.

Curiosity spiked.

How many times had I swum in these waters and never known about this hidden tunnel? I left caution at the waterfall and followed without a second thought, seeking the adventure Ares offered—the escape. I stayed near as the tunnel stretched on and finally opened into a larger space.

We rose to the surface, both gasping for air. I was so relieved to find oxygen that, for a moment, I struggled to process the surrounding scene.

The island.

The firelight.

The stars.

I spun in the water, still abnormally warm. The temperature difference from my body to my face—exposed to the chill of February night—was extreme.

Ares was able to stand, and I clung to him to get a better look at the area without treading water. He, too, was warm. I hugged him closer, our skin pressed together.

I didn't let it cross my mind that he was absorbing my energy; I'd slept long enough to fully recharge after the break in the Alpha bond this afternoon. He could bleed me dry for all I cared. It was worth it to have him pressed against me like this.

I wrapped my arms around his back and looked up.

The cave opened to reveal a cloudless night sky—the starlight rained down on us as we lingered within the water, gently swaying to the music Ares had set up on a stereo placed on the island of sand and rocks in the center.

"Music with lyrics," I said. Not the acoustic guitar instrumental the farmers played in the lift and on -1, but music I could sing to if I'd wanted.

Ares had decorated the cave with red lights here instead of blue, and it bounced from the walls, reflecting in his eyes with a dangerous hue.

"How did you get the speaker in here?" I asked, puzzled.

"Drones."

"Drones? How long have you been planning this?"

His smile was boyish. "Since I found this place. One day I was looking at the screens in the Observatorium and zoomed in close enough to see the pools. I studied my father's maps and figured there might be a tunnel which connected these pools to the cave pools in -1. And surely enough…"

"I'm glad you've been making good use of your time in the Observatorium," I joked, resting my head on his shoulder as he moved us through the star kissed water.

"I have a curious mind," he said. "And I wanted to do something nice for you. It's been a stressful few weeks, and after everything that happened earlier… I figured now would be the perfect time. But we don't have to talk about that. I don't want to bring the mood down."

My heart beat against his chest and I was sure he knew just how fast it raced. I didn't try to hide it.

"It's amazing," I said. "Thank you."

I placed a kiss on his cheek and his nose scrunched as he grinned. His expression was so gentle, I couldn't bring myself to look at his face for too long. That smile would be the death of me, I was sure.

"I can't believe we can see the stars from here," I said, changing the subject to hide my blush, but Ares didn't follow my lead as I gazed up, past rock and stone, to find the night sky.

"Your eyes wear them well," he said, his breath warm on my cheek.

I stopped breathing for a moment. My body weakened, not from a drop in my energy, but from his words.

"You'd rather look at my eyes than the sky?" I was taken aback by my own nervous laughter. "You once told me that nature was your thing. What happened? Did you two break up?"

Ares' face was so serious I barely recognized him—less boyish. Leading The Farm had matured him, but he was still *my* Ares. "I guess I found something more beautiful."

Oh… My heart.

"More beautiful than this damn planet?" And I once again

focused on him instead of the stars. My cheeks were on fire. He should have pinned me to the wall with the other torches. My heart raced at the thought.

Where had this version of Ares been hiding?

He traced the water on my lips with his finger, brushed the wet hair from my face, and whispered at a pitch so low and raw that I forgot my place, "I'd set the world on fire to see the flames dance in your eyes."

My body clung to him, but I was sure that I was sinking. Falling. Flying. All of it at once.

The world, which Ares loved more than anything—his peace, his safety—he'd risk it all for me.

"*Do it,*" I thought with nerves still fluttering around in my stomach, not realizing I'd actually mind jumped the words to him.

"*Maybe I will,*" he replied through the unexplained connection we shared when our skin touched.

I wanted him to know exactly what was on my mind as I kissed him in the steamy pool, buried 25 meters underground.

"*I love you.*"

He pulled back just long enough to say, "I love you too, Alpha." And then his lips and hands were on me again.

Every step back to the barn was a regret.

I made sure not to touch Ares as I thought about what I

had to do next, and it didn't involve falling asleep by his side, as he suspected.

I would have spent longer in our underground oasis, but sleeping this afternoon had gifted me the luxury of time, so when Ares admitted he felt sleepy, I suggested returning to the barn with the promise of more night adventures in the future.

I focused only on the missing hybrids as we stepped over Solace—giving us a dirty look—and climbed into bed. Ares propped his arm under my neck like my own personal pillow. I couldn't bear to think of leaving him there.

His breathing steadied. I counted his soft snores.

I assumed he was falling asleep when he finally whispered, "Tell me about the cottage by the sea."

My body paused as though my heart had stopped beating, and the blood ran still. It had been a while since I last thought of a life outside The Farm, on the other side of the war. I'd been so preoccupied with training, teaching the hybrids, and helping Ares that I'd momentarily forgotten my plans for our life when The Farm was no longer needed.

The idea swept over me like a dream.

"When the war is won, and vampires no longer roam the earth…" I swallowed. It seemed like the start of a poor joke. "When our only responsibility is to ourselves, we'll take a small bag of our favorite items and leave The Farm forever, for a peaceful life. We'll find a cottage overlooking the sea, on the border of a quaint little town where the hybrids can settle down. We'll make the cottage our home." I closed my eyes, listened to Ares' breathing shallow, and focused on the Alpha bond that connected us—far stronger than I'd experienced with any other hybrid.

"We'll have a garden big enough for Solace and the wolves, maybe even a field, and we'll throw parties where the hybrids come together to eat and dance, telling the stories of our success. In daylight we'll laugh as loud as we like, because no Day Walker will roam the earth. And we'll sing to the moon as a reminder of what we've been through and everything we've overcome—because we can—because no Night Walker will ever interrupt us again. And we'll cuddle until we fall asleep, exactly as we are now, but to the sound of waves distantly crashing outside our window, with no care in the world… completely at peace."

The lump slid down my throat as I gulped.

I wanted to tell Ares that this was an order and a plan he must abide by. He had to hold on to his humanity—to make this dream a reality. But his gentle snores occupied the space between us, and I feared waking him.

My body snuggled closer for a few more minutes of heaven, but better judgment told me I shouldn't stay.

He stirred as though reading my need to leave, and I slowly untangled our legs and arms, removing myself from the bed.

REAP

The winter air kissed my skin in Ares' absence.

I redressed quickly, tucked my feet into my boots, and threw my towel-dried hair into a small bun atop my head.

Solace opened an eye to watch me. I ran a hand over her head. "Keep him safe for me? I'll be back soon."

The wolf wasn't fond of me, and it had never seemed so apparent as she turned away and sighed.

I pursed my lips.

"I want to stay here, too," I said to Solace, my heart aching from the truth in the words. "Don't judge me for leaving again." But there wasn't time to stay and make friends with Ares' wolf, as much as I wanted her to like me.

I let myself out of our stall once more, pushed the barn door open just enough to slip through without making a noise, and disappeared into the starry night.

CHAPTER TEN

ARES

I squinted through groggy eyes the following morning, taking several minutes after the alarm woke us to recall the previous day's events. I pressed my nose into the back of Lora's neck and inhaled the smell of lilies. I'd never grow tired of it.

The dead, missing hybrids. The farmers in the interrogation rooms. The necklace I'd found in Marshall's room. The team member who'd edited the drone footage to make it look as though the hybrids had never left the tent.

I groaned into the pillow, pulling Lora closer for just a few more moments.

"Good morning," she whispered, turning to snuggle into my chest.

My heart faltered. I couldn't cope. Why weren't we able to stay like this all day? "Good morning, Alpha. Did you sleep okay?"

I felt her nod.

"Wake up, lovebirds." I dragged one eye open to find Jayleigh already out of bed and standing at our stall door, propping her chin on her elbow as she awaited our reaction.

"We're awake, Jayleigh," I grumbled. She did this every morning. "Pick on Hail instead."

She laughed, ignoring my suggestion, and let herself in, sitting on the floor beside Solace. "Hello there, my wolfy friend," she beamed, a smile as large as a morning sun—which was yet to make an appearance. "Did Ares' snoring keep you up last night?"

"I don't—"

"Or was it the sound of their kissing?"

"Jayleigh!" I released Lora from my grasp and turned to face the intruder. Jayleigh lay stomach down on the floor, her long ginger hair already neatly braided, and it roped out beside her as she petted Solace's chest. "Fine, you win. I'm up."

"You're all getting so lazy," she said, tutting at us. "Remember our training days where we'd wake up at four?"

Only too well. "How could I forget?"

"It's half-past-six, Ares! That is a lie-in."

"So you like to remind us." I stood, rubbed the sleep from

my eyes, and gestured my hand toward the door. "I'm up, Jayleigh. Your mission was successful. Now, please, go and wake up Hail."

She bounced to her feet and offered us a sneaky smile as she left.

"Snoring… I do not snore." I shook my head as I changed clothes and prepared for the day ahead.

"You do, a little." Lora rose from the bed, nudging me as she crossed to her draws.

"You're supposed to be on my side," I said, "not hers."

"I don't take sides, Ares. You're all my hybrids." She tried to fight her smile, corners of her lips quirking up. "I'm just saying it how it is."

Was she making jokes again?

I filled Lora in on yesterday's events as we finished getting ready, and by the time we stepped out of our stall, Jayleigh had forced Hail out of bed.

"The farmers are rebelling against us?" Lora's eyes were wide, her face unreadable. "Why? What reason have we given them? They never rebelled against Marshall or your father. Do they hate us more than they hated them? Don't they understand our methods? Do they oppose our approach?"

"I think it's less to do with what we stand for and more towards what we are." I'd concluded so yesterday evening, whilst eating dinner with Jayleigh and Hail. "The farmers created us, and now we're leading them. It must feel a little backward."

"But it wasn't our choice. You never asked to replace Marshall."

I shrugged, noticing a slight ache in my neck. I must have been tensing my shoulders in my sleep, or the pressure of yesterday was getting to me.

My hand slipped into my pocket and felt for the two necklaces still knotted together. Lora needed to know, but telling her would mean admitting I'd been in Marshall's room, hiding, and I wasn't sure I could take the pity first thing in the morning.

I'd tell her later.

Tye sat in the middle of the barn, waiting for us, whilst Diego closed his door. Jayleigh leaned back against the bars of Hail's stall, and she watched Diego's arms flex as he lifted a bench and brought it to the center to meet Tye's. His eyes met hers as he swung a leg over and lowered himself into a sitting position. He nodded to the space next to him, and she took it.

I raised my eyebrows, looking to Lora for confirmation of what I just witnessed, and we momentarily forgot our concerns about the farmers' revolution as we smiled.

"Finally," I said.

"It took long enough," Lora replied.

We'd been rooting for something to happen between Jayleigh and Diego for weeks. I'd purposely coupled them in tasks, and Lora could sense through the Alpha bond that the attraction was there. It seemed the only ones fighting it were Jayleigh and Diego themselves. But now… now they were sharing a bench, and I couldn't be more excited for them.

"What are you two grinning at?" Hail finally emerged from his stall and crouched to pat Solace's head.

We both nodded in Jayleigh's direction but said nothing, scared that if we made too much of a fuss, we might scare them and send them running like a flock of nervous sheep. No, not sheep. The couple were too deadly; with Jayleigh's stealth and Diego's strength, they'd be The Farm's most feared couple.

It wasn't common knowledge that Lora could release her energy in an explosion of uncontrolled helplessness. And, of course, we'd kept my Gen. 3 issues quiet. Nobody would trust a leader destined to lose his humanity if his animal alter-ego pushed too far.

Lora and I were dangerous for sure, but Jayleigh and Diego had an intensity about them. Whereas we lacked control, everything about them screamed order and self-reservation, even down to how they interacted with each other. I envied them.

Lora headed towards the benches for our routine morning debrief, and I followed with Solace and Hail on my heels.

We each shared information, ensuring that everybody stayed in the loop, and we decided to grill Tim and Wilson on their knowledge of the farmer's plans during the council meeting after breakfast.

The farmers' cafeteria on -2 was open to all. The hybrids were first to eat throughout the day, and we made our way to the silo just before 7am to bypass the queue of eager Omegas.

I collected my tray of porridge and headed for our usual table in the far corner, then searched the faces in the room for one in particular.

Lora noticed my change in behavior and caught on to what I was doing. She joined in as we ate, waiting for a certain black-haired being, with yellowing eyes and a posture which didn't seem quite human.

"He's usually here by now," I said to Lora, but it attracted the entire table's attention. Jayleigh's eyes darted around to make sense of the situation and her distraction allowed Hail to steal the crusts of toast from her place.

"Hey!" she swatted his hand away.

It was already too late. Hail was chewing on her leftovers as he said, "You never eat the damn crusts, so what's the problem, Broski?"

Jayleigh rolled her eyes. "I told you, you can just call me Bro."

Hail laughed and continued to speak with his mouth full. "Whatever."

I tuned out what they said next, deeming it an unimportant breakfast chat.

"The Venos are never late," Lora said into my ear, her breath tickling my neck. "They're too obedient to be late."

Those were my thoughts exactly. "Something's wrong," I said, only just loud enough for our circle to hear. My gaze landed on the tablet, the screen lighting up in an orange hue. "Crap." My blood ran still.

Everybody looked at their own tablets as they alerted with the same amber warning and small vibration.

"Orange?" Hail murmured to Jayleigh. "What does that color mean?"

I jumped to my feet, tripping off the bench and hurrying towards the staircase, which would take me to level -3. The pack followed, their footsteps echoing against the walls as we descended the stairs.

"It means a hybrid is out of control." Jayleigh's voice bounced from the walls as we spiraled deeper into the ground. "They're mutating in unsafe circumstances."

"So why are we going down instead of up?" Hail yelled back as we ran.

We finally reached the door at the bottom, and I swiped my tablet to let us into the corridor, heading for the Observatorium. I planned to locate the hybrid on the screens, ask the farmers for information and better understand why they weren't tasering the hybrid, but as we neared the screened room, I scrapped all plans.

REAP

Looking through the windowed panels of the doors which separated us, I found the Veno hybrid I'd been searching for.

Dickward was wild.

He thrashed about the room, upturning tables and ripping computers from their desks.

My mind spun with the traumatic memories of Phase 2. My body stilled as I laid eyes on the Veno, seeming much larger now than I remembered.

I'd only seen him mutate once before, and it hadn't ended well for Jayleigh or Tye. Both of them suffered serious injuries. I'd bested him and knocked him unconscious whilst in my animal state, but that wasn't an option now, with my humanity at risk.

We watched in horror as the shifter hybrid—a werewolf with snake scales in place of skin, and beady yellow eyes—lunged towards a small group of farmers who huddled in the corner. Dickward's posture was inhumane. His back arched and arms stretched forward in a gorilla-like stance. His clothing had ripped as he'd mutated. It was more proof that his animal state was larger than it had been the last time I'd seen it.

I tuned out the commotion behind me and focused on Dickward. He'd listen to my order. I was the leader of The Farm and the Veno Alpha had to obey. But I was stuck in a state of panic, memories of the last time he'd mutated flashing before my eyes, and I was too slow. Lora opened the door, charging in without a second thought. The energy flashed around her in brilliant white light as she evolved, sending chairs sliding across the tiled floor and momentarily blinding the humans in the room.

She kept her power controlled so that she didn't injure anybody—containing it, filling her eyes with raw electricity. She was a perfect storm.

Dickward turned to face her and the farmers scrambled behind her like she was their shield.

I wanted to be her shield.

I wanted to protect her from all things bad in the world, but Lora could look after herself. She'd wiped out a building full of Night Walkers. But she looked so fragile next to Dickward's werewolf frame as he leaned over her.

The rest of the pack followed her, placing themselves in front of the farmers to protect them from the Veno Alpha, but I couldn't follow. Stuck in a bubble of fear, my body wouldn't allow it, so instead, I watched with a strange sense of self-pity.

Seeing the pack gather and usher the humans to safety on my side of the door and talk reason with Dickward only made my heart ache. I wanted to join them, to be a part of it. I craved that unity—to fight alongside them without the worry of what I might do and who I could become if I lost control.

I'd only ever felt that unity once, whilst I was a true Beta and in control of half the pack, leading them to Lora on the other side of the fence. I'd had the Alpha hormones. It had forced the pack to see me as one of them. I wasn't a Gen. 2 or an Alpha, but I'd felt like both for those two days, and it made me only the more bitter now.

I had once known what it felt like to be included.

But I was an outcast once again—the freak who couldn't mutate or evolve.

I was a liability.

Lora tried to talk Dickward down as the farmers, safely tucked by my side, wiped their foreheads on their sleeves and their tears from their eyes. I should have reassured them that everything was in control, told them to take the day off, and ensured everyone was okay, but all I could do was watch my pack work so seamlessly without me.

My gut twisted.

Jealousy?

I was missing out. I overlooked the danger my family was bringing upon themselves, focusing only on the resentment inside.

Missing out on what, exactly?

They were helping me—preventing me from mutating.

I rubbed my face with my hand, hoping it would make me see the situation for what it really was and not whatever toxic thoughts my animal alter-ego seeped into my system. Being scared and angry, two emotions which loosened my control over the inner animal, were a frightful mix. *Calm down.* My head pounded. The nails of my fingers bit into the warm flesh of my palms.

"Ares. What's going on?" My uncle's voice appeared behind me, and absorbed in my own hazy thoughts, I flinched, swung out on instinct, and jabbed his nose with such power it crunched.

Dr. White wailed.

All I could do was stare as the blood ran down his face, pooling; staining his white lab coat red.

So shocked by my own actions, I glanced down at my fist. It had felt nothing more than a minor bruise to me. How had I inflicted such pain with one small move?

My gut twisted.

I'd never acted that way before—not in my human state, at least. My gaze flickered back to my uncle, and the sight transfixed me.

Dr. White held his nose. Several of the by-standing farmers helped him recover, whilst others placed themselves before me in the same way Lora had done to protect them from Dickward just moments earlier.

I'm the monster.

I wanted to apologize, but my mouth wouldn't form the words, saliva thick like glue and sour. I looked at the blood again and my stomach churned.

REAP

My mind wasn't processing the fight between Dickward and my pack in the Observatorium, and it didn't process what Dr. White said to me, either.

It only repeated a single word as I spun on my heels and broke free.

They're stronger without you.

Run.

They don't need you.

Run.

You'll never be one of them.

Run.

Run.

Run.

CHAPTER ELEVEN

HAIL

Lora kicked ass.

We'd been learning how to use the energy, but the Alpha could do *way* more than us.

I'd only just learned to project the electricity from my body and hold it in my hands. It took a lot of focus; despair, too. I thought only of losing Donnah as I pulled the energy from within me during training.

Lora's ball of energy was bigger, brighter, and busier. It zapped about as she warned the mutated Veno dude to calm down, and when he didn't listen, Lora stretched her arms out.

The ball of energy grew. Sparks of lightning formed from her fingertips, and I forgot we were in danger, captivated by the magic in Lora's hands.

Then the Veno charged at us. My attention snapped back to the attacking hybrid, and I stood my ground. I was ready for a fight. It had been too long since I'd last smacked someone, but I didn't get the chance today.

Lora pushed the ball of energy out, and it formed a bluish shield around us.

The Veno bounced from it, and the shock knocked him down until he returned to his human state.

It was the Veno Alpha, Steven—or Dickward, as Ares often called him.

I looked around in shock.

Nobody seemed quite as surprised as me. Jayleigh told me to close my mouth or the static would catch my tongue. I didn't know what she meant, so I looked to Ares to explain, but I couldn't find him anywhere.

Lora fought to reel the shield of energy back into her core whilst I leaned over Tye to look through the door. The farmers were still out there, moving about quickly.

Something seemed off.

They raised their voices, probably worried about us being shut in this room with the Veno, but they weren't looking in our direction.

Finally, the shield went down and Lora collapsed to the ground. She held a hand out to reassure us, so I walked towards the door to check out the confusion in the hallway.

The doctor stood on the other side, propped against the wall with his head tilted back and people surrounding him.

I opened the door.

"You okay?" I asked. All heads turned in my direction, looking up at me in shock. None of them were Ares. "What's up? Where's Ares?"

The doctor pointed down the corridor and spoke through the tissue on his face. "You need to find him, Hail. Get Lora."

I looked back towards my Alpha, still sitting on the floor after using so much energy. "Lora's not doing great right now. I'll go."

The doctor peered through the door and nodded. "Listen to your tablet. Once we're able to, we'll search the cameras and tell you where to find him."

I nodded, still not sure if I was missing something, but not wanting to ask more questions. This seemed too important.

I jogged in the direction the doctor had pointed, turning a few corners and hoping it would lead me to the bunker. A few minutes later, my tablet alerted me to a call from somebody named C. Wilson. I pressed the green button, and the voice instructed me through the tunnels, annoyed whenever I turned in the wrong direction.

He led me up the stairs, higher than I'd ever taken them before, and I ended up in a large room filled with trucks.

REAP

"This is the garage next to the Guesthouse," C. Wilson said. "There are no cameras inside, but we believe Ares is still in the building, so it's safe to assume he's in one of those rooms, my guess being Marshall's, which is on the top floor at the far end." I opened the door to the house and my eyes widened at the sight of the large kitchen, unlike anything I'd seen before. I continued to stare as I followed the voice's instructions through the house and reached a door.

The voice told me to knock, so I did, but there was no sound on the other side.

I waited a few seconds.

"I don't think he's here," I said, knocking again—just once more.

Ares' voice was small when he finally replied, "Hail?"

"Bro, are you in there?"

"No," Ares muttered.

I laughed and said to the voice on the tablet, "Found him, thanks." The voice shouted orders, but I cut him off. "Let me in, Bro."

There was a pause, a moment of silence, and I wondered if he'd somehow left the room. Had he jumped from a window? Or was there another exit?

It was too quiet.

"Ares?" I asked. "You don't have to let me in if you don't want. I just need to know you're okay. Tell me you're fine, and

I'll leave."

I was about to call the voice on my tablet again to see if they had spotted Ares outside the Guesthouse when I heard footsteps on the other side.

He approached the door with caution, and for some reason, it made me nervous.

My mind turned hazy.

It's happening again.

I tried to focus on the door handle and not the colors in my mind.

He stopped on the other side. I heard the jingle of keys and watched as the handle slowly turned and the door opened. I stared at him in horror.

My mind became numb.

It's not real. It's not real.

He looked at me, and I swore I could hear Donnah singing again. Everything turned red and blue.

Had I taken my tablets this morning? I couldn't think of anything but the vision before me, barely noticing the cold sweat building on my skin and the ringing in my ears. I focused only on calming my mind.

It's not real.

Then I blinked, and everything was back to normal.

"Hail?" Ares looked confused by my reaction. He'd been speaking whilst my mind danced to Donnah's music. I didn't know what he'd been saying.

I smiled and played it cool.

"Ares! Thanks for opening up, Bro. I thought you'd jumped from a window or something. So this is Mad Marshall's place, huh?" I peered inside, shocked. I'd expected it to be dark, messy, and smelly.

It wasn't.

I ignored Ares' questions and let myself inside. He told me I looked shaken. He asked if I still saw things that weren't there, but I didn't want to tell him what I'd seen when I looked at him. It didn't matter because it wasn't real. It was just the venom, still playing with my mind after all this time.

The visions I couldn't yet shake.

"I was just surprised, that's all," I said. "I didn't expect you to let me in."

Ares stepped backwards, towards the window. I didn't know if he believed me, but he didn't push further, and he changed the subject instead.

"Is Lora okay?" he asked.

I nodded. "She's amazing. Knocked that Veno out without even touching him, but she collapsed afterwards from using too much energy. You know how it drains her to hold the entire Titanium pack together and keep you human, and to project her energy like that was just a little too much—"

"What did you say?" Ares cut me off. He turned back from

the window to face me, his forehead wrinkled with pain.

"Lora collapsed," I repeated. "She's okay, though! She'll bounce back after a little nap. Sleep fixes everything, Bro, I'm telling you. It recharges the batteries."

"You said it drains her to keep me human." Ares stopped blinking, his eyes welling up with water.

Shit.

I forgot Jayleigh had told me to keep that a secret. She'd only found out because she'd been snooping through Lora's notes as she filed Dr. White's paperwork. I was supposed to keep it to myself.

"I didn't say that," I said, backtracking, slowly retreating towards the door. This would land me in so much trouble. Jayleigh was going to kick my ass.

"Hail, please." I'd never seen Ares so broken, so needing. "Don't lie."

I stopped moving, unsure of what to do.

Making Ares believe that he'd imagined it was mean. I knew what it was like to question everything going on around me, and he looked torn enough as it was. I couldn't do that to my best friend. "Okay. I did say that, but please don't tell anyone that I told you!"

Hopefully, we could keep this between us and forget it. I crossed my fingers behind my back.

Ares was stunned, dropping his face into his hands. "She's

been keeping me human. It's just like Benji said. Our auras fuse, and it drains my darkness. Well, he failed to mention that it drains Lora's light, too!"

I didn't know who Benji was, but I didn't feel it was the best time to ask. Ares' voice rose. The pain in his voice shifted into a low growl.

"This whole time, I thought… I thought I had it under control, but she's been…" A darkness I didn't like twisted in his eyes. "She's been keeping the monster at bay. All this time, it was her. I've never been in control. She's been controlling me."

Ares stormed past me.

I spun to stop him, reaching out for his arm, but he shoved me into the dresser.

"Bro, wait!" I called after him in a panic, racing down the stairs. Damn, this guy could move fast when he wanted to. "Where are you going?"

"To clear the air," he bit back.

Good, because I was really struggling to breathe.

CHAPTER TWELVE

LORA

A Veno died, and like the dead Titaniums, the body was yet to be found.

Steven's anger was understandable. It was justified. I knew the loss he was experiencing and the feeling of such betrayal. I wasn't sure how the Veno's Alpha bond worked—whether he sensed his hybrids on a spiritual level and caught glimpses of their auras—but losing them was just as painful, judging by his reaction.

He was in his human state now, clothes back to size but still torn, and he was yet to wake.

I'd tried to hold most of my power in, not wanting to injure the Veno, only catch him by surprise and disarm him, but

REAP

I was still learning to master my abilities and I feared I might have done a little more than taser him.

Diego and Tye carried Steven onto the balcony as we waited for him to regain consciousness.

I would never consider the Veno Alpha a friend, but I had to admit that he differed from what I'd expected. We could work together now that we were no longer rivals. We had shared experiences, both of us surviving our own Alpha Arena, and I found a new form of respect for him because—unlike me—he'd won on purpose.

He was the only other Gen. 1 I'd known and not killed.

I had no reason to kill him today.

He'd only mutated because of the anger at losing a pack member and not knowing how, why, or where they'd gone. We both needed justice for our fallen.

When Steven did finally wake, it was silent. There was no change in his raspy breath, no sign that he'd regained consciousness, and no sign of him losing control of his anger again.

I only knew he'd woken because I felt him watching me. My skin crawled, not knowing how long he'd been staring at me. I offered him a small smile. He wasn't a being of many words, and honestly, I preferred not to hear him speak. His voice made me just as uneasy as his glare.

Wilson informed us that there had been an incident with

the farmers whilst we'd been taking control of the mutated Veno situation, but reassured us that everything was under control and White would be with us soon. He also explained that Ares was with Hail and pointed towards the screens as they maneuvered the corridors of -3, making their way back to the Observatorium with haste.

I didn't ask where they'd been. I could ask Ares myself.

He burst through the doors, and my body—still not fully recovered from the incident—weakened at the sight of him.

The shadows.

His aura…

Ares appeared to be painted black—a broken pen spilling ink onto the white pages of the Observatorium walls.

His eyes settled on me and he stormed up the ramp, Hail trailing behind and trying to drag Ares away.

"Ares? What's going on?" My voice didn't shake, didn't break, didn't show how truly scared I was of the look in his eyes.

My mind screamed *danger*. But maybe that was the inner animal trying to keep me safe, because this wasn't Ares. This wasn't the boy I'd cuddled this morning or the boy who'd have sacrificed his humanity to save me. He wasn't the same person who'd once cried, huddled on the floor of the barn, upon realizing what The Farm was.

I didn't recognize the person before me.

REAP

The shadows of his aura stretched out, taking hold of the railings, climbing the walls, and licking the skin of those surrounding him.

"When were you going to tell me?" His voice clapped through the room, bouncing from the shiny walls. All eyes turned in our direction. "I thought I was in control of it, Lora." He laughed to spite his words. "I thought I could hold it back."

"What are you talking about?" I reached out. If I could touch him, hold him, I could calm the madness and tame the monster, and we could have a reasonable conversation.

"Don't." He snapped his arm away. He'd never shied from my touch before. If anything, he'd been too greedy for my affection. It hurt. This form of heartache was unfamiliar to me. I knew the pain of betrayal, but the sting of rejection was something new.

My mouth opened, but I said nothing, too shocked.

"Don't touch me," he spat. "I don't want to hurt you, Lora."

My heart stilled. "Ares?" It was all I could manage.

All energy vanished from my body, feeble, and stars danced in my vision.

How did he know?

I'd told nobody except White and—

No, there was no way he knew about that.

I recalled Wilson's story of the farmers in the corridor and wondered if Ares had somehow sucked the information from White whilst we'd been with Steven.

It didn't matter how he'd found out. The hows were irrelevant. The only thing that mattered was that he knew and was not happy about it.

"I can explain—"

"Well, please!" His voice raised, louder than I was comfortable with. *My* Ares didn't talk like this. "Be my guest."

And I stood there for an eternity, biting my lip to stop it from quivering. I squeezed my thumbs and searched for a glimpse of Ares within the darkness.

I couldn't find him.

CHAPTER THIRTEEN

ARES

I thought we were past the lies.

I'd lost count of how many times Lora hid things from me. We were supposed to be a team: Alpha and Beta versus the apocalypse.

But team members don't lie to one another.

Lovers don't hide things.

We were supposed to work through our problems together.

As Lora stood speechless before me, I quickly realized that we had never been equal in her eyes. She was, and would always be, the leader of the pack—an entitlement she'd earned—whilst I was the leader of The Farm; a burden I'd inherited.

I didn't deserve my title. I'd never earned a thing, only

taking what they gave to me—I wasn't worthy of it; not like Lora.

She would always be the better of us, and as she struggled to find the words to explain the situation without making herself out to be the bad guy, I concluded we could never be equal.

This relationship could never work because Lora didn't accept me for who—what—I was. My Gen. 3 traits might have once been what attracted her, but now they were nothing but a burden and, of course, she felt the need to fix me.

My humanity wasn't her responsibility.

Saving me was draining her, and I'd never asked for it. Even if she'd offered, I'd have turned her down because saving my humanity wasn't worth risking her health. It wasn't worth weakening her bond with the other hybrids.

I wasn't worth it.

I was who I'd always been—a helpless boy with an evil monster inside. I was an animal.

I shook my head, still waiting for her answer. "Who are you to control me?" I tried to keep the rage back, sucking my tongue against my teeth as my alter-ego began to merge through the barrier that separated us. "I didn't ask for your help, and I never asked to be salvaged, Lora. Somehow, I would have found a way without your input. But no, the mighty Titanium Alpha must save the day because, God forbid, I become the hero in my story." I inched closer to her; close enough to smell the salt of the tears rolling down her cheek. "I never needed you to rescue me. I just needed your acceptance, but you can't even offer me that. You've been altering me behind my back." I drew in a shaky breath. "And that's all the proof I need."

"What do you mean?" I could just make sense of her words as she trembled beneath me.

"I'll never be enough for you because I'm not like you, and it doesn't matter how hard you try to make me into one of them." The pack watched in concern for their Alpha as I nodded towards them. "I'm never going to change. Do you know why? Because I'm a Gen. 3, Lora. I can never be the person you want me to be."

I'll never be the person you deserve.

I turned before she had the chance to reply.

I couldn't stand to hear her sob, apologize, or talk sense, because I'd cave if she tried.

I understood that there were reasons for her lies, but I wouldn't allow myself to hear them—in fear that I'd wrap her in my arms and kiss her until I stole every last flicker of light.

Maybe, in the strangest of ways, walking away before she could explain made me the hero.

I saved her life by not touching her. So I vowed to never touch her again.

CHAPTER FOURTEEN

ARES

I moved with no destination in mind, weaving through the corridors of -3, feeling as though the white walls were closing in on me.

Memories of these halls invaded my mind, thick and fast. Images of Dr. White and Uncle Flynn as they chatted, Mom holding my hand, her graying hair swishing from side to side. Nothing of significance, but it was everything—familiarity when all else felt lost.

I turned another corner.

Heads turned in my direction and flitted away as I entered the bunker. I'd seen the farmers act the same way with Marshall, and now they feared me as they'd once feared him.

REAP

It was surprising how quickly news traveled in this place. The farmers liked to gossip.

They knew I'd hit my uncle. It wouldn't have surprised me if they already knew what had just unfolded in the Observatorium.

I forced my mind away.

They likely saw me as a monster, a replica of my brother and father before him. I didn't need to prove anything to them.

"Ares!" Dr. White called from the other side of the bunker. My pace slowed. I wasn't sure if I could look my uncle in the eye after what I'd done, but I needed to apologize.

I turned and he approached with caution.

"I'm not Solace, Dr. White," I said. "I don't bite."

My uncle pursed his lips as he considered. "No, I suppose not, but you have a rather powerful swing, Ares." I had to hide a laugh, not sure why I found the situation amusing.

Doc's nose angled, broken. The skin changed color around that area, and one of his eyes had swelled so he could barely open it. His glasses perched atop a white bandage.

"I'm sorry for hitting you," I said.

He nodded. "I'm sorry for sneaking up on you."

I nodded, too.

We both lingered.

I should have said more, but my mind went into overdrive. Too much had happened. Too many thoughts buzzed around in my head: memories of the bunker, trying to stay in control, the pain in Lora's face, *the urge to run*, the missing hybrids, memories of Dr. White teaching me to write, the smell of Lora's tears, *the primal need to hunt*.

"Excuse me," I rushed past my uncle before I could hurt anyone else.

Dr. White's eyes lingered on me. I sensed his gaze and his worry.

"Ares!" Chipper's voice filled the bunker, and the anger flushed through me in a higher dosage.

"Now isn't a good time, Chipper." I turned away and prayed Dr. White would take control of the situation.

"But you promised me a tour."

"I did," I called back. "But not right now."

Why had we ever invited The Sanctuary to join us on The Farm? Chipper was testing my patience, and he knew it.

I didn't wait around to hear his reply.

Trees, water, and earth. I needed to be in nature and away from people.

There were too many farmers between here and the stairs. Chipper ensured the lift was not an option, so I made a brisk jog for the Biome.

I sealed the doors, entered the artificial rainforest, and ran into the trees. I screamed in agony, throwing my head back and arms to the sides. Had this been a real rainforest with wildlife—

birds—I'd have scared them away with the inhuman noise that erupted from me.

It was the only way to release the anger without welcoming my alter-ego. I yelled until I ran out of breath, and even then. When black areas spotted my vision, and I felt my lungs might crumble, I finally fell to the ground.

She lied.

After everything that had happened in the past few days, this was all that mattered.

She lied again.

She thought she was doing right by me again, but she only built more walls between us.

I didn't cry. Too enraged with fury. Too exhausted.

Every part of me wanted the earth to open up and swallow me whole. Everyone would be safer that way.

I propped myself onto my elbows, not bothered by the drool that spilled from my mouth, formed from the bitter taste of my regret.

You fool.

Things had been going too well. It had been smooth running up to this point. It had almost been easy—too easy.

I'd been in a bubble. I was too naïve for this, caught up in advanced technology and false encouragement.

Even Lora's hesitation when replying to me last night had been a warning sign. I'd asked if she trusted me, and it took a second too long for her to decide. She shouldn't have needed to question it. But I became so wrapped up in the moment, and too excited to show her the hidden pools, I'd overlooked her reaction.

She didn't trust me, but I couldn't blame her—I didn't trust myself either. Especially not now.

I crawled towards the stream, washing my face in cold water, and then I turned onto my back and stared up at the fake sky above.

A low hum emanated from my tablet as it vibrated on my arm. Somebody called, again and again, but I ignored it each time. There were cameras in here, so they knew where to find me if they needed me.

I stayed put for a while.

Eventually, the craziness in my mind settled, and I looked around, realizing that I laid across the large boulder Mom had once sat me on whilst she plastered my wounded finger. I'd forgotten that memory until now.

Floppy—Marshall—had given me a map, and I'd showed Mom as though it were the greatest gift in the world.

And…

What had Mom said whilst she'd been trying to distract me, to divert my attention from my wound?

To wave at Dad through the hidden camera. He'd watch on his secret screens…

REAP

I turned in the direction she'd pointed, scanning the walls for clues.

In my time leading The Farm, I'd never seen Father's secret screens or heard them mentioned. But they were called secret for a reason.

The camera would still be there.

I waded through the shrubs, weaving between banana trees and coffee plants, toward the wall, peering up at it in wonder.

There was no camera there. It was blank. No sign of cables or light reflecting from the lens. Nothing. Unless… the camera used the same masking technology as the rest of The Farm's drones.

Of course it would. They wouldn't leave a camera in plain sight for anybody to find.

I sighed and tilted my head. A camera on the wall would still leave shadows. It was hopeless.

I'd have to find another way to find Dad's secret screens, but how? I paced backwards and forwards as I considered, legs brushing through leaves. Without recollection, I returned through the city of plants to the boulder next to the stream, and my gaze fell to something on the ground beside it.

My hand reached into my empty pocket.

Mom's necklace. It must have fallen out whilst I was lying on the large rock. Its chain still knotted with the second necklace, pulling them both to the dirt.

I stared at it, and I blinked as I processed what I was seeing.

The pendants laid at a 180-degree angle to each other, one backward whilst the other remained facing upright. The slight differences in shape made sense now.

I picked them from the ground and pieced the pendants together, snapping them into place, and studied the peculiar shape the interlocked jewelry made.

Whoever had left the second necklace for me to find had intended for me to work this out. It was a part of their game, their message.

But what were they trying to tell me?

Why the secrecy?

Did it have something to do with Marshall? I'd found the second necklace in his room.

Or was it about the farmers' revolution? I couldn't see it being a coincidence that someone had left the necklace for me on the same day the farmers killed the hybrids.

My frustration grew as I battled my mental list of questions. I exhaled through my nose, and my gaze wandered back towards the wall with the hidden camera.

What if somebody else knew about Father's secret screens? The same person who'd left me the necklace in Father's old room.

What if this person wasn't trying to play games but help

me?

Were they leaving clues on how to get there? And if so, why not tell me in person?

I closed my fingers around the necklaces.

If there was one thing I needed, it was a distraction, just as I'd distracted myself with finding The Farm's leader during Phase 1.

I would work out what this all meant—what games the owner of the second necklace wanted me to play.

But Lora's games? I still needed more time to process and accept those. I couldn't forgive her anytime soon.

CHAPTER FIFTEEN

LORA

I gasped for breath. The world closed in on me and I could only listen to Ares' words, watching the shadows of his aura stretch so far they filled the room in darkness, and force back the emotion.

Bottle it up. Close the door. Shut everyone out again.

Because the alternative would be to release my anguish in a hopeless burst and turn everybody to ash. That was not an option, so I fought to keep it inside and let Ares spit his venom.

He could have been a Veno with the heartlessness of his words, and when he and his shadows left the room, I sank to the ground, not caring if the others would see it as weakness, heartbreak, or anything else.

REAP

I no longer choked on the density of his aura, but my own regrets.

Why had I kept it from him?

Why did I think that the truth of his slipping humanity was something he didn't need to know? *The same reason you hide where you go at night.*

I needed space, so I picked myself from the ground and looked to each member of the pack, not focusing on their expressions long enough to understand what they made of the situation, then swiftly descended from the balcony and through the door.

I turned a few corners into an area of -3 I wasn't familiar with and then leaned against the wall. The air was cooler here, thankfully. I let my head fall back and my eyes close.

How had we fallen from such a height? Last night, I'd have sworn I was on top of the world. Ares had claimed to love me enough to light the world on fire, yet he wouldn't allow me the chance to explain myself.

His inner animal was becoming more dominant, demanding, and the only way to stop it was to delve deeper into trouble. To tell more lies. To betray his trust once again.

Unable to hold the tears back, I stopped fighting and let the full weight of what had just happened crash down on me—a tidal wave washing over me with no remorse. This was my doing. I deserved every word Ares had spat at me. My chest ached with heartbreak, and no matter how much air I tried to inhale through my sobs, it never felt enough to fill my lungs. I was losing control.

The lake… I needed to get to the lake.

Thankfully, before the energy could build past its limit, footsteps alerted me to somebody's approach, and I quickly wiped my face with my sleeve. The fabric would clear away my tears, but it wouldn't hide my bloodshot eyes or the puffiness of my cheeks, which were sure to have swelled up by now.

"Oh, Lora," White's voice was like a comforting hug as he rounded the corner and saw me standing against the wall, staring into oblivion. The white walls of level -3, so different from those of the barn, did well to numb my mind. "I heard what happened and I'm so sorry. A hot temper runs in the family, and I'm afraid to say that Ares is much like his brother and father in that respect."

I shook my head, still too ashamed to face White. "It's not his fault," I said, my voice void of life. I didn't blame Ares for the way he reacted. Wouldn't I have done the same? I'd betrayed his trust.

I *had* done the same, worse, any time I lost faith in those closest to me.

"Well, anger management techniques are not something I would usually suggest for a hybrid, but under Ares' circumstances, I might deem them appropriate." White offered a friendly smile.

"I don't mean the anger," I corrected White. "He had a right to be angry. We've been so wrapped up in trying to fix him, to restore his humanity, I never thought to question if it's still what he wanted. From all my time of knowing him, I thought he'd try anything and everything to remain human. But people change, and their wants change, and Ares... Ares has changed." I gulped the words out. "I should have asked him."

"My dear." White stepped closer now, joining me against the wall and crossing his arms over his chest. "You made that decision as his Alpha. It's your right to choose what is best for your pack members and make decisions based on what you believe to be favorable to them."

"But they're not animals, White! They can decide for themselves." I blurted, looking at the doctor for the first time since he stepped into the corridor. My mouth hung open as I witnessed his bruising. "What happened to your face?"

"Don't worry about my face. As with most things, it will heal in time. Instead, why don't you tell me how you're feeling?"

I stared at the peculiar angle of his nose. This wasn't an accident. I'd thrown enough punches in my time to know a fist would leave that kind of injury. "Upset, guilty, distracted, angry, self-loathing... would you like me to go on?"

"And why do you feel these emotions?"

"Because I kept the truth from Ares," I said. I should have

added 'impatient' to the list. White knew, so why was he asking? To cause me more pain; draw it out; make me suffer for hurting his nephew? "I should have told him what I was doing. I should have given him the option to choose between staying human and merging with his animal state. It wasn't my decision to make."

"And why didn't you give him the option?"

"For the same reason as you…" The answer hung in the air between us.

The doctor pursed his lips. We'd agreed not to speak about our night meet-ups in unsafe areas, but my need to share the blame was too strong. White may not have been altering Ares' aura, but he was working to change Ares' just as much as I was. We both feared Ares losing grip on his humanity, and the desperation had led us down a much darker road. In doing so, we might have lost a little humanity of our own.

It was highly unethical to be experimenting on somebody without their permission. I tried to justify it, to make myself feel better about it, by convincing myself that we weren't physically experimenting on Ares. I was only stealing DNA swabs in his sleep so that White and I could manipulate them. But the guilt ate at me. If Ares ever found out about that…

"Do you regret it?" White asked. It was a vague question, most likely because of the spying cameras around us.

I fiddled with my sleeve, picking at a seam.

REAP

He was no longer talking about what happened with Ares in the Observatorium. He knew that answer; knew that I would go to the ends of the earth to keep Ares in control.

My gaze landed on the bruise of White's left eye, bloodshot from the impact. He winced a little as he noticed me studying, and my gut twisted.

Ares did this.

A sweat broke out over my skin and the guilt choked me again.

Oh, shit.

"No," I said, only wishing I *did* regret it—I was just as much a monster as Ares' alter-ego. "You know what Ares is capable of when he's not fully in his human state. If he lets the animal take control, then... then I can't be with him. I can't watch him deteriorate, or hurt the people I care about. I will never stop loving him, but if he loses his humanity, it will end our relationship, and that's something I can't bear to imagine... I can't lose him."

"So there's still hope that this is fixable, if you believe that your relationship has not yet ended? You still believe that you can make him see sense?"

It was a silent agreement. Despite everything that happened today, we would continue our program. It was likely that Ares needed it now more than ever.

"Yes." I straightened up, pulled the wrinkles out of my

clothes, and tucked my hair behind my ear. "I can do that. I can make him see sense. Thank you for finding me. You're the only one who understands."

"That's what I'm here for, Lora," White said, squeezing my shoulder and offering a sympathetic smile. I turned away, my feet the only sound within the hallway as I formed a plan of what I'd say to Ares. But as I rounded the corner, White called my name and I retraced my steps.

"Lora!" I poked my head around the wall, facing White and his bruising. His broken nose was evidence he knew exactly what Ares was capable of. "Be careful."

My gaze dropped away from White's.

I couldn't imagine what might happen if Ares refused to see sense—the lengths I would go to.

Since the Alpha Arena, I'd claimed that love is a distraction, but now I knew it was so much more. Love is hope and acceptance, but above all else, love is a burden.

Love is a responsibility.

And it was my responsibility to keep Ares from doing something he'd never come back from. I couldn't let him lose control. And if I had to sacrifice my own humanity in the process of saving his, then that was a burden I would carry.

Because I loved him, and I knew he would do the same for me.

CHAPTER SIXTEEN

LORA

Ares was somewhere above ground.

I'd already followed his scent to the Biome, and then back to the lift, not needing to track the path he'd taken, but wanting to get a feel for his head space before I saw him. Knowing where he'd gone after our argument told me he'd wanted space. Only five people had access to the Biome.

I pushed the button to 0, sensing through the Alpha bond he was distant—far enough to be above ground—and clasped my hands together as I waited for the lift to escort me back to fresh air and cloudy skies.

The doors opened, and I inhaled, holding the breath in my lungs for as long as I could.

I would never again complain about the freezing temperatures of the morning or the heat of the sun in the middle of summer. After being holed up underground for so many hours of the day, I found time to appreciate the living world around me before making a brisk jog in Ares' direction.

Training had resumed today, and the hybrids continued their routine lessons as I passed. Some stopped to stare, and guilt tickled my stomach. I should have been spending more time with the Omegas. If losing four hybrids yesterday had taught me anything, it was that I needed to do better, but I couldn't do anything until The Farm had its leader back—until I had my Beta back. I offered the hybrids the best smile I could manage under the circumstances, the nerves, the worry of what might happen once I found Ares.

I tracked him past the hybrid camp and the Veno barn, towards the Guesthouse and The Sanctuary's camp. Part of me doubted he'd be with Chipper. He wouldn't have the patience for the nosy human's questions, especially after the encounter he'd had with White—if he could hit his own uncle, then the annoying stranger would stand useless to Ares' rage.

My theory proved correct as I drew closer to the Guesthouse; Ares' scent led me to the front door. I knew he was in there. I could sense him.

I reached for the door handle, my fingers hovering over it but never touching.

REAP

Would he even want to see me? What if he denied me again—turned me away and cast me out?

What was he doing in the Guesthouse in the first place? Was he busy? Would I be interrupting?

My hand retreated from the handle. I could come back later.

Only, this was important.

I stared at the wood of the doorframe for a long while, battling with the fear in my mind.

It was my responsibility as an Alpha, if nothing else, to convince him. Ares' humanity was at stake.

I took a breath, squeezed my thumbs, and built the courage to open the door. My hand reached out once more, and this time wrapped around the cold metal handle.

I could do this. It was just a door.

"Lora?" A voice stopped me from entering the house and I sighed in frustration before turning. I'd been so close.

"Chipper," I seethed. "How are you settling in?"

His arrogance replaced any kind of friendliness he'd once offered. "I'm not settling in. You have promised me a tour of the underground world, yet nobody will show me around. How can I possibly settle in when I don't know what you're up to down there?"

I did my best not to snap. "I'll get somebody to—"

"No," he said. "I need a leader to show me around,

somebody who can answer my questions, not one of your puppets or lousy farmers."

"Excuse me?"

"If you want to use my people for your war, then I have every right to be included in what goes on below ground. Something's going on around here. Being a leader myself, I know when things aren't running smoothly, and something has rattled you since the moment my people arrived."

Shit.

I sighed, not liking the truth. "You're right."

My gaze danced from Chipper to the Guesthouse, and then back again. Ares would have to wait. Maybe it would be better to give him more time to calm down, anyway…

I looked at my tablet. It was a little after ten. We still had two and a half hours before The Sanctuary's kitchen—a marquee in the middle of their camp, kitted out with cooking equipment and some of The Farm's most experienced chefs—would serve lunch. We thought it would be best that The Sanctuary didn't interact with the hybrids too often. A fight between hybrids was even. If a fight broke out between a hybrid and a human? There was no question on who would win. The Sanctuary didn't train like the farmers, not yet. They wouldn't stand a chance.

"We have enough time before lunch. I could show you around now, if you'd like?" I said the words through gritted teeth, hoping the human would see just how much the interruption aggravated me and offer to postpone.

Chipper's face lit up. "Fantastic. Let me gather the group."

"Just you," I said, snappy. "Level -3 is too busy right now. I'm happy to show you around today, and your group is welcome to explore once everything has settled down."

Chipper understood what I was suggesting. There was something going on. My honesty seemed to earn his respect and his posture changed from upright to something a little more relaxed. "Of course. Thank you," he said.

I nodded, took one last look at the Guesthouse, and then regretfully led Chipper away, promising myself that I'd speak to Ares at lunch. Just a few more hours.

Chipper wasn't as annoying as we walked past the hybrid camp and I went into more detail about the training done above ground: target practice, building stamina and strength, mental challenges. This was Phase One training.

"And what happens when the hybrids pass Phase One training?" Chipper asked as we loaded into the lift.

"Let me show you."

Pushing the button for -3, I said goodbye to the sky once more and felt the life draining from me. I hadn't expected to be returning to the bunker again so soon.

I talked Chipper through different areas of the bunker as we passed, explaining their roles and purpose, although I suspected he already knew what to expect after spying on The Farm for so many years whilst under the vampires' control.

"This is what we call the bridge." I opened the doors for us to enter. "To your left are all the compatible animals for cross engineering, and on the right we have the Phase Two training grounds."

I wandered towards the window to watch the hybrids in combat. We'd cleared away the incubators a few weeks ago, used their parts to build new equipment, and transformed the space below into a high tech training facility. We taught the hybrids about the vampires, both Night and Day Walkers, during Phase One, so learning how to fight and disarm them was the aim of Phase Two.

The challenges used holograms and drones which could accurately replicate both types of vampire, and we encouraged the hybrids to explore their different states within the safety of the enclosed training rooms.

"Come with me," I said, motioning Chipper through the door at the far end of the bridge, towards the metal staircase.

I tried to force out the lingering memories.

Ares had been so excited to show me the infirmary once we'd returned to The Farm, especially the zoo, and he'd taught me about the animals contained there. I'd wondered how he'd learned so much. He must have spent a lot of his childhood exploring the room with his parents or uncles.

REAP

Then he'd shared his plans for a new Phase Two in the room opposite. I'd strolled with him past hundreds of hibernating hybrids as he explained his vision—the same hybrids who now played out his dream.

I gulped back the memory of his enthusiasm, wondering if I would ever see his eyes light up in the same way again.

CHAPTER SEVENTEEN

ARES

I'd always been too sentimental to touch anything in Marshall's room, not wanting to disrupt how he'd left it. His fingerprints still painted the handles of the furniture, like invisible artwork etched on the wooden grain. The sheets were exactly how he'd placed them, and to go around touching things would erase him from the room. So I'd left things exactly as I'd found them—except for the wardrobe, which I opened occasionally.

That all changed today.

I charged into Marshall's room in search of answers, not knowing what I was looking for, but sure I'd know it when I found it.

REAP

Although hurried and eager, I didn't destroy the room. I opened one draw at a time, emptied its contents, and returned each item with care. Upon finding the draws empty, I moved to the bookshelf, and then the desk, and the bedside tables.

My tablet rang multiple times over the next few hours—Dr. White, Jayleigh, Wilson, Hail, Tim—I ignored every call, continuing to search even once I'd been through the entire room, skipping lunch, and deciding I must have missed something.

My mind often drifted to Lora, annoyed that she hadn't come to clear the air—glad, worried, and scared of what might happen if she did. But every time the rage and the betrayal resurfaced, I forced my thoughts back to the pendants in my pocket.

Eventually, the light outside the windows vanished. I sat on the floor in the middle of Marshall's room with my head resting on his bedpost and my legs outstretched, and I listened to my stomach complain.

The room was hopeless.

There was nothing here for me to find. But I couldn't bring myself to leave. I wasn't ready to face the consequences of my actions just yet. I needed to talk to Dr. White and explain what I'd been experiencing, to ask him if there was another way to control the inner animal without draining Lora's energy, and to apologize again for breaking his nose.

And I needed to find Lora.

I wasn't happy about what she'd done, but I could understand her reasons. She hadn't kept it from me to spite me, but to help me, and I couldn't be mad at her for it.

We needed to talk.

I looked at my tablet, surprised to see the time was 21:13.

I blinked at it.

That couldn't be right, surely?

I'd been so taken to finding clues about the necklaces and the secret screens that I'd lost all sense of time.

The Titaniums would be back at the barn now.

I made plans to grab some food from the canteen on -2 and then talk to Lora before bed.

No wonder my stomach was so upset.

The farmers were in their rooms as I escaped the Guesthouse and made a brisk jog for the silo to escape the rain, which had started throughout the day.

I raided the fridge of the abandoned canteen, sat on my usual bench, and ate in silence.

What happened to Dickward? Did they contain him and was he okay?

I'd missed so much, and I regretted not answering the calls throughout the afternoon. They must have been important.

I washed my plate, left it to dry, and then returned to the lift. Instead of pressing the button for ground level, as I'd intended, I made a split second decision to visit the Observatorium and catch up on the day's events. It would only be a ten-minute diversion, I figured.

So I made my way to the screened room, sure the farmers would be happy to fill me in. I needed to apologize to them, too. I'd scared them just as much as Dickward had this morning.

I stepped through the door; the room filled with an expectant hush and I used it to my advantage. "I'm sorry I've been absent," I said, "and I'm sorry for this morning. I shouldn't have lost control like that. It was irresponsible of me."

Nobody replied. It would take a while to rebuild their trust.

"I just want to take this opportunity to thank you all for your hard work. It doesn't get said enough, but I'm extremely grateful for your efforts." Still no movement from the farmers. "Okay." I nodded. "Just pretend I'm not here, I'll just be…"

I pointed to the balcony and then escaped for the higher level, right to the back where the farmers couldn't see—glad to be out of view.

I sat at the desk and logged in, searching for today's incidents, then watched The Farm as the program loaded.

The farmers who'd entered the missing hybrids tent yesterday were still within the interrogation rooms. I pinched my fingers over the bridge of my nose. Crap.

Hybrids had died. And instead of finding out how they'd vanished, questioning the farmers, I'd been hiding in Marshall's room—because I was having relationship issues…

Lora had once told me we couldn't lose sight of the war in favor of each other, yet that's exactly what I'd done.

I needed to squash this.

It was stupid to fight over something so simple. Lora had been doing me a favor, so why was I punishing her?

I turned back to shut down the monitor—I'd ask the hybrids for updates instead—but as I drew my gaze away from the screened wall, something caught my attention.

The barn.

The door sliding ajar, and Lora slipping out.

I watched her make for the silo.

Good, she was coming to find me. She was ready to talk this through like a reasonable adult.

I waited for her and planned exactly what I'd say when she got here.

I'm an idiot. I'm sorry. I love you.

She crossed the screens as she moved from the bunker to the corridor.

I should never have said those hurtful things. We'll make this work without draining your energy.

Suddenly, I was eager to see her, even if she wasn't able to smile after all I'd said this morning. Just to see her face was enough.

And then she turned down a different corridor.

REAP

I stared at the screen and frowned, watching her pick up speed, continuing to make the wrong turns. She wasn't coming to find me at all.

Where was she going?

A sickly feeling grew in the pit of my stomach, though I wasn't sure why.

She vanished behind a door labeled 'Cupboard,' with a large warning sign underneath which read, 'Corrosive Substances—No Unauthorized Personnel.'

I blinked at the screens for a few moments, waiting for her to reemerge.

Three minutes passed.

"Wilson?" I called to Greenman as I descended from the balcony. "What do we keep in that cupboard?"

"Which cupboard?" Wilson asked as he looked at the screens, but I sensed he knew which room I meant.

"The one that Lora just entered. Screen 208."

"Oh." He swallowed. "I'm not sure. I've never actually been in there."

"Do many people use it?" I asked, the tone in my voice suggesting I'd know if he was lying.

I didn't have that kind of power, but Wilson wouldn't risk it; the cameras could tell me what I needed to know if he refused. "Only Dr. White, and recently, Lora."

"And how often does Lora use this cupboard?" I held my

breath, not sure if I wanted to know the answer.

Wilson paused, reluctant. "Every night. She's usually in there for an hour or two, and then she returns to the barn."

My heart dropped. So, not only had she been hiding that she was restoring my humanity through her touch, but she'd been sneaking around behind my back, too.

Every night. She waited for me to fall asleep and then she left.

Why? What else was she hiding?

CHAPTER EIGHTEEN

LORA

I closed the door, waited for the lock to click before flicking on the switch, and the strip-lights blinked to life.

There wasn't much time.

Ares was on -3, and not in the Guesthouse as I'd presumed. I thought I'd be able to sneak back here and destroy the evidence before seeing him again. He'd been hiding away all day, still too angry to face me—too angry to answer his calls.

Another Titanium had died as I showed Chipper around the Phase Two training grounds. This time, I knew the hybrid as soon as I felt the rift in the Alpha Bond. It was Yiri.

I'd taught her to tie a fisherman's knot just days ago—even Chipper had met her. Yet, there was no evidence of her death or where she'd vanished to. Her records no longer existed. There was no footage of her leaving her tent.

We had tried to tell Ares, but he didn't answer.

His carelessness struck a nerve within me, and so I ignored him as he ignored his responsibilities. My energy was better focused on finding Yiri's body, but after an afternoon of searching, combing through data, footage, and records, there was no sign of her.

Waiting for the hybrids to fall asleep that night was painful, and I rushed from my bed with a new sense of urgency once I sensed them resting, and hurried to the silo—but I knew then that Ares had left the Guesthouse, his scent still lingering in the lift.

It was okay, though. I wouldn't be long. After thinking about my talk with White earlier today, I decided we must continue our work, but I had to hide my part in it. A list formed in my mind as I followed Ares' scent through the corridors of -3 until I branched off to the lab.

I wasn't sure where Ares was, but my guess was the Observatorium—the worst place for him to be. I prayed he'd been looking at his computer whilst I tiptoed around, but I sent White a message, just to be safe. He'd be ready for bed, but this was important. I needed the backup.

Now I stood at the entrance to our secret lab. The room was small, as expected of a cupboard which stored chemicals and equipment, closed off behind locked cabinets.

There was a chair at the back of the room which I spent too much time occupying, beside it a bookshelf spewing encyclopedias and textbooks which I'd put back in haste, wanting nothing more than to return to bed and snuggle into Ares' chest.

I slid the bookcase to the left to reveal the real reason I was here tonight.

The hole in the wall gave me access to a room only a few knew about. White had allowed me access once it became clear that I was using my energy to keep Ares in control of the animal state, and together, we'd been trying to create a synthetic energy for Ares to take like medicine, in order to keep his shadows away.

I switched on the lights, and the lab glowed in a dull blue haze, so they didn't interfere with the Titanium frogs in the center of the room. Their tanks were large, filled half with vegetation, and half with water as they spent just as much time in the water as they did on land. I'd usually feed the frogs around this time of night, but now I didn't have the time.

I washed my hands, grabbed gloves from the box, and keyed in the codes to unlock the test chamber. The door popped open, and the air released in a cloud of icy fog.

Last night's experiment sat in a tube. Liquid energy. The answer to Ares' problems, or so I hoped.

White had taught me everything he knew, which he'd learned from Samantha and Flynn. They were both scientists. Biochemists, I recalled. White had always been a psychologist until the war, but being on The Farm with his sister gave him more insight into the world of biology. I'd joked that Flynn had been the real reason White developed a sudden interest in the subject, which he'd shrugged off with a small laugh.

He knew the basics, which he'd taught me. My determination to find a cure for Ares meant I was eager to learn. Tired, weak, but full of fight.

White had started work on a cure whilst we'd been saving Hail from the vampires, alongside a few farmers who trained in this area of science. The cure had started as a hormone replacement until I informed White that it was the Titanium energy that Ares was lacking—it was most likely the reason he couldn't evolve—so we'd switched course.

We studied the glowing frogs, trying to work out how they generated electrical currents, and I projected my energy into a container of plasma.

We ran multiple experiments, aided by the scientists who knew what they were talking about, fusing Titanium frogs' DNA into plasma—fusing my own cells into plasma.

I followed the instructions left out for me whenever I was here alone, which was most nights recently, but skipped the caution signs because I'd read them so many times I could recall their warnings.

We'd come so close. Thirteen days ago, we'd placed an experiment under the light and it shone just as brightly as my energy. The plasma consistencies were as desired. The only thing wrong with it was the temperature. As we'd placed it among Ares' DNA, the test tube exploded.

We'd almost saved Ares' humanity but fallen short because the plasma was 0.5 degrees too hot. It was a small margin, especially for a girl like me, with no academic training, but I couldn't doubt what we were doing or think of the consequences of getting it wrong. I had to remain positive.

I tried to see this as a good sign—that we were on the right path. Trial and error was a tiresome task.

Now it had been another two weeks, and we were no closer.

I stared at the test tubes in my hands and wondered if it was all a waste of time and supplies. Even if we'd found a cure, Ares might have refused it.

But until I spoke to him about his decision, I needed to hide all the evidence that I'd been involved with this. Who knew what he'd do if he found out?

His reaction to this morning had been bad enough.

I pulled out the large test tube that held the suspended orb of my energy, which floated in goo like the universe's smallest star, sparking lightning in every direction. I replaced the current label—'Lora's energy'—with a new one which read 'Titanium Alpha energy'. That way, if Ares ever stumbled across the lab, the label would be too vague. It could have been Benji's energy, or another Alpha before him.

I hurried through the computer files, renaming anything that could count as evidence that I'd been here, acting behind his back, guilty as ever.

My finger hovered over the delete button of the video files.

What if I came clean and told him everything? Would he understand? I could show him our work, and he'd see I did it in good intention; that I was only trying to help.

But I'd have to explain the sneaking around and the fact that I'd hidden so much from him. This was much worse than transferring my energy to him. This was hours upon hours of research, meetings with White and the scientists, and studying.

Ares would mutate if he found out, and then I'd lose him forever.

I clicked the screen. Deleted the video logs. Discarded the evidence.

There might have been something useful in those entries, but it wouldn't matter if Ares had already lost his humanity in finding them—it would all be for nothing.

The videos disappeared, and I logged out of the computer as my tablet lit up with a call from White. I answered, only to find that the doctor wasn't talking to me. He was calling Ares' name and asking him to listen.

My heart dropped to the pit of my stomach. A warning—White was telling me to finish up and get out.

Get out. Get out.

But there were no other exits. I rushed to the door, racing to reach the cupboard before Ares did. I switched off the lab's lights and ducked through the gap in the wall.

My blood boiled with panic.

The adrenaline needed an outlet.

Then came his voice, emotionless and demanding, asking White to open the door.

I pushed the bookshelf back into place as the door handle moved.

It was too late.

I forced back the need to evolve, the need to fight my way out, and the energy which charged my veins. Still, I couldn't shift the uneasy feeling in my stomach, which convinced me that this was all so wrong. Ares couldn't find out.

I couldn't be here.

But I had no other option. They had me trapped.

CHAPTER NINETEEN

ARES

Dr. White scanned his finger against the security lock without looking me in the eye.

My uncle was involved in whatever Lora was doing inside. He'd rushed towards me as I made my way to the cupboard, conveniently being in the right place at the right time, and tried to steer me back towards the Observatorium whilst claiming that I needed to catch up on the death of a new Titanium hybrid.

I told him I was busy and he could update me as I walked, but he trailed behind me, insisting. He tried to call me back, acting like a child who wasn't used to hearing the word *no*. He reminded me more of Marshall in this moment than he ever had before. It was the first confirmation they were in any way related.

He scanned his fingerprint—the most high-tech lock I'd seen on The Farm, besides my childhood bedroom—and waited for my uncle to open the cupboard door, but he turned away. I was glad. I didn't have to see his bandaged nose and purple eye, a visual reminder of what I could do if he got in my way. He stood out of arm's reach as I twisted the handle, opened the door… only to find Lora sitting in the cupboard with a book in her hands.

I paused.

The cupboard was exactly what the sign said it was. There were storage units against the walls and shelves lined the higher areas. Lora sat at the back of the room on a plastic chair like the ones in the infirmary, her gaze lifting from the pages as I stood in the open doorway, and we stared at each other for what felt like an eternity.

The relief was so strong I almost crumbled from the ease of pressure.

Her eyes remained on me, her expression stern and much like the unreadable Alpha I'd first met on The Farm; guarded after this morning's argument, and she had every right to be. I'd overreacted. Just as I'd overreacted about her sneaking to this cupboard to read.

"Ares." Her voice was full of expectation. "What are you

doing here?"

My mouth hung open. How could I explain this without digging myself into a hole or making it sound as though I was having trust issues?

Not that it was a lie.

The trust would be hard to rebuild.

"I—um." I looked back to Dr. White, who held his hands in the air as though to say *keep me out of it*. "I saw you enter the cupboard, and I became curious. I couldn't understand what you'd be doing in here at this time of night, so I came to find out… that you come here to read." It sounded so petty—stupid—as it left my lips. "And I wanted to apologize for this morning. I was completely out of order for how I reacted and everything I said. I understand why you kept it from me, I do, but it was such a shock and the animal was—"

"It's okay, Ares." Lora stood, placed the book on the shelf, and walked towards me. "I'm sorry too. I shouldn't have lied to you."

She stopped before me, close enough to touch, and I had to force myself not to reach for her. "I won't let you transfer energy to me anymore." I flinched away from her. "Not if it's draining you."

Lora looked down at her outreached hand. "It doesn't hurt me, Ares."

"But it weakens your connection to the other hybrids." I

shook my head. "It distances you from them. I've been thinking about it all day, and how you reacted so badly to the hybrids dying yesterday. You weren't at full strength when you felt the split in the Alpha bond, and that was my fault."

"There's a lot to talk about," she said, her eyes bagged as though she could sleep here and now. "Why don't we go back to the barn and we can talk about this in the morning?" She offered me a convincing smile and switched off the light.

We were okay.

She didn't hate me for what I'd said this morning.

"I'm sorry," I repeated.

"Me too, come on." She ushered me from the cupboard and as we turned, I saw Dr. White's shoulders sag.

"Wait," I said, keeping the door ajar with my foot. "What were you reading? Why don't you bring the book back to the barn? It won't bother me if you want to keep a light on to read in bed."

"Oh, it's nothing, just a hobby I've picked up over the past few weeks—"

"A hobby? You sneak out of the barn every night to practice your *hobby*?" I flinched at the sarcasm in my voice, the accusation behind it. Lora stilled. Her smile faded. "Wilson said you come here every night, that sometimes you're in here for hours."

"Okay," she nodded and looked at Dr. White with an

expression I couldn't quite place. "Since we've been spending more time on -3, I've developed an interest in biochemistry. Seeing the animals in the infirmary, and meeting the scientists—it sparked a curiosity in me. So White showed me the bookshelf, full of your mother's old textbooks and reports, and I've been studying."

Dr. White stepped forwards. "Lora has been researching the Titanium frogs and how they generate energy."

I looked between the pair, a strange nervousness in the atmosphere surrounding us. I could feel it. Lora studied my face a little too obviously—looking for reassurance—trying to see if I'd fallen for her lies.

Because she was lying, or bending the truth. I'd seen her lie enough times to recognize it now. That look in her eyes.

And my uncle was backing her. Saving her. Just as he'd tried to lure me back to the Observatorium. Now they were both trying to get me to close the door. To step away from the cupboard.

But why?

What were they hiding?

"My mother's textbooks?" I asked, playing along. "Can I see them? I don't have much to remember her by, other than…" *memories of her as a Day Walker, the necklace in my pocket, and flashes of my childhood whenever the inner animal awakes.*

Lora and Dr. White shared a look.

REAP

I could smell their uneasiness.

I didn't wait for them to respond. I flicked my foot, opening the door wide, and reached for the light switch.

My first instinct was to reach for the book Lora had been reading. Surely enough, it was a textbook on the Titanium frogs, notes scribbled along the pages in my mother's handwriting.

I picked up another book. And then another. It was much of the same.

My fingers clung to the spine of a journal as I turned back to Lora and my uncle, who remained in the doorway. "You didn't mention it," I said to Lora.

She bit her lip; the silence lingering in the air as she paused. "I didn't want to give you the idea that my mind was somewhere else. But this helps."

"I didn't realize the frogs interest you so much." I ran a finger across the bookshelf. "Enough to sneak away in the night…"

I looked back to Lora as she replied, "I have an enormous amount of energy inside, Ares. More than any Alpha before me. Losing control for one moment could cave the whole of -3. Is it so difficult to believe I'd want to know where that power comes from and how my body generates it?"

No. It wasn't difficult to believe.

Lora felt so much guilt for the people she'd killed in the past. I understood how knowledge could relieve her mind, just as it had mine in my first few weeks after hibernation.

But that's not what this was about.

I sighed. Maybe I was thinking too far into it.

Still shaken over this morning's argument, I was reading into everything, and maybe even trying to look for problems. It was self sabotage.

I shook my head and dropped my gaze to the floor. What was I thinking? We didn't have to be holed up in a cupboard like this. We could cuddle in bed.

Let it go.

I put the journal back on the shelf. Returned the pile I'd stacked on the chair. Then I turned to leave.

And, as I stood approached the bookcase, I glimpsed something behind. A sliver of white light.

I took a double look.

Reached once again for the bookshelf and pulled.

The legs of the bookshelf scratched the floor as I dragged it forward, adding to the other marks I hadn't noticed before. And it moved to reveal all of Lora's secrets.

CHAPTER TWENTY

ARES

White noise filled my ears as I stepped through the narrow doorway. Lora called my name, and Dr. White told her to calm down, but the ringing blocked it all out.

I was underwater and moving against a current, which tried desperately to keep me out of the hidden room, pulling me back, blurring my vision and the pressure... I was in too deep; it built in my head and willed my brain to implode.

The light I'd seen came from a tank of frogs in the center of the room. They were the first thing I noticed before I could understand what the room was, and I walked towards them with little recollection of moving.

Titanium frogs.

Just as Lora had said.

She'd been studying them.

They were smaller than I'd expected, staring up at me with glowing eyes. I met their gaze and then looked past them to the rest of the room.

Lora was in front of me now, her mouth moving, but I couldn't make sense of the words as she pushed her hands against my chest to stop me from moving any further.

I looked over her head at the equipment around the room. Glass containers, microscopes, more chemicals, and… something else on the wall… glowing just like the frogs.

I pushed past Lora to study it.

Trapped inside a glass cabinet was a series of test tubes, each containing a liquid which held a ball of energy. I read the labels.

I processed.

I moved along.

And everything snapped into focus as soon as I read the words on the whiteboard.

Hypothesis: Ares can use a synthetic copy of Lora's energy to control his animal state.

My legs threatened to collapse. I held onto the closest thing to me, fighting to stay upright, but the metal equipment table moved with me as I tried to find my balance.

I fell.

Scalpels and test tubes scattered to the ground, glass smashing and metal bouncing around me.

I scrambled backwards across the floor on my elbows and back—away from Lora, who I could hear clearly now as she tried to help me to my feet. "I'm sorry. Oh, God. Ares, I'm so sorry."

"Stay away from me!" I dragged myself until my back hit against the wall, yet it still wasn't far enough.

Not only had Lora been lying to me, but she'd also been hiding this from me. She'd been hiding it because she knew it was wrong—that I'd have a problem with it. She knew just how much I resented my mother for experimenting on me, yet Lora had snuck from the barn every night to create synthetic energy to *fix* me.

Bile rose in my throat.

I didn't need fixing.

Heat spiked the back of my neck and my blood pounded faster and faster. I was going to mutate.

I needed out.

My hands were slick with blood from the glass on the floor. I hadn't felt the pain as my flesh sliced open, which suggested the inner animal was very much present within me, and I felt nothing as I pried myself from the ground.

"Ares, please. Say something!" Lora cried. Screamed at me. Tried to break through.

I felt everything and nothing all at once.

Hatred.

Rejection.

Guilt.

The need to run.

Betrayal.

The need to break free.

Loss.

Devastation.

Complete hopelessness.

The need to kill.

My mind filled with noise as my human and animal states battled to be heard, fighting for control over my body.

Too loud. Too loud.

All too much.

And then, just for a moment, there was an element of calm. All the noise faded into one stream of sound. I could no longer hear Lora's voice. My mind focused only on the scream —the scream that came from my throat as I held my hands over my ears and squinted my eyes closed.

It knocked the air from my lungs.

It gave me enough peace to control myself and allow my legs to remove me from the situation before my inner animal could do it for me.

I couldn't look at Lora.

Lingering any longer would be dangerous.

I ran.

Through the gap in the wall, out of the cupboard, and past Dr. White, who'd remained outside for his own safety. Down several corridors. In search of four walls and nothing else. I needed containment. I needed a prison to lock myself away in, because when the animal took over, I couldn't be near the farmers or the people lying to me.

Across the bridge and into the infirmary; I knew where I was going before I could process why. It didn't matter so long as I got there safely—killing no one. *Oh, crap*.

The memories started coming thick and fast.

I just needed to hold out for a little longer. Swallow the sickness creeping through me.

I turned the corner, passed the empty classrooms and dorms, to the room at the end of the corridor, and flew into my childhood bedroom.

Empty.

Just a bed and blank walls.

Silence.

Exactly what I needed—what I'd always needed, in fact.

I broke the quiet with another scream; the anger bursting from me in a pool of deception and confusion.

We'd never known what would happen to me as my human and animal states merged into one, whether I'd lose control of my humanity altogether or whether it would take a backseat as the stronger state took over.

I'd thought only of the negatives—the things I'd lose, but never the things I'd gain.

Like my memories.

Before, I'd seen them in flashes. They were wisps of gold in the darkness, gone as soon as they'd arrived, but I could see them now. I could focus on them—remember the context and where and when.

The merging of my two alter-egos wasn't a banishment of one. It was just as its title suggested—a merging. I didn't lose my humanity, nor was I imprisoned within my body.

And, in the same way, my animal state didn't push my humanity aside.

I was both of my alter-egos at the same time—aligned, reborn, whole—as I'd been as a child.

This was the way I was supposed to be, nature's intention.

I screamed again and this time I was sure the sound was mine, not questioning my voice any longer. There were no questions at all, in fact.

My humanity was still intact, working alongside my inner animal instead of the two states battling to be heard. I hadn't lost my humanity; I'd gained myself. I was certain of who I was for the first time since hibernation, sure of my place and the role I was to play.

And I smiled, because all at once, it made sense; why my parents had experimented on me; Gretta, and what had happened the day I met the Day Walker in the interrogation rooms; why my bedroom was void of love.

I remembered what the necklaces were—Mom's necklace and my own. The pendants connected to form a key, fitting into the engraving above my childhood bed and unlocking the steel frame from its place over the staircase.

I didn't know who'd left my necklace in Marshall's room for me to find, but they'd done it as an act of love, a welcoming. They were calling me home.

And I was ready to return to level -4 and embrace my destiny; to embrace who I was.

Who I'd always been.

Different.

A monster.

And that was okay.

CHAPTER TWENTY-ONE

LORA

White didn't deserve the orders I barked at him. This was my mess, fault, and responsibility, but I couldn't fix it alone. I needed his help.

If Ares mutated, then we were all in trouble, and the farmers needed warning of the situation, so I told White to return to the Observatorium, issue a lockdown, and track Ares from the cameras whilst I tracked him by foot.

I ran off before White so much as blinked. He appeared to be in shock, and I prayed he'd heard me.

There wasn't time to worry about White. He'd snap out of it soon enough.

I followed Ares' scent until I reached the bridge, and as I

crossed the glass corridor which separated the zoo from the training grounds, the Alpha bond snapped me backwards.

A fear stronger than I'd ever experienced claimed my body.

I couldn't move. The shadows of Ares' aura seeped through the Alpha bond and leaked into my soul. The darkness which infiltrated my veins took control, paralyzing me from my feet to my fingers.

He'd mutated.

I was stone. It was all I could do to blink through the tears. No other part of my body would listen as I willed myself forwards.

And I wanted to bawl and punch my fists through the windows of the bridge; to hurl my body from the heights and crash into the concrete below with every joule of Titanium energy within me.

I wanted the room to shatter in sync with my world—to test the limits of my mortality, because Ares was gone and without him... how could I hold myself together?

I had rooted my humanity within his.

I'd found myself the day I met him, but now he was something else and I didn't know what that made me.

I'd tried so hard to prevent this from happening, and in doing so, I'd only encouraged it. I'd caused it. In trying to save him, I had ended him.

The shadows swirled through my body, keeping me from

doing something devastating, pausing me in place. *Ares...* I searched for him, reaching for him on a spiritual level and following the connection which bound us. It had once been so strong. Now, it was nothing more than a whisper.

I found only darkness in his place.

Ares losing his humanity didn't cause me pain like losing the other Titanium hybrids; it didn't leave me with scars, but the emptiness was just as savage. I wanted to wear him on my skin like the others. I wanted that invisible reminder of him like a hidden tattoo.

Maybe it was too soon? Maybe it would take time?

But as I stood there, suspended by the shadows, I figured I'd lost all sense. I wasn't in pain because Ares hadn't separated from the Alpha bond—because Ares wasn't dead.

The darkness I felt when I searched *was* him; the shadows of his aura multiplied to new levels, and they released me as though he were prying his fingers from my body, one by one.

He wasn't dead, but he wasn't himself, either. He radiated power. So much power that I couldn't locate where it was coming from. It surrounded me, fogging my senses.

I collapsed to the ground, panting and swallowing back the tears. What had I done to him? What had become of him?

Dazed, I crawled across the bridge, reached my tablet to the security lock, and collapsed through the door as it opened. I pulled myself to my feet, my heart pounding in my ears.

REAP

Now wasn't the time to be feeling sorry for myself, or for blaming myself. I had to act—to accept my mistakes and move on. Fixing Ares should never have been my priority. My mindset was the problem, and I needed to shift again. I needed to find him.

I took my sorrow and guilt and used it to drive me forward, my feet pounding against the tiled floor as I ran through the hallway. Ares' scent led me to the right, and I figured he'd returned to his childhood bedroom—the one he'd told me about but never shown me. I was sure this was the first time he'd been back since White had reintroduced him to that section of his past.

I scanned my tablet against the lock of his door, but it flashed red. Unauthorized.

I scanned it again.

Red.

I called White.

No answer.

I called Wilson.

"Shoot," he said on the second ring.

"I need you to grant me access to Ares' childhood bedroom," I ordered.

"Are you sure that's a good idea? We're tracking the data from his clothes, and they're off the charts, Lora. This isn't like his human or his animal state. It's something else entirely."

"It's… not like his animal state?" I wasn't sure I'd heard correctly, but it made sense. Our tablets would flash orange if Ares had mutated outside the regulated zones. "Then what in hell has happened to him?"

"We don't know. There are no cameras in his bedroom. You know this."

"Grant… me… access." I separated each word with clarity and aggression. The seconds were hours. I needed to see Ares.

"I'm working on it," Wilson's tone was sharp, unphased by my urgency.

I knocked on the door, calling Ares' name, asking him to come and talk. He had every right to be angry at me, and he didn't open the door.

"I can't change your access, Lora. The system won't allow it." Wilson seemed panicked now.

"Shit!"

I ended the call.

The anger surfaced. The only way I could hold it back without mutating was to evolve, so I let the energy push through. I focused on everyone I loved and projected the light through my fingers as I switched into the higher state; the power bursting from me and frying the security lock of Ares' door as I pushed all of my power into it.

I hastily twisted the handle, opened the door, stepped inside.

REAP

But Ares wasn't there.

I studied the room, although there wasn't much to take in.

Empty.

Ares' tablet lay on the pillow of his freshly made bed. Other than that, there was no evidence he'd been there at all… but the smell. His scent had changed. It was Ares for sure—chopped grass and mint—but the grass was mud soaked, and the mint wasn't as fresh as it used it be. The muskiness in the room made me feel someone had picked Ares at the stem and left him in a cold, dark room to dry out.

An engraving on the headboard caught my eye, and I ran my fingers over it. Odd, but nothing of significance. I tried to move the box-like bed, but it was stuck to the ground. I searched for a hidden door but found nothing.

I stood in silence in the middle of the small room, hanging my head back. Helpless.

Defeated.

He was gone.

Panic bubbled in my chest, and my shock resulted in laughter. My body convulsed as I drew in sharp breaths, gasping through painful giggles, and the sound echoed from the blank walls in mockery. I laughed until I cried; the giggles giving way to deep sobs, and I sank onto the plain white bed and let the pillow absorb my tears.

Just like the missing bodies of the dead Titanium hybrids,

Ares had vanished.

I could no longer locate him through the Alpha bond.

I was at a complete loss.

CHAPTER TWENTY-TWO

ARES

Level -4 was exactly as I remembered it, save for the hundred-or-so incubators lined across the back wall, which hadn't been there when I was a child.

My eyes were drawn to the secret screens in the center of the room, directly in front of the steps I descended from, and the man who'd kept this level running whilst the rest of the world forgot it existed.

"Uncle Flynn." I recognized him immediately. He'd barely changed from the person he'd been in my memories. Familiarity shone in his large eyes, a birthmark still occupying his right cheek, his hair longer but still as dark as the night. "Uncle Danny thinks you're dead—the entire farm thinks you're dead,"

I said as I slowly crossed the room, my body feeling different, but not at all out of control. I stopped before him and the screens. My eyes adjusted to the dim lighting.

"It had to be that way after losing your parents. I needed to continue their work," he said. There was no surprise in his voice. He'd beckoned me here, after all. He'd been expecting me. *This* version of me.

"For the greater good."

"Exactly."

I glanced towards the bodies suspended in incubators, then the pin-board on the wall next to the stairs, which displayed several of Marshall's drawings and paintings from over the years, and my schoolwork from my infantry. Two people worked at their desks, dressed in white coats. They didn't acknowledge me.

The room felt calm.

I couldn't believe it had been lying underneath the chaos of The Farm for all these years. It didn't seem to belong to a land of such mayhem.

"Take a seat, Ares," Flynn reached an arm towards the chair.

"No." I couldn't rest now, not with all this newfound knowledge. "I'm happy to stand. I need to stand."

"Of course." Flynn nodded.

"Mother's experiment failed." I gestured towards myself. "As I'm sure you've already realized."

"Oh, yes." Flynn laughed. "Who do you think has been cleaning up after you, Ares? That's why I left your necklace out for you to find. I figured you'd work it out eventually—that we've been here, waiting for you, I mean."

I nodded and ran my fingers over the steel of the control unit. My Father had cautioned me to keep my hands off it when I was last here, even though I was too short to see it. One wrong flick of a switch could expose us to the farmers above. I recalled Father's bitter voice with clarity… some things I'd like to forget again.

"Marshall never knew about -4, did he?" I said.

"Marshall didn't know about you, so he did not need to know about what we do here. It would have defeated our purpose. We're here to monitor your every move and override the primary system whenever necessary."

"Thank you."

"You don't need to thank us, Ares. Your mother's experiment may have failed; however, we still believe you are the key to winning this war. The alter-egos may have collapsed, your ulterior self absorbing your mutations, but you still have the hybrid power and control within you. You are better equipped now."

"So, what do you suggest I do?" I asked. "The hybrids and farmers will not accept me. They've already proved just as much. I cannot lead them." My words were harsh, although I couldn't blame them for trying to change what they didn't understand.

Unlike Flynn, they didn't see me for who I was, and how could they when they only knew half of my story?

"I suggest you wait until morning and then show them why you've always felt different."

I understood the context of his words, if not the full plan.

"And, about Uncle Danny… did he know? Has he known all this time?"

Flynn pursed his lips, looking flustered for the first time at the mention of his ex-lover. "Danny never knew, Ares. He suspected, and knew Samantha had experimented on you for a reason, but he never knew that reason. He had his theories, though."

I nodded, my movements feeling somewhat different.

I'd asked many questions about why Mother had made me a Gen. 3, and every time, my uncle had failed to answer. He'd told me that some truths were better left uncovered. And it was because of this. It's because I was—and always had been—a monster. So much of a monster that he'd been too afraid to ask the truth. And how could he have explained that to me without ruining the experiment?

Everything I'd believed was wrong.

Mother experimented on me because she'd cared. She had loved me enough to do this for me. The experiment was to help me—to give me the control I was so desperately lacking.

REAP

Everything I thought I knew was a warped version of reality, two different puzzles pieced together to create a completely new image. I'd done the best I could with the given information, but it was all patchwork—filling in the blanks.

Now I knew better.

Now I knew everything.

CHAPTER TWENTY-THREE

LORA

"Lora?"

I blinked. Blurry figures hovered above me, surrounded by harsh lighting. Where was I? Certainly not the barn. The mattress below me was plush, and the pillow surely made of clouds.

"Lora," Jayleigh repeated, but it wasn't a question this time.

The pack stood within the confined space of Ares' bedroom, and I scanned each of their faces, although I knew I wouldn't find Ares among them.

"Dr. White told us what happened." Tye stepped forwards to offer me a hand from the bed.

What happened... I'd fallen asleep in Ares' bed, hoping

he'd resurface from wherever he was hiding, but nothing had woken me.

There was no sign of him.

"What about the council meeting?" Diego asked, and Jayleigh shot him a look of warning.

My mind focused elsewhere.

I tuned out the conversations as the pack led me to the Observatorium. I kept fading in and out of the conversation, searching for Ares through the Alpha bond, but hitting a wall of shadows every time.

The farmers gestured to the screens as they told me there had been no sign of Ares since he vanished from his room.

Time moved, but I remained still.

I couldn't process—couldn't function.

"I know this is a lot," Diego said, "but The Farm still has to function. We need a leader."

"I can step in if you'd like." White ascended the ramp to my rescue. The bruise over his nose had darkened overnight, and the bags under his eyes suggested he'd slept as little as I had since I last saw him. "You have more important issues to address."

I nodded. "And you have more experience running The Farm than I do."

"Then it's settled."

I tried to focus on the meeting as the council discussed

more downed drones outside the fence, but I lost track of the conversation. I felt Ares' ghost stab at my heart and twist whenever they mentioned his name. It hurt to hear the council talk about him like he was gone, and it hurt even more to hear them talk as though he were still there, because I knew he was neither.

My confusion and loss overwhelmed me.

The tears fell, and everybody stopped to stare while I sobbed in silence.

Hail joined me in crying.

Jayleigh offered us both tissues and an awkward arm squeeze in the act of comfort. Tye gave me a genuine hug, and I didn't push him away. White stood in the corner, wiping his eyes on a handkerchief and hoping nobody saw him.

"So, where do we go from here?" Steven hissed, void of emotion.

I could have killed him there and then.

Chipper, who had somehow slipped into the meeting without my recognition, added, "We can't stop for the sake of one individual, leader or not—"

"Get out!" I snapped, an uncontrollable fire lighting me up from inside. "We did not invite you here to lead The Farm, but to offer you safety and security. You have no place in this meeting."

Chipper flinched. He was yet to see what I was capable of.

REAP

"I don't mean any disrespect—"

"Get out…" I repeated. This time, it escaped me like a growl.

Chipper straightened his coat, pursed his lips, and backed away from the table. "I can see when I'm not welcome. I will lead The Sanctuary back to our beach caves immediately." He said and scowled at me, his expression turning sour. "Thank you for your refuge over the past few days."

And with that, he removed himself from the meeting.

We stared, and I waited for somebody to tell me I'd acted irrationally—that I should call him back to apologize.

Nobody said anything until Jayleigh muttered, "Good riddance."

So, The Sanctuary packed up and left within the next couple of hours, seeming just as eager to leave as we'd been for them to go.

I offered them food for their journey and nothing more—not even plastering a smile on my face to wave goodbye. Instead, I watched from the Gate Tower as they began their journey, following the crumbling road, and not thinking about the dangers they'd face on their return home.

I wasn't thinking much of anything, in fact.

I stood atop the podium as the gates closed behind them, looking out over the fields and forests beyond the road until I lost track of my place. For a long while, all was quiet. Still.

Numb. Not even the birds sang. I should have noticed it then.

I should have felt alarmed, but I found comfort in the silence.

Only the screams sometime later brought me back to reality, and I froze.

Where did they come from?

Who did the screams belong to?

And then, through the trees at the far end of the field, the people of The Sanctuary reemerged, covered in blood, and their faces washed in terror. It was a nightmare come to life as vampires slaughtered humans before my eyes; bitten, beheaded, limbs torn from their bodies.

Day Walkers.

I tried to steady my breathing. I needed to think. Think. *Think*.

The footage in the Observatorium had insisted the road around The Farm was clear. They should have been safe. But that didn't change the fact that Gretta's Day Walkers were here and taking out The Sanctuary with no mercy.

I was too far to intervene. I couldn't open the gates and I let the Day Walkers in, and I certainly couldn't leave.

I called White.

"Are my eyes playing tricks on me?" I said into my tablet, my voice quivering. "Am I awake? Am I losing my mind?"

"It's very much real, Lora." White was somber through the

chaos behind him. The farmers within the Observatorium yelled, asking for orders and demanding answers. "Raise the alarms," he ordered them.

Moments passed, and the sirens wailed, sending shivers through my bones with each drawn out warning.

War, they cried. *Waaaar. Waaaar.*

"No… no…"

The situation was death and destruction—lives taken right before my eyes. War…

An army of Day Walkers stood at the bottom of the hill, less than five acres away. I wasn't close enough to see their red eyes, but I didn't need to. I recognized them for what they were; heartless, monstrous beings.

Not now.

I couldn't face it. Not after Ares losing his humanity and going missing. Not after the deaths of five Titanium Omegas, and the farmer's rebellion. There was too much occupying my mind. I couldn't face the battle before me.

I wasn't prepared—none of us were.

But that's why the Day Walkers had chosen this moment to attack, right? They'd been waiting for The Farm to fall to its most vulnerable position. The vampires knew we were on our knees, barely holding ourselves together. They'd been expecting it, waiting for it, biding their time.

"This can't be happening," I said, forgetting that I was still on the call to White despite the noise coming from his end of the phone. "We're not ready."

White was quiet for a moment before replying, "I don't think we have a choice, Lora. They're here, and there are so many of them. We have to give it everything we've got. This is the moment we've been waiting for."

No.

The hybrids hadn't finished their training. We were supposed to have an army, to infiltrate Gretta's nest when she'd least expected it, not the other way around…

How had this happened?

We'd stationed drones.

We should have seen the Day Walker army leave their nest.

"I don't understand." But my gut twisted as I recalled Wilson's announcement about another drone issue. I'd bypassed it, so taken by my emotions.

"It's too late, Lora. We need to act now," White said.

I nodded, watching more vampires stalk from the forest. It was too late. It didn't matter what was supposed to happen or what we'd planned.

This was how it would end.

By the end of the battle, only The Farm or the Day Walkers would stand. Only one would live to see tomorrow.

"They're coming," I whispered. "Prepare the hybrids."

CHAPTER TWENTY-FOUR

HAIL

The alarm blared again.

My tablet flashed green—another color code I didn't understand.

I stood in the Observatorium with Jayleigh, Diego, the doctor, and the Veno Alpha, and they were panicking. I'd zoned out a little, wondering what had happened to Ares since he'd lost control, and the next thing I knew, everyone was shouting.

"Chill, Bro." I held my hands out to Jayleigh, knowing that look in her eyes. "Whatever is happening—"

"Chill?" Jayleigh repeated, grabbing my shoulders and squeezing. That brought me straight out of my daydream. "We're going to battle, Hail. The vamps are here, and they're here for blood. They've already wiped out The Sanctuary."

"The... what?" I looked at the screens, watching a crowd building in the field below the gates.

They were back. They'd returned to take my mind again.

"It's time to get revenge for what they did to you." Jayleigh pulled me from the screened room and into the corridor. Diego followed close behind.

We entered a long queue of hybrids and the farmers placed a weapon made of solid metal in my hands.

My very own dagger.

Jayleigh helped secure it within a holster over my chest and then refused the weapon offered to her, claiming to have one in her pocket already. She pulled out two daggers to show me as the queue charged forwards.

We ran for ages at a steady incline. When we reached the end, through a slanted mechanical door, we were no longer on -3 but just behind The Farm's gates.

"Bro, this is happening," I said and turned to Jayleigh as we took our places on the frontline. I didn't have time to process why we'd been in the queue or where we were running to, but Lora was standing atop the Gate Tower, wind whipping her short hair behind her, and facing us with fury in her white, glowing eyes. The Veno Alpha was climbing the Gate Tower to join her.

"It's happening," Jayleigh replied, taking a deep breath.

REAP

"Are you ready to kill some Day Walkers?"

I was ready for a scrap, but these things were already dead. I didn't like my chances.

I gripped my dagger with both hands.

At least I'd be with Donnah again by the end of the day if things went horribly wrong.

"Sure," I said, my jaw tight, "let's kill some Day Walkers." And I switched into my evolved state. I was thankful for the extra training I'd squeezed in over the past few weeks, now able to evolve without mutating first. It had been slow progress, as my mind liked to wander.

Whispers surrounded us.

Through the gates, I could see the dead people running forwards.

It was time.

I turned to Jayleigh and squeezed her hand in mine.

"I'll see you on the other side, wherever that may be," she said through her smile, her eyes glowing with anticipation. I envied her for enjoying this. Her confidence was assuring, relieving my nerves just a little, but it wasn't enough to ease my racing heart. Each beat sounded in my ears like a drum.

Jayleigh squeezed my hand in return, before turning to Diego and kissing him with a passion that could end the apocalypse, and I had to look away—not at the other Titaniums, who appeared just as scared as me, and not towards the gate. I glanced up.

Lora watched us, her eyes searching for somebody in the crowd, but I was sure that Ares wasn't here. He was better off staying well away. Safe. Although whatever had become of him was likely just as violent at the dead things outside the fence.

Lora nodded as she caught my eye. I didn't nod back, not knowing what she meant. But then Jayleigh marched forwards, leading the crowd of evolved Titaniums through the gates whilst the mutated Venos lingered behind, waiting for their Alpha's orders.

We charged through the gates.

I ran as fast as my legs would take me, off the road and onto the field, yelling at the top of my lungs—my voice rasped with a fearless edge.

You got this, Bro. Make some dead people even more dead.

I smelled the human blood, even from this distance. It sent a wave of anger through my body as I projected my energy into a ball and waited for Lora's command. Her voice floated through the minds of the Titanium army at the same time.

"Fire!"

I took aim and launched it forwards. The lightning beamed through the air and hit a red eyed being in the chest, and I laughed in victory as I plunged the dagger through his heart. His whispers didn't affect me. He couldn't move as I withdrew the weapon, and his skin turned a lifeless gray.

REAP

The body fell into the grass.

Maybe this wouldn't be so bad?

I drew from my year of training and leaped towards my next red-eyed target.

They were fast, but no different to fighting another Titanium hybrid in training—so long as I stayed in my evolved state. That's what I told myself, anyway.

Jayleigh battled beside me, laughing as the bodies piled up around her. She was a killing machine.

"Good work," she said to me through her ducking and striking.

"You too!" I called back, still not great with the mind jumping. My energy was better focused elsewhere—in my hands as I pinned my dagger back into the holster and threw a ball of lightning. Right on target. I swiftly retrieved my dagger and thrust my arm forwards. The vampire's blood soaked my hand as I made contact, and I yanked backwards, wiping the blade and my fingers on my clothes. Then on to the next.

I'd barely received a scratch. Covered in mud and blood, and surrounded by stench, I was in the heart of the battle, and it was going so well it almost seemed easy.

And as the thought crossed my mind, my sanity slipped. I could usually control it in my evolved state, working out what was real and what was a dream, but this vision felt so real that it stopped me dead, knocking the air from me.

Danger surrounded me, but I was stuck, unable to defend myself.

"Jayleigh!" I called out, unable to tear my eyes away from the nightmare before me as a vampire lunged for me. Panic claimed me. I couldn't fight back, unable to blink the vision away. Thankfully, Jayleigh threw a dagger into the Day Walker's neck as it closed in on me. I heard it drop to the grass.

All the while, I stared.

It's not real. It's just a dream. Snap out of it, Bro.

But I couldn't look anywhere else.

He had me.

"It's not real!" I shouted, forcing myself to take back control and fight. There were too many vampires around to be losing my mind. There was too much at stake.

It's just another vision. It's your mind playing tricks on you.

But Ares taunted me from the forest, lingering within the treeline nearest the fence.

Not the real Ares.

It was the Ares from my hallucinations—the one I'd seen in the Funhouse, and who had opened the door in the Guesthouse yesterday—who'd haunted my nightmares ever since returning to The Farm.

Just a vision, Bro... just a vision...

I had to blink, and it would go away—only, this time, it didn't. "It's not real!" I yelled again, slapping my face with my hands.

In the corner of my eye, Jayleigh ended her fight. Her movements staggered, and she became as lifeless as the Day Walkers around us. "Oh…"

"What? Are you hurt?" I asked, trying to force my eyes back in her direction, but I couldn't. "I would help if I could, but I'm slipping again. I'm sorry—I forgot to take my tablets—"

"You don't need those tablets, Hail." Jayleigh was beside me now, grabbing my wrist while the war raged on around us.

"What—"

Diego interrupted my sight on Ares for a moment, tackling a Day Walker to the ground, and then he moved on to the next, and my eyes reconnected with the Gen. 3's.

"It's real. I see him, too," Jayleigh said.

No. No. I'd rather be losing my mind.

"His eyes are red. You're not imagining it, Hail. Ares is one of them."

CHAPTER TWENTY-FIVE

LORA

Focused.

Steady.

Prepared.

Steven was everything I wished I could be as he stood beside me, watching from the Gate Tower as the battle raged on below us. I'd lost two evolved Titaniums so far. I'd gripped my hands against the metal frame and gritted my teeth through the pain, but I couldn't lose concentration. My hybrids needed me.

I mind jumped to those most in danger, warning them of approaching Day Walkers they hadn't yet seen. I was the eyes and ears.

It felt wrong.

REAP

I should have been fighting alongside them.

Dying alongside them.

I wanted to be in the battle's heart, destroying our attackers for ending innocent lives, yet I knew I couldn't, for my life held too much value. One wrong move would kill seven-hundred Titaniums, but I could have been explosive. The Day Walkers wouldn't have stood a chance.

To go to war with an empty heart would be a powerful weapon… but to go to war with a distracted mind was suicide. I had to fight my own battle on this podium to keep Ares from my mind. Everyone depended on my focus.

Ares was still somewhere within The Farm's boundaries. He was safe, for now. He didn't need my thoughts or concentration.

Dickward was still in his human form beside me, but the sounds he made as he lost members of his pack were monstrous. He would mutate, I realized, and I hoped he'd see me in a high enough position to follow my orders when he tried to attack me.

Or, I could save myself whilst I still had the chance…

I glanced again at the battle, everybody seeming in good stead to cope without my backup as I jumped from the Gate Tower to the narrow walkway on the opposite side. I landed with such force that the metal crumbled beneath me, bending and contorting around my feet and fist.

We lost two more Venos to the Day Walker invasion, and Steven threw his head back to the sky, a howl erupting from deep within. It ended in a raven-like caw as he ran out of air.

I turned my attention back to the field.

The remaining Titaniums—those who couldn't evolve—lingered behind the fence. If the more experienced, evolved Titaniums couldn't take down the army, the farmers planned on sending the Omegas out. They were using all of their resources.

It only meant one thing.

This really was the last battle—the one that would end the Day Walkers or humankind.

Energy sparked around me at the realization.

The Omegas were no warriors. They wouldn't hold up any better than the farmers if they came face to face with a Day Walker. But it wouldn't come to that.

I watched on, mind jumping to Titaniums on the field. I pinched my thumbs.

More Venos fell to the ground, unable to match the speed of the Day Walkers. Steven's outbursts became more frequent as he lost too many Venos to count. His Alpha bond wasn't as strong as a Titanium's, I figured, for if I'd lost as many hybrids as he had, I'd of passed out from the pain by now.

Feet thundered behind me, but not those belonging to hybrids. Wolves. Solace led her pack onto the battlefield to aid our efforts.

REAP

The wolves didn't nearly make up the number of lost Venos as they ran under the gate. I could only see them in the corner of my eye while watching the battle.

"Hail!" I panicked, shouting his name instead of mind jumping, but Jayleigh was quick to his rescue as he turned, frozen.

"What are you doing?" I asked, more to myself than anybody else. I panicked for him and prayed, "Get it together, Hail."

It was as though a vampire had compelled him despite being in his evolved state. The battle surrounded him, but he didn't move. Didn't flinch.

Then Jayleigh turned, too.

Both stood in the field, unaware of the surrounding dangers.

My gaze followed their line of vision to the forest near the fence, and a figure standing among the trees. The wolves were running in that direction.

"Behind you!" I mind jumped to Jayleigh as a Day Walker approached. Jayleigh snapped back into action, flipping the vampire in one swift motion and plowing her daggers into its chest.

And then, head first, Steven dived from the Gate Tower and into the bloodbath, his human form shifting into that of a Veno mutant before he reached the ground. He was an avenging beast as he charged into battle on all fours. He'd lost too many of his pack. Unable to hold himself back, he put every Veno at risk.

I knew that same urge, enticing me forward, but I had to remain on this podium for the safety of my pack.

"Relax, Hail." I attempted to ease his mind. *"You're doing great."* But he was still motionless—beyond my help. He didn't react as I spoke directly into his mind. Jayleigh protected him against attacking Day Walkers, their numbers growing as more bodies emerged from the treeline.

Some were children.

And then I recognized faces among them; the Day Walkers had turned members of The Sanctuary.

It had been almost an hour since I'd heard their screams for help. The Day Walkers hadn't killed all of them, but used those innocent humans to grow their army.

And it was my fault.

It was because of me that Chipper decided to leave.

They had every reason to despise me… to seek revenge… to target me.

"Nobody is expendable," I said aloud, reminding myself, because I'd been so distraught in losing Ares, I hadn't stopped to think of the people around me or the lives I'd put at risk.

I'd sent The Sanctuary away.

And I would have blown The Farm to pieces had the

shadows of Ares' aura not paralyzed me yesterday, whilst he'd lost his humanity. I didn't care.

I'd have killed my own hybrids, crumbled -3 and everything above because of heartbreak.

And as the wolves returned from the figure in the trees, I felt it again—that same recklessness beckoning me forward.

The shadows of Ares' aura consumed me, and I gasped. I welcomed them. It didn't matter that they were arms of darkness wrapping themselves around me, only that they were here… Ares was here.

Despite better judgement, despite everything I believed and everybody I cared about. I leaped from the podium. I risked it all, and I didn't look back.

I jumped.

Even as the stability of the Gate Tower under my feet vanished, I didn't question what I was doing. I was entering a battlefield full of inhuman creatures who knew what it would mean to kill me—I was risking all humanity, not just my own.

But, for the first time in a long time, I felt I was following the right path—a path towards the cottage by the sea.

A small beam of energy escaped me as I landed, freezing the surrounding Day Walkers and sending the mutated Venos flying backwards, but not affecting the Titaniums. I ran, desperate to see Ares. I had to know I'd not lost him completely. There had to be some trace of his humanity still present within him.

My feet pushed into the soft ground, the grass now churned up from the battle, and I moved faster than ever.

The energy sparked from me in static anticipation. It crackled around my ears as the bitter wind blew my hair from my face.

I followed the shadows to the figure in the trees, and he stepped into the sun to meet me.

And, much like Hail, I froze.

I should have prepared myself for everything and anything. I'd always presumed that Ares' inner animal was a deadly, vicious creature, but that was exactly the problem.

I'd always believed that Ares' alter-ego was just that—an animal.

His red eyes mocked the sun with a superior vibrancy as they landed on me. And when he spoke, why did it still feel so familiar?

I should have run.

I should have balled my energy up and shot it at his chest —it's what anybody else would have done.

But that voice…

It was pristine, drizzled with honey, warm and seductive. It traced my skin like the shadows of Ares' aura as they reached for me, pulling me in.

"Lora." Just one word—my name—was enough to disarm

me. I'd have shed my energy, my weapons, and my clothes if he'd asked.

He smiled because he knew. Of course he did… he'd always been able to read me.

"Ares." The shadows snaked around my body, no longer cold and haunting but a wisp of shade on a summer day. It was welcoming and delightful, and I wanted to sink into everything he was.

Ares was no animal. He was no monster; just misunderstood.

He stepped forward again, and I waited for him, counting down the seconds until I could feel his skin on mine.

Why had I ever tried to prevent this… this captivating, beautiful being before me? He still had the same softness within eyes, gentle freckles upon his cheeks, and that scrunch of his nose as he smiled.

He wouldn't hurt me. Even after everything I'd done to him, after every fight we'd had, I knew this with absolute certainty.

This was still Ares.

It was in the way he looked at me, and in the way he moved. He was still the person I fell in love with. Despite it all, he would never hurt me.

"Come with me," he motioned into the woods. "I have a plan to finish this, but I need your help."

I eyed the darkness behind him. The Day Walkers were already on the field. I had nothing to fear from the trees.

"How?" I asked, taking one small step towards him.

He offered a reassuring smile, and my heart burst. "I've found a loophole."

Of course. Hiding in the woods and finding loopholes had always been Ares' style.

I took another step.

"Lora," a wary voice appeared behind me—Jayleigh's voice. "Lora, you need to back away from him right now. That is not Ares." I sensed her approach, closer and closer, and Hail with her. "Take my hand, Lora. Come back to us."

I shook my head, seeing only those familiar shadows surrounding Ares.

I'd been so scared to say goodbye to those gray eyes. I'd feared them glowing blue for the rest of our lives, but never—*never* had I thought of how beautiful they'd look in red. He was fire and danger, and I loved it.

"It's okay," Ares said, turning towards Jayleigh and Hail with a hand out to steady them. "I'm not here to hurt anyone."

"You may be a Day Walker, but we won't fall for your mind games." Jayleigh spat on the ground next to Ares. "Lora, turn around. Now."

"It's okay, Jayleigh," I said, holding my hands out to show my control. "It's still him. I can sense it through the Alpha bond. It's still Ares."

Jayleigh stepped forwards, placing herself between us. The shadows of his aura wrapped around her too, but she didn't feel them. She looked directly at me and said, "You can't be down here. You're putting everybody in danger."

"No, he won't hurt me," I said, but she was already dragging me backwards. Hail took my hand and gave Ares a cautious glance, not saying a word. He led me away as Jayleigh swept the area, clearing the path back to my podium.

"Ares!" I reached my hand out to him, feeling the energy charge through me. *Don't separate us. I've only just found him. I can't lose him again.*

I'd meant to mind jump the words to Hail, but I projected the energy differently instead. It was a controlled zap which screamed 'get off of me', and Hail ricocheted backwards as my power shot through him.

Jayleigh turned at the sound, only seeing half the picture.

She saw Hail slamming into the fence and Ares rushing to help him.

I turned to tell her it was okay.

But it wasn't.

Because Jayleigh had always been the deadliest of the group—the best aim, with the sharpest instincts.

She was the hybrid The Farm had striven for.

She was a warrior, the ultimate weapon.

And whilst I'd recovered and taken a second to work out what happened, Jayleigh had already processed her own version of events and done exactly what she'd been made to do: defend her people, act, and kill the vampire.

I screamed, my heart pouring through my throat, and watched in horror as Ares' legs buckled beneath him. He fell to the mud with one of Jayleigh's titanium daggers lodged in his chest.

"For the greater good," Jayleigh spat.

CHAPTER TWENTY-SIX

LORA

"No… no… no… no..." I didn't realize the words were coming from my mouth as I rushed forward to catch him.

I reached him in time to stop his head from hitting the floor.

"No…" His shadows laced around me, embracing me for one last time. "No… no… Ares. Look at me. Oh, God." I placed my hand over his heart, just below the dagger, and blood soaked through the shirt whilst I stared in horror.

I yanked the blade out, holding my breath.

I sensed his shadows through the Alpha bond, so he was still a hybrid. Titanium wouldn't kill him.

He could survive this.

He just needed to heal—and heal fast.

He could heal from this, right? Just like he'd done when Marshall stabbed him.

"Breathe." I couldn't follow my own advice. I gasped, air catching in my throat. Jayleigh might as well have taken her second dagger and stabbed it through my heart.

"Is that an order?" he choked, blood spewing from his mouth as he fought to give me a small smile.

The blood was red, just like any other Titanium or human, and my heart faltered because it was proof that he wasn't a vampire.

Of all the orders I'd ever given, this was the most important. I nodded, wiping the tears that rolled down his cheek, and I savored every one.

"Help!" I called out, not knowing who I was shouting to—Hail, White, Wilson, anybody... Nobody came to our aid.

It didn't matter to them that this was still Ares; they only saw red eyes. Maybe things would have been different if his eyes were gray—or blue, even. But not red.

Red made him one of them.

They couldn't see, as I could, that this was who Ares had always been. This was his true state.

Beautiful.

"Help, please." I yelled again, hopeless, but my voice rasped. It wasn't far from the noise a Veno would make. As I applied more pressure to his wound, my hand soaked red, the pain became clear on Ares' face. He squinted through it, wheezing. My tears claimed my next plea, "Help…"

It didn't matter if my voice attracted unwanted attention.

It didn't matter. It didn't matter. Nothing mattered.

Ares was dying in my arms.

I was losing him.

I sobbed to his chest, covering myself in his blood. "Why aren't they helping?"

"It was always going to be this way, Lora," he spluttered, the blood now coming thick and fast from his mouth, staining his teeth. When he couldn't speak any more, he mind jumped, *"I never was warrior material."*

He'd given up.

"No… You're supposed to live—Alpha and Beta versus the apocalypse, remember?" I said, glad to mind jump, knowing my voice wouldn't hold up. My words would have been inaudible. *"You're going to live. I'm going to make sure of it. I promise."*

But the wound didn't appear to be healing. Why wasn't it healing?

His red eyes no longer glowed. The hope was gone, and he rested a hand over my cheek as I continued to put pressure on the wound, as though to comfort me.

In his last moments, Ares was comforting me.

"Whatever happens next… don't forget me," he said, as if it

could ever be possible. I would hear his voice in every question and smell his scent in every summer rainfall. Under every shadow I sought shade, it would remind me of his aura.

I shook my head so fast, so painfully fast, and took his hand as it slipped away. *"Never."*

I couldn't process it.

The numbness returned. The energy within me ran wild.

"Find our cottage by the sea, Alpha." He squeezed my hand with all the effort he had left. *"I'll meet you there."*

I gulped, blinked through the tears, squeezed his thumbs. *"It was never about the cottage, Ares. Surely you know that… it was you —you are my freedom. It was always you."*

But his grip loosened. His red eyes rolled back to stare into the endless sky, and the shadows of his aura leaked out into the world around us.

He was gone.

As soon as the dagger impaled Ares' chest, the Day Walker army fell too, and the battle ended. I hadn't noticed or stopped to wonder why—I'd blocked everything out but the sound of his voice. It was only as I felt the energy rush through me at a rate I'd never experienced before that I looked around, and even then, I didn't take it all in. I couldn't.

I ran, jumped into the air, and allowed the energy to push me higher. I cleared The Farm's fence with ease. It was as though I was flying, but I didn't feel weightless and free inside.

The drop in my stomach as I fell to the ground on the other side was more fitting. The world closed in, dragging me down. It could swallow me whole.

The tablet on my arm vibrated and White's face lit up the screen, but I didn't have the willpower to answer it, so I let it ring out. White would have seen it all. He'd sat there and let Ares die, ignoring my cries for help.

Thinking about it only increased my growing fury.

I knew where to go—to the only place I was completely harmless to others. To the same place I'd gone the last time I thought I'd lost Ares. A lake. Not the same lake as Phase Two, but it would provide me with the security I needed.

I pushed my legs to move faster than ever before and pressed my feet into the soft ground, kicking dirt up behind me.

I longed for the icy water all the more as the lake came into view. Maybe it was the frog DNA that attached me to the depths whenever I lost sight of myself, or the knowledge that I was safe to expose myself within the water. Unlike electricity, the Titanium energy couldn't travel through the lake. I'd learned in the early days that water absorbed the electrical currents. It neutralized me. I wasn't harmful here.

I dived in and broke into a front crawl, heading for the center.

Was I suffocating because I lacked oxygen or was I

drowning in my grief?

The water lit up around me. I couldn't hold the energy much longer.

Surfacing, I gasped for air, and then I let myself fall.

Down… down…

I recalled how Ares had pulled me beneath the water just nights ago and then forced the memory from my mind, unable to face it.

I begged the water to drown me, wanting the pressure to push at my skull and burst my eardrums. I needed to feel something other than loss.

And then my feet touched the bottom, and it was all I needed to explode—as easy as flicking a switch or tapping my tablet screen, but as deadly as a bomb.

The energy shook the water surrounding me, most likely producing gigantic waves on the surface. I was a tsunami. The sand and stones beneath my feet churned up, and the entire lake lit in white as I screamed, I screamed, and screamed…

The water stifled the noise, my mouth producing bubbles.

Eventually, the sound turned into one high-pitched ring, like a siren, warning the fish to stay away.

Dangerous. Do not approach.

My lungs burned, and I rose to the surface only when I was sure I'd pass out if I waited any longer. My tears mixed with the lake's water, and I hovered in place for so long… too long. I'd released my energy, and now there was nothing left. I was a shell. A hollow, emotionless shell.

I floated on my back and let the tide I'd created carry me to the shore, where I rested on the bank and stared at the sky. And that's where I slept.

I awoke sometime later and wished to fall back to sleep.

The sky was grayer; the clouds were thicker, and now I could feel the rift in the Alpha bond. I yelled in pain, forcing myself into a sitting position and squeezed my thumbs. I cried, sobbed, and pulling at my hair.

It was torture.

But it was Ares. It was the last piece of him setting himself free, so I embraced it. I encouraged it—savored it.

I remembered our first kiss, how he used to stutter in my presence, and how he'd catch my eye from across the barn, refusing to let me go. The smaller things, like tucking the cover behind me at night to stop the draft, opening doors for me, and always asking if I needed anything.

Alpha… I'd never hear it the same again. Never hear his voice again.

The boy with so many questions—risking his life just to know a little more. I wondered if he'd got the answers he needed; about himself, The Farm, and the war…

I wished for answers now, too.

Why?

Why didn't I appreciate what I'd had? I should have told him I loved him at every chance and treasured every night beside him instead of sneaking away.

I'd thought that Ares losing his humanity would be the end of mine, but in reality, it was losing him that allowed me to finally regain sight. I'd been poisoning him, leaking my venom into him with every lie, and then retaliating whenever the side effects kicked in. He'd never been the issue—my self absorbed beliefs had been the problem all along. My need to take responsibility had caused this.

I'm sorry, I thought as the pain eased and his shadows completely disconnected from the Alpha bond. He finally had the things he'd always wanted—freedom and acceptance—but it was too late. *I'm so sorry. I love you.*

The only response was the newly formed scars on my skin and the gentle ripple of waves hitting the shore.

CHAPTER TWENTY-SEVEN

HAIL

I fought to pry myself from Jayleigh's arms, but she was too strong. "Ares!" I called out. He was on the ground. His blood covered him, Lora, and the muddy area around them.

Lora was shouting. She was asking for help.

I needed to help.

"It's too late, Hail," Jayleigh said. "He had you under his compulsion, just like Lora. There was no other way for us to get out of this alive. Lora would have gotten herself killed."

"You killed him! He's our friend. Friends are supposed to help each other, not kill each other," I said.

"He was a Day Walker." Her tone showed her disgust. "You better than anyone know what they're capable of. He would have lured us into his trap and tortured us for fun, then turned us into one of them." She nodded towards the vampire bodies surrounding us.

Of course I knew what the dead people were capable of, but that was the thing—if it wasn't a vision, then I'd seen Ares transition between red and gray eyes for the past three months. "Ares wasn't dead. He didn't even smell like a vampire. We could have helped him…"

I stopped fighting against Jayleigh as Lora sobbed over Ares' chest, holding his hands to her forehead. Her body sparked, her skin glowing.

"Back off," I warned Jayleigh, recognizing the despair in Lora's eyes as she rose from the ground. I was no stranger to the reckless thoughts born in pain and loss.

Jayleigh didn't need telling twice, knowing she'd be the target of Lora's anger if she sought revenge, and ran down the field towards the trees for shelter.

I lingered, ready to help my Alpha, but she didn't stay to seek comfort. White energy sparked around her and I flinched back, not wanting another flying lesson anytime soon, but Lora didn't seem to notice me against the fence as she sped past and leaped into the air and vanished within The Farm's boundaries.

Ares' body lay less than ten meters away and I couldn't bring myself to look. The guilt ate at me, despite my evolved state.

REAP

My tablet flashed blue, and I watched the field move into action as senior Titaniums ordered Omegas back through the gates. I didn't help. Instead, I glared at Jayleigh, who smiled at the younger hybrids and congratulated them as she rounded them up.

Had she processed what she'd done? That she'd killed our friend? This wasn't just some vampire dude—this was Ares. Or did she not care?

I struggled to make excuses for her.

She was no better than Marshall, killing without reason but claiming it's for the good of the people, or whatever.

My scowl continued as she crossed under the gate and vanished from sight. She didn't look back, didn't pause to say goodbye, or even blink in our direction.

My nostrils flared. I'd never been more ashamed to call her my closest friend, and all the trust between us was gone.

I remained on the field long after all Titaniums had filtered back through the gate. The Venos still roamed around in their mutant states, not listing the Titaniums or Steven's tablet—Ares was the only one they sometimes listened to.

Their behavior was odd, dragging the bodies of their dead into a line across the field. Nothing the Venos did made sense to me, but this was one of the strangest things I'd ever seen them do. Because of their size and arched backs, the mutated Venos needed at least three legs to walk, so they used their beak-like mouths to move the bodies, or pulled the dead Venos along the grass with their spare hand.

Once the Alpha finished rearranging the bodies, he let out that horrible bird-like howl and charged down the hill, his pack following, and they vanished into the woods. The rattling of their breathing faded with them.

"I wonder what rattled them," I said, hoping Ares' body would enjoy the joke.

If I turned a little, I'd see him in the grass, but I forced my eyes away. How could I say goodbye when I didn't know who I was saying goodbye to? My friend. A Day Walker? A Bro.

It didn't matter what he was or what Jayleigh might say about it.

I couldn't walk through those gates without saying goodbye. I couldn't close him out—I'd never been able to before, no matter how hard I'd tried. And boy, had I tried in those early days.

We all knew the dude was gonna wind up dead at some point. It shocked me he'd made it past his initiation—Phase Two and life outside the fence had been a bonus.

I walked forward, not looking at the body on the ground until I stood before it.

His red eyes stared at the clouds, so I couldn't even convince myself he was sleeping, but the blood on his face was a sure giveaway, too.

REAP

I said nothing, but I stood there until it rained.

I didn't know what to say. We'd never been the sharing kind, but I always knew he'd have my back. Sharing my heart now would seem weird considering it's stuff I would never have said to his face.

After losing Donnah, I'd wished I had the chance to say goodbye, but she already knew everything I would have said because I told her every day.

She knew exactly how I felt. I'd always believed it better that way, especially because of training—never knowing which day would be our last. I had prepared myself.

But Ares never knew how much his friendship meant to me or how he'd brought me back from such a dark place.

If, as Jayleigh said, Ares was a monster, then he was the monster who made me feel human again after losing Donnah.

I scoffed.

What made somebody a monster? The color of their eyes? What they *ate*?

Ares had never been a monster to me—far from it—and looking at him now, I decided he could never be a monster.

I would always remember him for restoring my faith in humanity, even when I believed all love, friendship, and Bros were lost; and for standing up for what was right. He'd never feared death, not in his initiation, not when he jumped from the waterfall, and not when he'd stood up against Marshall. Or maybe he *was* scared, but he was so set in his morals that he'd decided it was worth dying for.

Maybe this was another of those moments.

He'd walked onto the battlefield with red eyes, knowing he'd be a target. What had he felt so strongly about that he'd been willing to risk his life for it?

Or was it just a mistake?

I sighed.

I was tired after the battle, still in my evolved state to stop the grief from swarming me, but I let go of the animal side. The exhaustion returned me to my human state, and the aches and pains from the battle became apparent as my animal hormo —whatever Ares called them—left my body.

Then I looked to the muddy field, the bodies, and let the reality of the situation sink in.

I considered moving Ares, like the Venos had moved their dead, or burying him, but felt it was only right to do that with Lora.

Dr. White must have been watching, because just then, my tablet gave orders to leave Ares' body and return through the gates as they needed me on The Farm. I doubted The Farm needed me, but I was sure that Lora would—to restore her faith as Ares had mine.

Nobody else would understand.

I took off my holster, and then my jacket, and crouched

beside him.

"I'll keep Lora safe for you," I said as I patted the hand I'd never shake again and placed the waterproof over Ares' body to shield him from the rain. "Sleep well, Bro."

CHAPTER TWENTY-EIGHT

LORA

Hold your head high.

I battled my sorrow as I walked through the crowd of celebrating Titaniums. The gathering split through the middle as I approached, and time slowed. My breath became shallow. The claustrophobia hit, and the hybrids swarmed around me, engulfing me in a bubble of their merriment.

They had every right to feel victorious, but the smile I shared with them was a fake. My eyes weren't shining with glee, but glistening from the aftermath of a breakdown. Panic. I needed out.

I could feel their happiness, their auras gleaming and their energy vibrating the air. I heard it sing, chanting; the battle is won, and the Day Walkers are dead. They encouraged me to join, but celebrating was the last thing on my mind.

I fake smiled some more and shivered through my wet clothes.

Of course, I was relieved to find my pack was with minimal casualties, and we'd somehow won the war. We'd live to fight another battle.

But Ares wouldn't, and my heart ached for him.

I scanned the crowd many times to find his face, forgetting that I'd never see it again. It hadn't fully sunk in yet. Even though I'd felt his departure through the Alpha bond, I still felt him with me, so close he could have been standing beside me, running his fingers over the back of my neck and whispering into my ear.

That was love. Its ghost would always haunt me, but I wouldn't let it rule me.

I thanked more hybrids as I passed. I smiled some more. More. More. I prayed for less—get through this, and then I could return to the barn, crawl into bed and lay in silence.

Tye and Diego waited for me near the gates. They each offered a hug but didn't ask questions. I wondered if Jayleigh or Hail had filled them in on what had happened, although neither was present.

"Food?" Tye offered. I'd not eaten anything since yesterday evening. After waking in Ares' childhood bedroom this morning, I'd headed straight to the council meeting and then to the gates to wave The Sanctuary goodbye.

I should have been hungry, but the thought of food was making me ill—or more likely, it was the flashbacks that were making me ill and putting me off food.

"No, thank you," I offered Tye the same smile I'd given everyone else. "Well done today."

"We know what happened, Lora," Tye said. "You don't need to act for us. We're here to help in any way that we can. I've never been fond of Ares, but it's clear to everyone around here that what you two had was real. We don't expect you to pretend it's all confetti and champagne."

I swallowed. "Yeah." Gulped back the tears. "Thanks, Tye." Forcing the words out made them sharp.

"We're here if you need us." He nodded in understanding, gray eyes glancing between Diego and I.

"I appreciate that." I nodded.

Diego's expression was solid, as ever. He, if anyone, would know where to find the girl who'd killed Ares.

I couldn't process it yet. I didn't know how to feel about Jayleigh or what she'd done, and I didn't yet know how to blame her. She was The Farm's yield, after all.

"Where are Jayleigh and Hail?" I asked.

Diego took a moment, studying me.

"Did I hear my name?" Hail's voice came from my left, and

he looked every bit as battered as I was. Blood stained the blonde mop on his head, the light rain dampening it just enough to weigh his fringe over the bluish skin of his under eyes. His shoulders slumped forwards, defeated and distraught.

I ran to him and Hail scooped me into his arms like I was nothing more than a child.

Hail didn't care that my clothes were soaked through with stagnant lake water, pressing my head against his chest and rocking slowly.

Neither of us said anything.

I forced back the tears.

"Does it ever get easier?" I asked, finally understanding everything he'd been through with Donnah—everything he was presumably still going through.

Hail shook his head. "You learn how to cope with it, but it doesn't get easier."

I exhaled, wondering how I could ever learn to handle this, and I tightened my grip around his waist whilst trying to recall if we'd ever hugged before. I should have, when he'd lost Donnah, but I was closed off then. It wouldn't have crossed my mind.

"I'm sorry for electrocuting you," I whispered into his shirt. Hail was at least a full foot taller than me.

He shrugged, his arms shifting. "I had it coming. I shouldn't have tried to pull you away."

I crumbled at the memory. "I wasn't under his compulsion,

Hail." My head pounded as I shook it, yet I couldn't stop. He had to believe me. "I don't know why his eyes were red, but he wasn't one of them. He wasn't a vampire. I know it—"

"I know. It's okay." He hushed me, stroking my hair. "You don't have to explain it to me. I know."

"You do?" I caved in relief.

"He never smelled dead. He didn't drink blood. His skin didn't turn gray when he died. I'm sure that he wasn't one of them."

My breathing ceased. I'd not considered it until this moment. "But his eyes…"

"Were red." Hail nodded, pulling back to look at me. "But Bro's eyes were blue when he mutated a few months ago. It means nothing."

"Means nothing?" Jayleigh's voice echoed through the valley as she came into view, and I broke away from Hail as she rounded the path towards the gates.

My body tore at the sight of her. She held one dagger in her hand, the other still missing, presumably outside the gates with Ares' body, and her cheeks were flushed, painted with blood splatters. The rest of us had retired to our human state now, but Jayleigh still buzzed with electricity, eyes glowing.

I opened my mouth to speak, but she beat me to it. "What the hell were you doing out there? We could have died because of you."

REAP

My mouth snapped shut. Fury raged within me.

Ares was gone, and it was her fault. I'd always respected Jayleigh for her attitude and mentality, but all of that burned as I witnessed the ravaging expression on her face.

"Don't you dare," I warned. "I wasn't in danger. Ares would never have hurt me and I could have protected myself against any Day Walker who crossed my path."

Why was I explaining myself? Why was she accusing me?

Why wasn't she apologizing?

My skin crawled.

Because she isn't sorry.

I'd never despised a member of my pack before. Not as Torn and Shyla had gone against my orders and tried to escape The Farm, or even when Keril had tried to challenge me within my first few weeks of being an Alpha. I had disliked Gen. 2s, clashed personalities with some, but I had always cared for each too much to hate them.

But right now? I hated Jayleigh, from her careless smile to the blood on her pale cheeks and fingers.

Was it Ares' blood?

No… she'd been too far away, but my mind couldn't focus on anything else, convincing me it was his, it was his; it was his blood on her hands.

It made me sick to the core.

"I saved your sorry ass." Jayleigh approached, and I had to

fight not to step backward, clenching my thumbs tighter than ever before. I could barely look at her, let alone stand so close.

Couldn't she see it? Didn't she understand?

Would she have acted so senseless if she'd returned to her human state? Was she still capable of compassion, or had her commitment blurred the line between what was essential and what was not?

A crowd gathered around us, the Titaniums curious to see another hybrid—a senior—stand up against their Alpha. I had to diffuse it before it got out of hand.

"Stand down, Jayleigh." I didn't have it in me to argue, but Jayleigh seemed to have enough fight for the both of us.

Hail reached a hand onto Jayleigh's shoulder, forcing himself between us. "Let's take a walk," he said.

I held in my sigh of relief, glad he could use their friendship to distract her from whatever she planned to do here. Embarrass me? Show me up in front of the hybrids?

It didn't matter.

I couldn't—wouldn't rise to it.

"We'll talk later," I said, needing to appear in control despite my world falling apart around me.

Jayleigh dragged her eyes from me as Hail led her away, down the path leading towards the heart of The Farm. She looked back every couple of seconds until she disappeared.

I stood with Tye and watched them go. He rested his hand

on my shoulder, and I finally sighed. But I recognized the suggestive look in his eye and recoiled as he said, "So… now that Nerd is out of the picture—"

"Don't even go there." I shot him a disapproving look and stalked away with no destination in mind, but ending up exactly where I needed to be.

CHAPTER TWENTY-NINE

LORA

In all my time on The Farm, I'd never been in this neck of the woods. It was most likely because the farmers tried to keep us away from the gates whilst we were in training, and I'd had no reason to explore this area of land. But my feet carried me away from the hybrids with a determination to lose myself in the trees.

Did Tye really feel now was the time to hit on me? Not only was he a Gen. 2, but Ares' body was still lying outside the fence, yet to be buried next to his Father's head and the empty grave placed there in memory of his mother.

We'd visited the cemetery twice over the past weeks, taking a truck to the eastern border of The Farm, which was mainly used to grow crops. It was a fair drive. The farmers who worked in the area lived within the old villages on this side of the fence, and seemed to have a somewhat normal life, growing crops, harvesting, and delivering them to level -2 once ready.

The cemetery was in one distant village, expanded for the farmers who'd died since living on The Farm, and we'd taken time to wander through the church grounds. We even looked inside the old building. I figured some still used it, the furniture well organized, floors swept, walls maintained. Religion seemed a beacon of hope for the outer communities within the fence, and I needed a little hope right now.

I wandered if I'd come from a religious family, and to which Gods I would have prayed.

I called on all of them now, asking for strength as I battled through the unkempt pathway of the woodland, thorns and hollies snagging at my ankles, twigs pulling at my clothes as though they were alive and trying to hold me back—to stop me from reaching the center of the woodland and what it hid from the world.

I prayed for forgiveness for putting my hybrids at risk. Although I'd sensed that Ares wouldn't hurt me, there was no saying that any other red-eyed being on the battlefield would have spared my life.

I prayed for Jayleigh, although I couldn't bring myself to think about her for too long before my blood boiled and my inner animal woke from her sleep, stirring in her chains.

And I prayed White would stop calling me.

My tablet vibrated against my arm; the sound of it ringing scared away the nearby birds, squirrels, and rabbits so I was truly alone.

"What?" I said as I answered, not caring that White had just lost his only remaining family.

For one moment, just one damn moment, I needed to be selfish. I needed a break from the pack, and the responsibilities of the war, and *not* to hear the doctor's voice. Thankfully, my tablet seemed to understand. The Gods were listening after all.

"Lora… losing… back to… cameras." White's voice cut out with loss of signal, leaving radio static in his wake as I entered an area no longer covered by the drones. The trees were too close for the machines to hover, branches woven together, and the canopy ahead was too thick to see through.

Perfect. Being off the radar was what I needed.

Ending the call with White filled me with great satisfaction, but I didn't stop moving to look at my tablet. I didn't notice the low-hanging branch or the twigs that reached out until they pierced through my cheek, drawing blood, and caught in my hair.

"Stupid," I muttered as I pulled my damp shirt to my face to wipe the blood, although the scratch would heal soon enough.

REAP

My hair, being at the uncomfortable stage between wet and dry, was easily knotted and made freeing myself from the twig a laborious task, so instead of removing each fine strand, I yanked. The hair split just as my tablet rang again.

I answered and continued moving, leaving the silver tuft behind. White's voice cut through the woodland like a chainsaw, ravaging. "Return—need… his body—" Too demanding.

"Sorry White," I said, "I can't hear you."

I didn't pretend to listen before ending the call and turning my tablet off. Taking a large breath, I sighed in relief.

Silence.

It was everything I needed to cut off the digital world.

Now I was free.

Free from cameras. Free from communication. Free from reach.

I continued further into the woodland; the trees grew thicker and denser, and the path I became hard to make out. I halted, studying the surrounding area. I was so far in that I could no longer see the entrance or the hybrids I'd left behind—could barely hear them, in fact—but I knew how to return if I wanted, and it had offered me a false sense of comfort.

The woods hadn't felt so dangerous, especially being off the grid, because there was something to follow.

A chill crept over my skin as I registered the ground.

If this was a restricted area, then why—how—was there a

path? Enough feet must have trodden through the grass and flowering snowdrops to create one. It didn't seem likely that the rabbits, foxes, badgers, or whatever else lived in the woodland used the path enough to dig it down to dirt, and humans and hybrids were prohibited from entering for safety reasons.

But the path was there, and it was leading me somewhere.

Answers, the thought crossed me and I almost laughed, caught aback by the familiarity.

It was as though Ares was now living inside my head. I'd never sought for answers other than those surrounding Ares' humanity. I'd followed orders all my life. But now? Now I had too many questions; about Ares, his eyes, The Farm, the missing hybrids, the farmers' revolution.

I eyed the fading path.

This could be it—where the farmers came to plan their attacks. It had to be done somewhere out of range. Somewhere we wouldn't find them. My stomach split as though the few contents inside had turned sour and curdled. What if this was where they brought the missing hybrids' bodies?

It was dark enough, dense enough, and it was off the grid.

My heart was going to burst out of my chest as I continued forward, wondering what I would find at the end. Another graveyard?

Answers.

I ran as fast as the trees would allow, not worrying about

REAP

the scrapes or tears on my clothes; the anticipation pushed me forward. A powerful urge stirred within me. I was onto something. I could feel it in my bones—in my entire being, as though it was the Alpha magic drawing me towards something of great importance. This was fate. It was the Gods returning my prayers. This was something I was supposed to find.

It was everything.

I broke through two large holly bushes, bleeding as though I needed to give a blood sacrifice to get past their threshold, and burst into a clearing canopied by evergreens which cast out the light. There, in the center, stood a small miner's hut.

I glanced around, expecting the rebel farmers to pounce at me, taser me, and carry me away for finding their secret meeting spot, but nobody jumped from the shadows. Within this bubble of darkness, all was silent. All was still.

Twigs snapped underfoot as I took a step towards the crumbling building and I flinched, looking around once again.

Nothing.

I was alone. And I was unprepared—so utterly unprepared for what I'd find within the minor's hut because I'd been so wrong.

About everything.

The hurt of the betrayal was intense, a painful reminder of everything I'd put Ares though and all the lies I'd fed him.

I'd take it all back—the synthetic energy, banishing the

shadows of his aura, right down to toying with his emotions in his first days—if what I'd put him through was a smudge of what I felt now.

And it was too late to make it right, because Ares was gone.

CHAPTER THIRTY

HAIL

Jayleigh glanced down at my arm with glowing silver eyes as my tablet rang. I wandered if she'd smash it, or chop my arm off, or stab it with her dagger. That seemed to be her style.

"Are you going to answer that?" she asked instead. "It's Dr. White, so it's probably important."

So, not as aggressive as I'd expected.

"No." I shook my head, not interested in anything the doctor had to say. "We need to talk. You're not worming your way out of this."

"Come on then, let's hear it. Tell me I was wrong for saving the lives of every Titanium hybrid. Then I can apologize, you can call me Bro again, and we'll all go back to our lives, holding hands and skipping about, singing nursery rhymes."

I stopped walking, forcing Jayleigh to stop too. "You killed our friend!" I closed my eyes, my rage seething within. I feared what my inner animal would do to her if I slipped.

A flash of Beckle's torn up face.

I opened my eyes suddenly. "I won't speak to you until you're in your human state again. You're too snarky, and I don't like it."

"Snarky. That's a good word."

"Jayleigh, please," I begged. She must have seen how painful this was for me, because she fixed her remaining dagger back into place and sighed.

"Fine." She closed her eyes, and when she reopened them, they no longer glowed. The guilt crept in slowly, sharpening the lines of her thin face as she sucked in her lips, and she sank to the ground without saying a word.

I sat next to her as she stared at the grass below her. We remained in silence for so long that I developed pins and needles in my toes.

"I don't understand," she said finally. "His eyes, they were red. I saw them. He was a Day Walker, Hail. A freakin' Day Walker. Shit!" She lay back, resting an arm over her face to hide her expression. "He had you both under his compulsion. He attacked you, knocking you into the fence."

I stayed silent for a moment, wondering if I should rest a

hand on her shoulder as I told her the truth. Nah, Jayleigh didn't like people in her bubble unless she was the one doing the touching, so I picked at the grass and chewed a little of it. "We weren't under compulsion. I was in shock." I knew shock from experience—from the day Donnah died. "And Lora was the one who threw me into the fence. It was an accident." Jayleigh didn't reply, didn't look at me, she didn't react at all. I wondered if she hadn't heard me. "It was Lora—"

"Yeah…" She cut me off. "I'm just trying to process it, Hail. Sorry. I'm going to need a moment."

"Do you want me to leave?"

"No!" The panic was clear in her voice, and she sat abruptly to make sure I didn't leave. Her eyes were glossy. "Unless you want to."

I was mad at her, angry, hurt, and in pain, but I'd never leave. Especially not now, when she needed me most. "I'll stay. But it doesn't mean I've forgiven you."

Jayleigh didn't respond. Her face stayed blank as she stared at the lake, but didn't seem to *see* it. I could only stand to look at her for so long, so instead I watched the water ripple—gray from the clouds above. At least the sky had stopped crying now.

"I'm surprised Lora didn't kill me for what I did," Jayleigh said eventually.

"I'm sure she's probably thinking about it." I nodded. "But Lora cares about us too much, and eventually she'll see that you were trying to protect us, even if you'd been wrong."

"I'm not sure she will." Jayleigh's gaze landed on me. "Do you remember how much you hated Marshall for what he did to Donnah?"

I spurted air through my nose. "I hated him with every piece of my body. Sometimes when I'm bored, I think about how I should have been the one to kill him. I think about how I would have done it. I'd have ripped out his heart probably, so that he understood how I felt every day…" I stopped as I realized the point that Jayleigh was trying to make. "But you're not Marshall, and Lora isn't me."

She didn't seem to trust my words. She looked at me through the corner of her eyes and tilted her head forwards. I knew that look. I'd seen it too often whenever I said something she thought was stupid.

"You'll need to apologize, though." I held my breath. "It's the only way Lora will forgive you."

Jayleigh clucked her tongue and I frowned.

I didn't know what to make of her response. Before I could ask, the shouting of her name distracted us as Diego rounded the hill.

"Why do you not answer your calls?" he slapped me across the back of the head as he rushed passed me.

"Dude!" I held my hands up in question. "What the hell?"

"The doctor called. He needs you to find Lora," Diego said

to me, his face solid.

"Why me?"

"I don't know, but it sounded urgent."

I looked at Jayleigh, who nodded that it was okay. I grumbled low in my throat. This conversation was far from over. I needed to know what Jayleigh meant by her strange noises, but I had to be there for Lora, too.

Lora had nobody.

"I'll stay here, you go. Be quick," Diego rushed me away, although his voice didn't seem to match his words.

"Fine." I rose to my feet, looking down at Diego as I said, "Look after her. She needs you now more than ever." I nodded my head towards Jayleigh.

Diego looked baffled. "Of course, she has my heart. Now get out of here."

I watched him lower himself to Jayleigh's level and tuck her into his chest. Had they always been this close? Had I been such a bad friend not to notice how attached they'd become? I knew they liked each other, but not *this*. Watching it made my heart ache. I longed for Donnah.

I turned away before I choked up, glad that my friend could finally dip her toe into the pool of love—and I hoped she didn't drown in it like me and Lora already had.

A little way up the path, my tablet rang again. I answered this time. "Yep."

The doctor didn't tell me off like I expected him to. Instead, he gave me simple instructions on how to find Lora. "Follow the light blue pin on the map of your tablet. It'll lead you straight to Lora."

I nodded as I broke into a jog, moving my hair, which had grown too long, away from my eyes. "Okay."

"Be quick. There's something she needs to see."

"Okay," I repeated. "But why not call her? Why are you sending me to get her?"

"She's not answering my calls, and you're the one person she'll trust most to bring her back."

"Okay." I ended the call before realizing the doctor might not have been done with his instructions, but he didn't call back, so I followed the blue blob on my screen towards Lora.

I entered the woods, ducking low beneath the branches as I cut through the trees.

I wondered what the doctor needed Lora to know.

Was she okay?

Probably not.

That was stupid. Lora would *not* be okay.

My stomach growled, and I hoped that we'd eat after I found her. It had been a long morning. If it even was still morning. The clock in the corner of my tablet said 14:49 but I couldn't read the time anywhere past twelve in the afternoon, so I figured it must have gone past lunch because we always ate

REAP

when the clock said 13:00.

Ares had tried to teach me how time reset itself in the afternoon. I never got it. There was too much math, but he'd always tried to help.

I thought about Ares and warm bread as I followed the map, only stopping when I reached the blue dot to find that Lora wasn't here.

I called the doctor back. "She's not here," I said, but the doctor kept saying hello in response, asking if I could hear him, and then speaking a load of mumbo-jumbo with strange pauses. I frowned at the tablet and ended the call.

"Lora?" I asked, ducking as I spun to see if she was hiding.

A noise came from my left, and I turned quickly, squinting into the shadows.

There was something in the trees.

"Lora?" I asked again.

A loud noise erupted from the branches and I stumbled backwards, scared for my life after the battle this morning. My first instinct was to evolve. To fight. To attack whatever jumped out at me at the same time it advanced.

I felt the energy in my fingertips.

I fought as the creature leaped from its hiding place within the trees, punching my arm out and only missing because I realized, just in time, that it was nothing but a large bird taking flight.

"I showed you, bird," I mumbled to myself as I pushed back my hair and turned to make sure that nobody saw.

I was still alone.

Still no sign of Lora.

But now, in my evolved state, I sensed something I couldn't in my human state. The smell of blood.

Lora's blood.

I ran forward again, following the scent in a panic, fearing the worst.

Something had her. They'd attacked, just like the bird, and pulled her deeper into the woods.

It couldn't have been a bird, but maybe a woodland cat, or a cow—they could be scary when they wanted to be. Or-

Somebody with red eyes.

The hairs on the back of my neck prickled with energy as I tried to work out where I was. Was this the same woods that connected to the lake? It was a long way away, but did the trees ever break? Could this be the same woods where I'd seen the girl with the red eyes?

I thought it had been a vision, just as I thought Ares' eyes had been my mind playing tricks on me, but what if…

What if it had *all* been real—everything I'd seen around The Farm over the past months? What if there was somebody with red eyes living in these woods?

I ran faster, following the smell of Lora's blood.

REAP

It ended in a circle of thick trees, covering a small building.

That must be where it lived.

It had dragged her in there, and now I had to get her out.

PART TWO

PRESENT DAY

HIM

I am everything they claimed I would be.

CHAPTER THIRTY-ONE

HAIL

I don't know what to expect as I lift the rusty latch and pull the door. It's weightless. It flings open and I'm not ready for what's inside.

The door to one-hundred secrets throws me off guard and I jump back, ready to fight anything that might pounce at me like the bird in the woods. It's a good thing, really, that I jump back instead of forwards, because on the other side of the door is a hole—not a hole like the one we'd dug to get Ares out of the coffin on his initiation, or Tim's bottomless eyes, or my stomach when I'm hungry—but a hole that must lead straight to hell.

Maybe the bird killed me after all.

REAP

Nah, the door to hell would be heavier, and I always imagined the entrance to be gates. But I'm still in my evolved state, so of course the door feels light, it's made of wood, and wood weighs like… nothing.

But enough about the door. I need to focus. I'm distracting myself from the real problem.

The hole to hell at my feet.

Luckily, the devil put a ladder inside the hole, so I won't need to jump. Maybe the devil won't be so bad, if he's considerate enough to fix steps into the ground so I don't fall. That doesn't seem like something he'd do.

I think over the possibility as I lower myself into the ground, watching the light vanish as my head sinks and the world swallows me up.

Lora definitely came this way. I can smell her blood on the ladder as I cling onto it. At least it means she was well enough to climb down here herself, but it doesn't make me any happier to be doing this.

Today is not going as planned.

Today sucks.

It might even be the worst day—next to the day I lost Donnah—of my life.

It's so dark that I can only just make out the outlines of my fingers as they grip onto the ladder. Some bars bend as I squeeze them. "Chill the nerves, Bro," I whisper to myself as I hurry my pace.

The sooner I reach the bottom, the better.

Unless…

No. It's not hell. It can't be. But by preparing myself for the worst, I hope to be pleasantly surprised by what I find on the other side of this ladder.

I look down, something catching my eye, and straight away I regret it.

There's a light down there.

And I mean *down* there… so far that I can see the brightness, but not the light itself.

This puts the training rope to shame.

I climb, one foot behind the other, for what seems to be forever. I climb past the light. And then another light. And another.

And when I finally reach the bottom, I'm relieved to find that I haven't climbed into hell but what looks to be a part of level -3 that I've never seen before.

It has the same white walls and the shiny surfaces that make my skin itch.

"Lora?" I call out. The sound bounces.

I can see my own glowing eyes reflecting at me when I look from one wall to the next.

There's only one exit, so I take it.

I'm sneaking, although I've been on -3 so many times over

the last few weeks that it should feel like home, but something seems off and I can't work out what.

Maybe it's the smell, taking me back to the Funhouse, and the day I'd seen the woman outside the gates.

It smells like death.

Noise bounces back at me and I press my back against the wall, not knowing what good it will do to help me blend in, but not knowing what else I *can* do. I stop. I wait.

The sound carries on.

It's constant, never getting louder or quieter, so I figure I must be coming up to a room full of people, and slowly, carefully, I walk forward.

I hear her, Lora, speaking in a voice so high pitched I don't recognize it for a while. It's only when the pitch changes, the tone challenging and much more like the one I'm used to, that I realize it's her. She's here, and she's not happy, but she doesn't sound to be in danger.

Another voice replies, deep and confident. I don't recognize it, and he doesn't rise to whatever Lora had been saying.

The words become clearer as I close the distance.

"This isn't real. It can't be real…" Lora repeats over and over again.

The male voice replies steadily. "Put down the dagger, Lora. I can explain everything."

Dagger.

It's the only word that processes. *Lora is in danger*. My Alpha needs my help.

I run through the rest of the corridor, not caring if they hear me coming. Maybe I can create a distraction for her to run away. I'm still tired from the battle, but I'm sure I have enough energy left to fight off whoever she's talking to, long enough for her to reach the ladder and start climbing.

I round the corner, not knowing what to expect—not expecting anything at all—and I halt at the sight before me. I crane my neck and try to make sense of the strange equipment around me.

Screens. Pods. Sciencey stuff.

I wish Ares was here to explain it to me. He was good with the computer things.

People in white coats.

People with blue gloves.

People with red eyes.

Lora has her back to me and is holding her dagger towards the man I'd heard speaking, but he's facing me. His red eyes lock with mine.

This *is* hell.

"Hail," he greets me as I charge towards him, but he's not like the other vampires I've met, and instead of attacking, he offers out his hand in greeting.

REAP

I stop again.

"What are you?" I ask, and the man smiles, not a creepy, threatening smile, but a... friendly smile, welcoming. He doesn't mention the fact that I just charged in here ready to kill him and his red-eyed friends.

I eye the room once more. It's like -3, but it isn't.

The lights in here are dim, the computers darkened to near black, and the brightness turned down on the screens on the walls.

There are lights coming from the pods behind him, too.

They're blue, or maybe it's the goo in the pods that's blue. And the man with red eyes is talking again, but all I hear is noise. I hear everything and nothing.

Lora is talking, too, but not to me.

She's following me towards the pods and I don't even realize that I'm moving until I sense my Alpha behind me, just as shocked.

I'm dreaming.

The man behind me is a vampire, and he must be putting visions in my head. He must have bitten me at some point.

I believe this more than I believe Ares hadn't been a vampire, because this can't possibly be real.

My heart won't cope if it's real.

It's a vision. It must be a vision. My mind is playing tricks.

But if it *is* real, today would turn from one of the worst

days of my life to one of the best, and I don't have luck like that. Nobody in this world gets luck like that anymore.

I blink.

The pods remain in place.

I blink again, waiting for them to disappear. They will disappear. Mind tricks always vanish.

"What is this?" Lora says. "What have you done to them? How is this possible?"

I'm wondering the same thing.

"They're training. Much like the incubators used in hibernation, these incubators allow them to move, perform, and train in safety," says the man with red eyes.

"But they're conscious."

"They don't sleep, Lora. Of course they're conscious. We've adjusted the incubators to fit their new… needs."

I'm blinking.

The pods and the people inside are not going away.

"Is it real?" I ask, eyes welling with tears despite being in my evolved state. "Are they really here?"

I press my hand to the glass of one pod in particular; the one I'd seen from across the room.

"They're real, and I'm going to explain everything to you," the man says. "Why don't you come and take a seat?"

But I'm no longer listening to the vampire. I switch off to his words again after hearing his confirmation.

REAP

They're real.

She's real.

My legs can no longer hold me. I blink out of my evolved state as I fall, hand grasping at the glass, only to be met by another on the other side.

"It's real," she says through the liquid that keeps her floating. That sweet, sweet voice. I'm a mess as I scurry back up the glass to face her, studying the fingers that reach for mine through the glass of the pod separating us, checking her neck for scarring, my eyes resting on the creamy white skin of her face.

Her face. Right here, before me.

Still so pure, despite the red eyes. Everything else is exactly as I remember, from the freckles on her nose that I've counted too many times, to the curve of her brows, to the blush of her cheeks.

She's blushing now.

How I'd love to kiss those cheeks.

"My angel," I whisper as I rest my forehead against the glass. She copies my every move, placing her forehead to the glass on the other side. If I focus hard enough, I'm sure I feel her skin—I convince myself so.

She replies softly, shyly after all this time apart, "I'm here, my love."

She's alive.

I don't believe it, even as I think it. Seeing it isn't proof enough.

And suddenly I'm laughing and sobbing, the hiccuping sound too loud for the hushed room around us, but I don't care. Neither of us do.

She's laughing too. Her smile is just as perfect as the last time I saw it, and the sound… I don't know enough words to describe her beautiful giggle. There aren't possibly enough words to describe it. It doesn't matter. I'll make more words.

It's real.

And she's singing to me as my heart explodes with a joy I've never experienced before. Love. So much love I could die from it. I could melt into a puddle on the ground and not care, just as long as they mopped me up and poured me into the pod with her.

This isn't a dream or a vision.

Donnah's here, and this time she's real.

She's alive.

Her voice fills my ears. It leaks into my soul.

She's really here.

CHAPTER THIRTY-TWO

LORA

Hail's face lights up as he reconnects with Donnah, just as doting as he'd been when they'd met. Time hadn't parted them; not even death could part them.

It was something I'd considered impossible before, true love—my vision tainted by my experiences in the Alpha Arena—but watching their love blossom in their early days had filled me with hope. It became something I longed for, but knew I could never have. But then Ares came along and changed everything, and I'm reminded of it as they both cling to opposite sides of the glass. Besotted, as ever.

Those old feelings of envy resurface, deeper, thicker, because I want it more now that I've had a taste of it.

I'd had it all, and I'd messed it up.

Still, I don't tear my eyes away from them. Hail has his world back. I can see the happiness in his eyes, his aura illuminating brighter than ever, as he pulls his face back from the glass to watch Donnah float within the incubator.

And she's not the only hybrid here. There are rows upon rows of the cylinder machines, each containing a Titanium hybrid I'd failed. Shyla, Jamini, Conna, Zayne. I walk further along the line, stopping short as I lay eyes on a face I recognize, but I don't know him well enough to remember his name. An Omega. Unlike the others, his body is limp in the incubator, floating aimlessly.

He is one of the missing Titaniums who'd disappeared days ago.

"They're here," I say, more to myself than anyone else. "They're…"

How?

The red-eyed man, who'd introduced himself as Flynn, repeats his earlier invitation, "Come and take a seat. We have a lot to discuss."

I nod, but find it difficult to steer my eyes away from the hybrids. *My* hybrids. But I can't feel them in the Alpha bond. They're no longer connected to me.

Because they're dead.

I swallow, observing the red irises in the room. My mouth

dries and I resist the increasing urge to run from the room of nightmares. I've been wearing each of these hybrids' souls on my skin like scars, mourning their absence and regretting my failures. And now I stand face to face with them again.

Some of them pause their training, whatever they're seeing within the incubators disintegrating as they meet my eyes.

They must hate me.

I had let them die, just as I'd let Ares die.

A cold sweat breaks out over my skin and I back up slowly, observing the exit and calculating how long it will take me to run from the room. But running has never been my style.

I squeeze my thumbs.

I owe it to the red-eyed hybrids to stay, and I owe it to Ares —to get answers to his questions.

"Talk to me, Flynn," I say as I sink into a blue plastic chair, pressing my damp clothes against my skin and feeling all kinds of uncomfortable.

Hail doesn't follow to hear the hows and whys, he remains by Donnah's side.

Flynn clears his throat, already seated, and leans back in his chair. "Okay." His gentle manner of speaking and the way he moves his hands while talking seems familiar, but I can't work out why.

"Are you a vampire?" I ask, despite the red eyes. I need to be sure of who... or what I'm dealing with. The smell definitely screams vampire.

Flynn smiles, and it's genuine—handsome, even. His teeth don't scare me as I would have expected. "I am a Night Walker, but you have nothing to fear from me."

My body tenses at his words none the less.

I study the kindness in Flynn's crimson eyes as he analyzes me. He's able to read my mind. I wonder what he sees in there, because I'm too numb to process my own thoughts. He continues to watch me as I turn towards the room, half looking for answers, and half looking for an escape. "This is where Ares came when he disappeared, isn't it?" I ask.

He nods slowly. "Instead of asking questions, how about I explain what we're doing here?" He gestures to the room in one smooth sweep of his hand. "I can tell you exactly what we are and what this place is, but first I need to tell you a story, or else you'll never understand."

I keep my mouth shut and nod, gulping back the realization that there is still so much I don't know.

"This is level -4. It's a secret bunker with five exits. The first is the one that you used. The second will take you to Ares' childhood bedroom, but you would need his key in order to reveal the stairs. The third and fourth lead you outside of The Farm via a long tunnel once used for sewerage, and the fifth is hidden behind the wardrobe within Joe and Sam's bedroom in the Guesthouse. The farmers do not know we're here for obvious reasons, but the story runs deeper than our red eyes. This lab was originally used to create a cure for Night Walkers. I helped Samantha set it up in secret. It was a project sure to be shunned if anybody found out."

"Flynn," I say, not because I want his attention, but because the name finally registers in my mind and I realize why his mannerisms seem familiar. "You're Ares' uncle, and Dr. White's partner. You and Samantha were the brains behind the metamorphosis."

Flynn smiles again and nods. "I am. And yes, we were. Alongside Gretta."

I gasp. "Gretta? As in… Queen of the Day Walkers? That Gretta? The same Gretta who killed Joe and Samantha and… you?" I thought she'd been a Night Walker undergoing experimentation, in order to turn her human again.

I already have questions, but I shut up and let him continue the story, praying that Flynn will answer them as he reveals the truth of The Farm's past.

"Gretta wasn't a Day Walker when we first created -4. She was a cunning biologist with a talented mind. We were young and full of enthusiasm and dedicated to our cause, and we were going to find the cure for vampirism. Foolish really. Only a few years later did it become apparent that, once dead, we couldn't bring a human back to life. Night Walker venom contains magic, and it's that magic which brings us back from the dead. Trying to remove the magic is like turning off a vampire's life support.

"So, eventually, we tried a new angle. Not a cure for vampirism, but an antidote to stop venom from killing humans. Venom is a powerful substance, if used correctly. Not enough results in a painful death, and too much results in immortality. We found an optimum, a sweet spot between the two, and created an antidote. We could introduce the venom into a human's bloodstream in regular small doses; a process called mithridatism, so that a Night Walker's bite couldn't kill in the event of an attack."

"But, if bitten, with the antidote already in a human's system, wouldn't it turn the human into a vampire?" I ask.

"Yes, it would turn a human into a vampire if they died, but it would allow the human valuable time to kill the vampire before the vampire could kill them." He seems to sense my disapproval, adding, "It wasn't perfect, but it was a starting point."

I piece it all together, my gaze lingering on Donnah as I reply, and I wonder what variation the hybrids have become. "Is that how you created the Day Walkers?"

The vampires in lab jackets at the far end of the room smirk, mocking my lack of knowledge.

"I wish it were that simple. You see," Flynn begins, "Joseph didn't know about the antidote. He was a stubborn soul, set on using the hybrids to attack the vampires. To tell him what we'd been planning—he would have considered it a waste of time and resources. We knew our only chance of convincing him would be to provide a ready antidote, one that he could use straight away."

"Stubborn runs in the family, it seems." I search the room for Ares, forgetting for a moment that I won't find him, and my heart shatters again.

Flynn rushes on with his story, trying to distract me. "In the early days, I'd been able to test the useless cure for Night Walkers whenever I left The Farm with earlier generations of Titaniums on their missions. But once we changed our tactics, to find humans to experiment on—to bring them back from the outside world and keep it quiet from Joseph? It was impossible. Our only other option was to test on the farmers, but we couldn't risk word getting out about what we were doing."

It seems like a lot of hassle to me, especially considering the increased speed and strength of a vampire. Humans still wouldn't stand a chance, antidote or not.

"So…" I will him to continue, but he's waiting for me to piece it together, oblivious to my exhaustion from the battle and everything that's happened since.

He understands soon enough. "So… we tested on ourselves."

Despite my tiredness, I conjure enough enthusiasm to show my shock. "Oh, wow." It seems mad. Three of The Farm's most valued scientists experimenting on themselves when the world needed them most?

What had they been thinking?

"We each tried a different variation of the vaccine, already proving to be successful during the animal trials. Testing ourselves meant we had to be fully certain of our work. But… the vaccination wasn't the only thing that Samantha should have been testing."

He falls silent as the muscles of his face tense, and he can no longer look me in the eye.

"Oh," I say as I understand, my mouth hanging open as my head drops back. I stare at the ceiling as the information sinks in. "Oh, shit." I bring my hands over my eyes and pinch down hard. "She was pregnant with Ares, wasn't she?" When I look back at Flynn, I don't have to hear his answer to know that it's true. It's written all over his face. "So Ares had Night Walker venom in his system the day he was born?"

Flynn nods. "Ares was born part human, part Night Walker, yes. He was the first Day Walker to grace the planet."

CHAPTER THIRTY-THREE

HIM

I'm as free as the breeze through the empty winter branches.

No rules.

No games.

I am smoldering fire, ready to set the trees alight.

I can do whatever I like. Nobody can stop me.

CHAPTER THIRTY-FOUR

LORA

I can't believe it.

I'm not sure I want to believe it.

Ares was the first Day Walker?

Ares?

I hate how it makes sense: how he always reacted so strongly to the sight of blood, and he never had the energy to evolve. I search for ways to deny it, but how can I?

"Of course, Samantha told Joseph everything once she realized she was with child, and their relationship fell apart as the trust between them crumbled, but they agreed to continue working together in order to keep their secret. Ares wasn't fully human, and we didn't know what to expect from him; if he'd become unpredictable and dangerous as he grew into his power. We couldn't risk Marshall's safety, so we raised them apart."

"You thought Ares might hurt Marshall?"

Flynn pursed his lips before answering. "We didn't know enough to be sure. If he developed a thirst for blood, there's no saying what he might have done."

"And did he?" I hold my breath.

Flynn doesn't answer my question right away. "Ares was just like any other child for the first years of his life. We ran tests on him daily, and this lab transformed into what it is today, the A.P.P.—the Ares Protection Program. Joseph installed extra cameras around The Farm and granted access to The Farm's databases, with the option to override the primary system when needed."

"Protection Program?" I ask, wondering why they'd thought it necessary. Surely Ares had been safe on The Farm? "What were you protecting him from?"

Flynn's pupils tighten, zoning in on my face. "Himself."

There's a sense of danger in the air, thick enough to taste. My hand longs to reach for my dagger, but I pick at a loose stub of plastic on the chair as I rip my gaze from Flynn's to the screens above, looking out over The Farm. I sift through the information I've received about Ares, and Day Walkers, and The Farm, and hybrids.

Himself. I swallow my fear.

"Was he… dangerous?" My voice is quiet, fearing I already know the answer. I can't bear to look at the red-eyed hybrids on at the far end of the room to consider possibilities I'd never have believed. But I know it's true. It's true and my heart can't handle it.

"He could be, if he felt threatened."

I've seen the evidence—the bruising on White's face, and everything else I'm still trying to process. My eyes flick to Yiri, her body floating lifelessly in the front row of incubators. "How dangerous?" My stomach is twisting, churning, bubbling.

Flynn nods, his brows creasing in concern.

"I need to hear you say it," I urge. Maybe I'd start to believe it if I heard it.

I could cry.

"Dangerous enough to lose control and forget everything he'd done."

My chest contracts, the air leaving my body and refusing to return. I gasp, clinging to the chair in hopes it'll stop my world from spinning, but it doesn't help as I try to focus on one of the two Flynns before me.

"He killed them." My voice is breathless. "There never was a rebellion. The farmers didn't kill the Omegas, Ares did. And you cleared it up."

Flynn gives me time, but an eternity wouldn't be long enough.

Ares had been mutating and killing hybrids and then forgetting everything as soon as he returned to his human state. No wonder his shadows were forever fluctuating.

"But he could always return to his human state? He shouldn't have been able to. We thought he'd lose his humanity if he mutated again."

Flynn hesitates.

"Tell me," I say, gripping the chair harder, for what could possibly be worse than this?

"He was killing hybrids and drinking their blood. The extra Titanium energy gave him the power to return to his human state, contributing to the energy you were already feeding him through your aura."

Feeding him.

It was all so twisted. So wrong.

This wasn't the Ares I knew. I refused to believe it was Ares at all. It was an animal.

"Had he always been this way?" I ask, needing validation. Was the Ares I knew real, or was the boy I fell in love with just a result of the metamorphosis?

Flynn registers my desperation. "The alter-ego was not Ares, Lora. It was a mutation—a failed experiment. The Ares you knew was his true personality."

I wish his words would fill me with relief, but they don't, because it doesn't change the fact that Ares had been killing hybrids.

Flynn is still rummaging through my mind.

"He was a good kid." Flynn slides his seat closer to the desk as he reminisces, his eyes landing on the pin-board behind me. "Smart, just like his parents, gentle, but troubled. He'd always felt different from the other children in the infirmary, more aware, faster reflexes, and so in tune with the people around him. The other kids segregated him, shunned him. I think that's why he took such a liking to Marshall—his brother was different too, being the oldest in the infirmary, and maybe Ares recognized him as being of the same blood."

"They were friends?" I question, distracted by Flynn's story just enough to forget what Ares had done.

The Night Walker chuckles. "Ares certainly tried, but you know what Marshall was like. He was a lone wolf. He took after his father in that way." Flynn's smile fades. "Maybe they could have been friends, but as Ares grew, we saw more of the vampire traits become present. His eyes turned from honey brown to red, his strength became abnormal, and he reported having a strange fascination with blood, so we took precautions."

My heart aches, recalling the sight of his childhood bedroom. "What kind of precautions?"

"We decided it best to keep Ares isolated within his room, this room, and the Biome—not only for his safety, but for the safety of those around him, until we found another solution."

Three rooms?

They'd caged him for being different—for being a result of their own experiment. He'd never been accepted, not by his family, or the people who'd made him this way, or me. All this time, he'd just been looking for somebody to embrace his differences, and I'd failed him.

Me, the Alpha who knows all too well what it means to be different.

Flynn's story pops my heart—it's deflating and I pull a hand to my chest in hopes to bandage the puncture. "So, how did he end up a hybrid? Was that the solution you came up with?" I ask.

Flynn looks away again and his face twitches. I've touched a nerve.

"Ares was born with Night Walker venom in his system. The antidote allowed Ares's cells to mutate as they multiplied, so as he grew, he generated his own venom, as a Night Walker would, yet he was essentially still human. He was never dangerous—not until…"

Flynn stands and turns away from me, focusing on the vampires across the room. I continue to pick at the chair, but nudge my leg against the desk to feel the dagger is still in my pocket.

If the conversation turns, I'm ready. I know exactly how

long it'll take to move my hand to the weapon strapped against my leg. It's a precaution—just like imprisoning child Ares. I don't know Flynn. I don't know what he's capable of or what he's comfortable doing to people who overstep their mark. He was a farmer once, after all, and rule number one is to not ask questions.

I focus on him, waiting for his discomfort to settle, but he starts to pace. I dig my nails deeper into the plastic of the chair.

Flynn finally speaks again, and I wonder if he's been reading my mind this entire time.

"Ares wasn't a prisoner. We didn't lock him away. And just because we kept safety measures, it didn't mean we loved him any less, but as the years went on and the pressure of the war grew, we had to focus our attention elsewhere. We didn't have the time to keep Ares entertained for hours, and shifts became more and more sparse."

Shifts.

As though treating Ares like a human was *work*.

"Marshall and Joseph were having more disagreements as Marshall grew older, and one day there was an argument. Well, more of a fight, actually. Samantha ran to diffuse the situation. I was caught up in surgery, and Danny was with the hybrids. We left Ares alone all day, without food, and when Gretta visited that evening…"

"Oh, God. Did Ares—"

REAP

"No!" Flynn knows what I'm about to say, the image of what Ares had done to my hybrids resurfacing. "No, he would never have done that before the metamorphosis, but when Gretta visited, he tried to escape his room. He pushed Gretta back through the door with so much force that she flew into the wall behind and split her skull."

I flinch. How old had he been by this point? How long had he been in isolation?

"He was eight, with the strength to outmatch any hybrid on The Farm, and he used it all on one fragile human…" Flynn pauses, distracted by whatever memory he has of this moment —whether he found them like that, or if he watched it on the screens—and it haunts him. "We never told Ares what he was, so it must have been instinct that made him bite Gretta as he watched her life slip away. He knew he could save her."

I feel only sadness for Ares as I listen to the story. It hadn't been his fault. He was just a child trapped in a box, needing to escape. I'm sure I'd have hated the farmers had it been me in his place, but Ares didn't, or else he would have left Gretta to die. He would have taken his chance and run through -3 until he found the lift or the stairs, and then he'd have risen to freedom; rolled in the grass, jumped through puddles, filled his lungs with fresh air for the first time in his life.

But he hadn't done that.

He'd injected his venom into Gretta to save her and started

his own bloodline of Day Walkers.

"His mutated venom turned her into something entirely new. She was feral; angry and raging. A real monster."

Like Samantha. She'd been a real monster, too. Scheming, manipulative, and blood-thirsty. It's the first time I've ever considered that Samantha had been more destructive than the Night Walker Queen I'd killed in The House of Nightmares.

"You wouldn't consider a Night Walker a real monster?" I know what I'm implying, but Flynn can read my mind. He already knows what I think of vampires.

He smiles as though I'd told a joke. "Night Walkers only do what they have to in order to survive. Don't believe what Joseph or Marshall told you. The Night Walkers never started a war, they—*we* just reached the top of the food chain, and humans started to fight back." He has to correct himself, as though even after eight years of living like this, he hasn't processed that he is one of them. "Of course, humankind has dominated the earth for centuries. Handing the power over to creatures of the night would never be an option for them."

I once again recall the Night Walker Queen I'd met inside The House of Nightmares—her bargain. She'd asked me to join her and Benji's pack, telling me I would care for what she had to say. She'd tried to be reasonable, calm, just as Flynn is now.

But then I'd killed her… I'd killed them all.

"Night Walkers didn't start the war?" I repeat, processing.

"Night Walkers are docile most of the time, living alongside the humans since the beginning. But as technology advanced, cameras and computers, the vampires found it more and more difficult to hide. You can't compel a computer to forget what it's seen. And once the humans discovered the vampires, they attacked. The vampires only protected themselves as any other species would."

Night Walkers didn't start the war… humans did.

"Day Walkers, however," Flynn continues, "They're out for blood. They want war. They crave death." Like Samantha as she'd gripped onto Ares outside the Funhouse. I remember the bloodshed around us as Day Walkers fought against the wolves.

How have I never seen the divide between the two species before?

The Night Walkers I'd encountered had never once laid a finger on me. They'd been creepy as hell and they'd tried to turn me into one of their own, sure. But instead of forcing their teeth into my neck, they'd asked my permission.

And what about the vampires that killed Zee in the woods? I could bet now that they'd been Day Walkers, too.

What if it was all true?

What if the Night Walkers had never been the problem?

We started the war to keep control of the planet. The Night Walkers are no different to lions, or sharks—only posing a more immediate threat because they have the power to rob our free will, feed on us, and turn us into one of their own.

We're trying to wipe out an entire species for our own personal gain.

A shiver crawls up my spine.

I've played my part in this war. I've killed Night Walkers—not fully understanding the terms.

I believed they were a threat. I believed that they'd pledged war against humankind, to feed on us, use us to their advantage, but what if I've been wrong?

They're just doing what they needed to survive, and we're killing them for it.

How many Night Walkers had I killed when I brought down The House of Nightmares? I'd killed the Queen, and therefore her entire bloodline.

I shift, uncomfortable in my chair.

"What happened?" I ask. "To Gretta?" The real monster. The one that humans created.

"We kept her in the isolation units and tried to fix our mistakes. We explained everything to Ares then, and once Ares saw what had become of her, how violent and power hungry she'd become, he suggested that the metamorphosis might be the best route for him to take in order to separate his vampirism from his human state. The plan was for the animal genes to neutralize his vampire mutation."

"He volunteered himself?" I mumble the words in

disbelief.

"He didn't want to hurt anybody else, and he didn't want to create any more Day Walkers."

Of course he didn't.

Flynn nods in response to my thoughts. "We overrode the primary system and wiped all footage from the Observatorium's database so the farmers and Marshall would never find out about Gretta or what we'd done."

"But then Gretta escaped."

"Oh… no, Lora. She didn't escape." Flynn looks away from me, to the ground as he says, "I let her out."

CHAPTER THIRTY-FIVE

LORA

"I'm sorry, I think I might have misheard you," I say, my voice steadier and more controlled than I feel. *Now* I grab for the dagger, and I grip the handle tightly, resting it on my lap underneath the desk. "For a second there, it sounded like you said you'd let Gretta out of isolation. The same vampire who you just called an angry, raging monster."

Flynn's voice drops. I wonder if a human could hear his words as he says, "Gretta was my friend and I couldn't bear to keep her within the mirrored walls of her cell another day longer."

"But you were okay to keep Ares in isolation," I snap.

"Ares was different," he says, mirroring my icy tone. All

friendliness vanishes as he glares. "For seven years I delivered bags of blood to Gretta's cell, some traced with new antidotes, tranquilizers, antidepressants—whatever we could think of to calm her. She became a test rat. She was losing her mind, able to see her reflection on every surface. Each wall was reflective glass so that we could see in, but she couldn't see out and compel us. To see a friend go through something like that…" He sighs. I have no sympathy for him or for Gretta. "We weren't making any progress and I couldn't continue to torture her, so we struck a deal. I would let her go, and she promised to leave The Farm and never return—to lie low, only feed when necessary; to control her impulses and act like a Night Walker."

I play my dagger between my fingers. "You trusted her to keep these promises, given her mental state?"

"Foolish of me." Flynn swallows. "She killed a quarter of the farmers on her escape."

"Including you."

Flynn nods. "Including me."

We fall silent. The air is thick with tension, and I need a break from it. I need a break from it all.

Hail and Donnah are still together. Neither of them have moved, both of them pressing their heads to the glass and staring into each other's eyes.

"She didn't bite you?" I ask, processing as I watch the couple across the room and the surrounding vampires. Flynn's vampires. "Gretta killed you, but didn't inject her venom, otherwise you'd be a Day Walker."

"The only evidence of her gratitude. Instead of biting me, she snapped my neck. Quick and clean." Flynn runs a hand through his hair at the back of his head. Can he remember the pain? I hope he can. "I died with Night Walker venom in my blood from the antidote I'd continued to take over the years. Apparently, it had been just enough to turn me. I was alone when I finally came around. The sirens were so loud, and I ran back to -4 to escape the ringing. Joe and Samantha never returned, and it became obvious why once I watched the screens. I shouldn't have let Gretta go. I should have killed her."

"And you've been hiding here since? Wallowing?"

"Not hiding—"

"I get it, Flynn." I stop him short and shock myself. A wave of regret washes over me as I utter my confession. Why couldn't I let him suffer? I'm bitter, but I recognize his actions. "You're responsible for all those deaths, and now… now you're trying to compensate by turning the hybrids that I couldn't save."

I can't blame him for what he's done. His past mirrors my own in too many ways. I understand it, the guilt. One mistake made with good intention can have catastrophic consequences. These Night Walker hybrids are his redemption, just as they'd been mine.

REAP

Did he let White believe he'd died alongside Joseph and Samantha because he was a Night Walker, and therefore the enemy, or because he no longer felt worthy of White's love?

Flynn scowls, but it softens. He knows what happened to me in the Alpha Arena. We carry a similar weight on our shoulders.

"My team has been injecting my venom into selected hybrids for years. Those we know are certain to die—those we can save."

Hail looks at us over his shoulder for the first time and I wonder if he's been listening in to the entire conversation.

"They follow my rules. My bloodline will not kill humans, only take what we need to survive. We use visions to soothe the human, to take away their pain, and to distract them from the horror of the situation and then make them forget it ever happened. Mind control is only for feeding. We never use our powers to our advantage. We're good people, not Day Walkers." The silence is so dense that I can hear my own unsteady breath. Is he expecting me to thank him? Is he trying to reassure me that his Night Walkers won't hurt us? "Well… the Titaniums that Ares killed are. He fed on them, injected them with enough venom to turn them, and then he snapped their necks. I was raising them on my rules, but when Ares died…"

My eyes find Yiri. Kind, gentle Yiri, floating in her incubator.

"I could tell the difference," Hail says from across the room. I jump, not expecting to hear his voice. My hand tightens around my dagger. "When the Night Walkers took me from The Farm, their visions were nice. They showed me images of nature, and food, and Donnah, and sometimes I could even hear her singing. But when the Night Walkers handed me over to the Day Walkers in the Funhouse… it was like a nightmare. The Day Walker used the visions to scare me, and he found it fun."

Flynn nods. "The only reason the Night Walkers within the fairground sided with the Day Walkers was to stop The Farm. The Day Walkers wanted their leader back, and knew the Night Walkers would be willing to join their mission if it brought peace. Samantha and Gretta tricked the Night Walkers into doing their dirty work."

I stop breathing.

Their leader…

So caught up in everything else, I've overlooked this. If Ares had turned Gretta, then she wasn't the highest member of the bloodline. Ares was.

Ares was the King of the Day Walkers.

I'd seen the vampire army die as Ares' life slipped away, but I'd been too emotionally wrecked to question it. The Day Walkers died because Ares died.

"But Ares was still part human," I say.

"Once Ares put himself forward for the program,

REAP

Samantha suggested she could separate the human side of him from the vampire by adding to his genome. He would have a human alter-ego, and an alter-ego made of vampire and animal genes, so we could trust him. If his eyes were blue, his animal genes were in control, but as soon as they turned red, we'd know that the vampirism had taken over." Flynn finally retakes his seat, folding one leg over the other as I'd seen White do so many times before.

I'm put at ease by the familiar gesture. I wish White was with me now, despite his ignorance.

"The animal alter-ego was supposed to suppress the vampire genes, and it did for a short while, but the more Ares mutated, the more they fused together. He continued to generate vampire venom, more and more each time he became angry, or uncomfortable, and it changed how the animal alter-ego behaved."

"The darkness of his aura… was I sensing the growing vampire magic? Was I watching the vampire within him becoming stronger? And that's why he needed my energy?"

"When he fed on your energy, you were feeding the animal alter-ego, giving it more power, but paralyzing the vampirism just as when he drank a Titanium Omega's blood. But no matter how much energy he absorbed, I fear his eyes would never have returned to blue. He is—and has always been—a Day Walker. There is no changing, suppressing, or altering that. The vampire genes will always triumph because it is the stronger species."

I gulp. His words make me uncomfortable, not just in the context, but in the nature of them. *The stronger species.*

"What would have happened?" I ask. "If Ares had died in training?" He'd come close on so many occasions.

"That's what the A.P.P. has been preparing for. I would have released the hybrid Night Walkers to detain him and return him to this level. They train in those incubators whilst I spy. I control drones, observe, and make sure that Ares is safe."

Safe?

"Really?" The anger brings tears to my eyes. My voice is weak. It makes me sound vulnerable and I hate it, but there's no hiding how I feel; Flynn can see past my shields. "So, where were you earlier? You did a crappy job of saving him when he needed you." My lips curl out as I fight away the breakdown building within me.

Flynn seems unaffected by my emotion, barely blinking at the accusation. "We were there for him in his initiation, overriding the system to feed oxygen into his coffin and keep him alive long enough for you to find him. We were there for him when he mutated in Phase Two, overriding the database so that the farmers assumed Ares had absorbed the venom from the drones. We were there for him two days ago when the darkness consumed him and he killed those hybrids."

"Okay!" I shove my chair back, knuckles turning white as I

grip my dagger against my leg. "I get it."

Hail jumps to my aid as he sees my discomfort. "Ares… Killed them?" he asks as he rests a reassuring hand on my shoulder. So he hadn't been listening.

"I know this is hard to believe, but you need to know who Ares really is and what he's capable of before you leave." His words make my skin crawl. "He killed the first four Titaniums before The Sanctuary arrived at The Farm. The stress was enough for him to mutate after he'd taken a shortcut through the hybrid camp to get to the gates on time. Beena,"—he points to the Night Walker monitoring the incubators—"used compulsion on a couple of farmers near the woods to clean up his mess and retrieve the turning Day Walkers for us, the same farmers you put in isolation units. Then I cleared the Omegas' information from the database and edited the camera footage."

Hail stares at the Night Walker named Beena, but she turns away from him without saying a word.

I'm still. So, so still.

Not wanting to believe it, even after having the time to process it, I try to think of another explanation, but I can't fight the memories.

Ares had seemed strange that afternoon. He had been stressed. But enough to mutate into his vampire/animal alter-ego? Enough to kill any hybrid who crossed his path?

My heart races. I swallow again, but this time my mouth is

dry, and it becomes painful.

"He killed the Veno hybrid in the early hours of yesterday morning, before you returned from the secret lab, Lora. He woke to find you were no longer beside him." My nails bite into the palms of my hands. "He'd gone searching for you, and this young Veno was returning from the bathroom. He didn't turn this one, but again, I wiped away all evidence."

I'm no longer able to force back my emotions. The tears sweep from me in a rush of regret.

I was so focused on finding a cure for his shadows, I didn't stop to notice that I was encouraging them, beckoning them out.

"Fast-forward to yesterday afternoon. You'd had quite an explosive argument, and Ares spent most of the day in Marshall's room. However, as he became more frustrated within Marshall's bedroom, he decided to take a walk and ended up on the outskirts of the hybrid camp once again—"

"Stop! I understand." I push away from Hail, leaning over the Night Walker at the other side of the desk, and glare so deep into his eyes that I might be able to control his mind.

Why is he putting me through this? It's bad enough that I've lost Ares, and lost these hybrids, but to find out how he'd killed them? I can't take any more. "You don't need to say it. I understand."

Thankfully, he stops talking and I drop into my seat, wiping my tears on my sleeves and then burying my face in my hands.

Eventually, Hail fills the silence. I'm glad about the distraction. I'm glad to have a moment away from the beams of Flynn's eyes, but Hail's words surprise me.

"Why doesn't the doctor know you're alive?" he says.

Flynn sighs and I hear him shuffle in his seat. "Danny doesn't know what Ares is," he replies, and it perks my attention. I look up.

After all this time—watching Ares grow, studying him for years—how could White not know?

"When he was born, Samantha told Danny that Ares was different, that we couldn't trust him, but she never said why. It's what Danny wanted as he prefers to remain neutral. He doesn't know that -4 exists. He doesn't know what happened to Gretta, and he still thinks that Samantha died on The Farm." We never told White about the finding Ares' mother in the Funhouse. "And some days, even that is too much for Danny. I've considered making myself known to him, but I can't do it. I'm no longer human. I'm the enemy, and I think that might be enough to finally push him over the edge."

The way Flynn mentions Ares' name has the back of my neck tingling. There's something I'm not understanding. I feel it, but I don't see what I'm missing.

Hail doesn't seem as alarmed as I am about Flynn, slouching as he crosses his arms across his chest. "I don't think you're the enemy, and I'm not upset that Donnah is a Night Walker, I'm just glad she's alive," he continues the conversation—because he's interested, or because he's giving me room to breathe, I'm not sure—but I eventually compose myself. "I'm sure that the doctor would feel the same too if he learned you were still here."

Flynn looks to screens above. I'm guessing he's located White. "But I'm not the person Danny remembers. I'm different from the memories he'll have of me… a new version of myself."

"So you're never going to see him again? Don't you think he'll want to hear your voice? Dude, don't be selfish. Let him make that decision for himself. If he doesn't want to know you after you've told him the truth, then you'll be no worse off than you are right now. At least you'll both have closure."

Closure. That's what I need.

Flynn studies Hail for a while, absorbing his words, and then his attention turns to me. I want to cower backwards into the shadows. "What do you think, Lora? Does it matter that I'm not the same person I used to be? That Danny will have to learn to trust me again—that he might not like the person I've become?" he asks. His smile is small. It's a warning, a test. "If you were Danny, would you want to know I'm still walking the earth?"

My mouth is too dry. The air gets stuck at the back of my

throat, and I swallow, despite the sandpaper texture. The room closes in, squeezing the oxygen out as it compresses, and I can't catch my breath.

The words.

Flynn's words.

I finally understand why they've been making me uncomfortable.

He's been speaking about Ares as though he's still here.

You need to know who Ares really is and what he's capable of before you leave.

Flynn's smile grows. He's been waiting for me to piece it together.

I swing to my feet but the blood rushes from my head and I'm left dizzy, stars painting my vision, and I'm too unstable to move. I rest my hands on the table—steady myself—blinking away the black spots.

Breathe.

The dizziness clears eventually, as does my shock.

In a split second decision, before I have time to think about what I'm doing—before Flynn has the chance to read my mind—I'm evolving, using what little energy I've managed to charge up to propel me forwards, leaping over the desk and knocking the Night Walker King from his throne.

I'm on top of him, my legs pinning him to the ground, and my dagger finally in use.

I position the titanium blade over Flynn's heart.

"Where is he?" I growl.

CHAPTER THIRTY-SIX

HIM

Who knew death can make you feel so alive?

CHAPTER THIRTY-SEVEN

HAIL

My mouth hangs open as Lora kicks the Night Walker's ass. I didn't see it coming. Neither did he, I guess.

She urges him to his feet and walks him down the tunnel with one hand on his shoulders, and the other pressing the blade of her dagger into his back.

And she's glowing—not like I've seen before.

Light beams from her entire being, not just her hair and her eyes, and I can feel her energy in the air.

Loose and wild.

I know how easily a mind can slip into a dark place after experiencing loss, and I won't blame her for anything she does over the next few hours, but I need to reel her back if I can, or help her regain control of that energy if nothing else.

Leaving Donnah so soon after finding her feels like a bad move. Every piece of me craves her company, but my Alpha needs me. My friend needs me. Ares would never forgive me if I let Lora go off the rails now that he's gone. So, I kiss the glass of Donnah's pod as I pass, promising to be back soon—telling her not to move.

Idiot.

She's stuck in that pod. Of course she's not going anywhere—or at least I think she's stuck. I never asked.

I don't linger to think about my silly words. Lora's light is fading as they move further along the tunnel, and I run after them.

One last glance back at Donnah.

She waves me goodbye.

My heart sings and its melody hums through my veins.

I catch up to Lora and Flynn as they reach a junction in the tunnels. "Which one leads us outside?" Lora asks.

"Outside?" Flynn's voice rises in panic, but Lora only tightens her grip on his shoulder, pressing into the sensitive point below his neck. "The sun is still up, Lora. I cannot touch daylight."

"That sounds like a *you* problem," she snarls and I wonder what I've missed. What had Flynn said to get this reaction out of Lora? Did she really care so much for the doctor, to drag

Flynn into daylight and show the world that he's still alive? That's what we'd been talking about—Flynn hiding from Dr. White.

The Night Walker sighs. "Left. It'll take you to the woods outside the fence. Turning right will take you to the nearest village."

Lora jolts him forward, and I follow at a safe distance. I don't trust the light warping from her body. It grows and shrinks.

I've never seen her so angry.

The tunnel slopes uphill like the one I used to get from -3 to the battlefield earlier today, and when we reach a barred gate at the end of the tunnel, Lora forces Flynn to open it. He types a code into the box on the wall and the circular gate clanks open, and she forces Flynn outside.

He whimpers, begging Lora with sharp words to let him remain in the tunnel, but she drags him forward.

The rain has stopped, and light creeps through the few leaves on the trees. I wince.

"Which way to the battlefield?" she asks.

"Left."

The blade has already ripped through his shirt, but Lora pushes the dagger into his skin as Flynn slows, and he unwillingly steps into a small patch of sunlight, flesh melting away.

REAP

He screams in agony.

I flinch at the violence, but I don't look away. Donnah is one of them now. I need to know what she can and can't do if I'm to protect her, and because of it, I'm glued to the yucky sight before me. I expected the skin to sizzle—like Teri's face had in Phase Two as she'd cried venom filled tears—but not this.

Not the blisters, bubbling and popping; not the dark blood that seeps into his shirt and stains it black; and definitely not the smell. It's nasty.

Vampires already smell bad enough, never mind when their skin is cooking.

Thankfully for Flynn, Lora pushes him back into shadows. The woods are thick, and the trees are almost enough to protect him the entire way to the battlefield; we only have to stop a couple more times as Lora forces him to walk through sunlit areas and his body works to fix the holes at the back of his neck.

Vampires heal faster than hybrids. I didn't know that.

The battlefield comes into view and voices merge as one person tries to talk over the last. The group of farmers outside the gate argue among themselves, not noticing us as we approach. They sound like the chickens next to the Guesthouse.

I need to show Donnah The Farm's animals—at night, of course. I imagine her sweet laugh as the hens *cluck-cluck-cluck* away to themselves. She's going to love them.

Lora and Flynn stare. The Alpha's mouth hangs open, and I can feel her nerves through the Alpha Effect. I want to throw myself in front of her, to protect her from harm, but I can't understand what she's afraid of. There is no danger here, just the steady rustle of the wind through the trees and the farmers crazily arguing as they circle the coat I'd placed over Ares' body.

I look between the farmers and Lora, her head snapping around to listen to the woods, like she's expecting to hear something other than the birds.

She's just on edge after this morning.

Flynn stares at the doctor. Is this the first time he's seen Dr. White in person since he turned vamp? His burns no longer seem to bother him as he gazes out to the battlefield.

Weird how love can cause and cure pain at the same time. I see the heartbreak in Flynn's eyes as he watches the doctor lean over Ares' body. The doctor yells at a group of farmers—demanding answers—and reaches to lift my coat.

I suck in a breath.

It's like a magic trick. I can't understand what I'm seeing.

It's a joke.

It must be.

Ares must have set this up. He always was a joker.

But how could he have set this up, when he didn't know that Jayleigh would kill him today? I don't understand it, but

REAP

there are a few things I know for sure:

    1- I'm not under vampire compulsion.

    B- I no longer have visions.

    C- Ares' body is not under my coat.

CHAPTER THIRTY-EIGHT

HIM

I'm unseen from the woods at the bottom of the hill, watching figures crowd the space where I'd died like vultures.

Death surrounds me, all descendants of my bloodline, but I carry only Gretta's body. I'll bury her when I'm far enough away from The Farm to be safe. She is family, after all.

There is one thing I must do before I leave The Farm for good—just one promise to make, and then I'll vanish into the shadows where I've always belonged.

She appears alone from the woods to my left. She is blinding, a deadly white light as she crosses to the crowd of farmers near the gates.

There she is, the only one that matters.

REAP

If only I could steal her away now—away from the poison that is The Farm, leaking twisted lies into the blood of all who enter its gates. The group points to the grass where I'd died. Thankfully, Lora had pulled the dagger from my human heart and I bled to death with my own mutated venom in my blood. I wouldn't be here to warn her if she'd left the dagger in place.

They will feed her stories about me; they will turn her against me, and if it's her choice to listen to their fabrications, then I'll respect it.

"Allora," I whisper her name, and it reverberates through the air, filling me with joy. Such a beautiful name. I've never paid it much attention, but now I can appreciate it fully. I have an eternity to play the sweet syllables from my tongue, savoring each with her by my side. We can have it all.

But not yet.

Lora stops as she reaches the group in the field, and they fall silent. She spins, unable to see me, but she feels me, hearing her name whispered through the wind. She knows that I'm here, waiting.

Uncle Danny reaches for her, undoubtedly to tell her I am gone. I am no longer human. I'm the enemy.

But that's where he's wrong.

I will not make myself the villain so long as The Farm leaves me in peace. I've never wanted violence and I do not call for war, but they will inevitably force it upon me, so I must prepare.

If it's a war The Farm wants, it's a war they shall get.

"Allora," I say once more in promise. *"We will be together again—I'll make sure of it."*

Across the valley, she falls to her knees, and it's the answer I need.

"I might be a King, but there's no need to kneel, Alpha. You will always be my equal, and together we will set the world alight."

CHAPTER THIRTY-NINE

LORA

He's here.

The voice travels in the wind, the farmers' chaos turning to silence in fear, rather than matching my relief.

He's here, and he's saying my name.

His whisper caresses my ear. It wraps me in a dangerous, sticky warmth that threatens to melt me. The magic is so thick I can taste its sweet touch on my lips. My insides have already fallen victim—my heart, my lungs—they've betrayed me, and I know it's wrong because Ares is now dead. He's a Day Walker, and he's everything they have taught me to despise.

I should draw my dagger.

I should project my energy.

I should not scan the trees for a hopeful glance at him, unless it be to target him, which is not the case. I'm searching for him because I need proof that he is standing and moving—even if he's not breathing.

I need to see him. To know that the dagger wound has healed. To see his face once more before he leaves and decipher whether he is still the Ares I know.

It's possible that he is like Flynn, and Donnah, and the other hybrids saved from death, acting more like them than the Day Walkers we've encountered. Besides, the venom in his system once belonged to a Night Walker, and Ares' magic was never fit for anyone else but him and his mutated body.

But I'm a fool to give myself hope.

"Allora." His whispers tickle the air in small echoes and I am torn.

I know he can't reveal himself. It's not safe, but I crave a glimpse of him.

The farmers on the Gate Tower will shoot him with titanium bullets if they see him, and they will expect me to help. They will make me kill him. Although it pains me, I'm thankful that he stays hidden. He hasn't lost his mind in death.

"We will be together again—I'll make sure of it," he speaks directly to my mind and my knees can no longer hold me. My face betrays me, revealing my shock as he can still mind jump—this time without touching me. He still has the hybrid genes. *"I*

might be a King, but there's no need to kneel, Alpha. You will always be my equal, and together we will set the world alight."

My energy warms to his words as though obeying, ready to take on anything that might come between us. I'm laughing and crying—a mess of a lethal weapon.

I could lose control at any moment.

But I reel the emotions in. The farmers can't know what I suspect he's confirming; they will attack at the first chance they get, and to reveal Ares' words will only make them more eager. He is the only Day Walker left, but he can easily create more, and that makes him the most dangerous being on the planet. He has already set the fire—I don't need to stoke it, so I keep his words to myself, stand, and tuck my hair behind my ears.

My best hope of helping Ares is to act presentable and distract the farmers from him.

White, ever skeptical, is looking at me through half-closed eyelids. He hasn't yet noticed Flynn, who remains buried in the shadows of the woods where I left him; under threat from the dagger in Hail's hands.

It's the perfect diversion—earth shattering enough for them to forget about Ares for the shortest time; enough time for my Beta to run. The drones will locate him soon enough. He needs to get out of here before the farmers send an assassination squad.

I'm thankful the other Titaniums still lurk within the gates.

Jayleigh wouldn't react well to learn that killing Ares had only turned him into what he was always destined to be. She'd try to finish the job, I'm sure of it.

The farmers would send her out to hunt him.

I needed to direct their attention sooner rather than later.

"Hail, please push Flynn into the sun," I mind jump to my fellow hybrid who frowns at me in response. He can't reply, as he's not evolved, but I see the concern written on his face as though he'd drawn it on with a thick tipped marker—eyebrows scrunched forwards, lips pulled into a straight line. *"Trust me."*

He does. He always has, despite everything he's been through and everything I could have done to prevent the events that destroyed his life. At least, by some work of a miracle, he has Donnah back—actually, less of a miracle and more thanks to the Night Walker I'm now ordering Hail to sacrifice for Ares' benefit.

Hail follows my orders and Flynn yells out in pain as the sun scorches his skin once more. It's bad. Facing the battlefield, and therefore the sun, the Night Walker's face takes the biggest hit.

The farmers turn at the commotion, puzzling over what Hail is doing, and why he has a Night Walker in a headlock with a dagger against his back.

Flynn's face is beyond recognition as the skin simmers like boiling honey. *"That will do perfectly, thank you,"* I say to Hail, and they return to the shadows.

He holds Flynn still as the skin heals, and I turn to face White, who is staring at the woods as though he's seen a ghost. He could be a ghost himself, his skin void of color, and I wonder if I've made a mistake in revealing Flynn to him so soon after losing Ares.

To lose a nephew and find out your dead lover is a Night Walker in such a brief space of time would be a lot to process. Especially for the man who'd rather trick himself into believing a less hurtful, false version of reality.

White doesn't act in the same way Hail did upon finding Donnah again.

The doctor recoils as though he's been shot, holding a hand over his heart. The gathered group of farmers don't yet recognize the injured Night Walker before them, but White knows Flynn too well. White stumbles into the group, falling as he scrambles backwards through the mud of the battlefield, and somehow finds his way back to his feet.

Then he runs.

He runs.

And he doesn't look back as his feet carry him through The Farm's gates.

CHAPTER FORTY

LORA

I stare at the ever shrinking knot in the wood above my bed. The morning light hasn't yet snuck through the gaps in the walls. We'd done a good job of replacing the planks I'd destroyed upon my escape last year. But now the rain filters through with the winter wind and small drops land on my skin as I lay there, craving Ares' morning kisses.

I can't sleep without him by my side. I've become accustomed to his body heat and cuddles, and I wonder when we're reunited if his body will feel the same against mine.

I imagine it will be cold, as though he's made of speckled granite, like his eyes used to be. I worry what my future with Ares might look like—whether he'll accidentally feed on me whilst half asleep, as one would sleep walk. *Will* he sleep? Flynn said that the Night Walkers can't.

Ares will be able to read my every thought. He'll be able to control me if he looks into my eyes.

That's not what stops me from sleeping, though.

I spend most of the night worrying about White. He retreated to his bedroom in the Guesthouse as fast as his human body would allow, not accepting visitors, food, or any word of the explanation I tried to share through the wood of his door.

I'd been right to think that exposing Flynn was too much after losing Ares, considering that White had refused to help Ares as he lay dying because of his red eyes. Discovering that Flynn also has red eyes would be devastating. White would see them both as a lost cause—more lives lost to the enemy.

Only... Ares has always been one of them.

I shiver, recalling how his lips had a tendency to find my neck. Was he ever tempted to bite?

Even with this new... situation, I'm certain I'll still enjoy the neck kisses, despite the danger of him finding my pulse. I still trust him. Stupidly.

Perhaps I won't when I see him in all his vampire glory. Maybe the world will come crashing down and I'll realize that Flynn was right—Ares is no longer the person I remember. This new version of the boy I love might be destructive, a killer, a variation of his alter-ego. I should tread on thorns every time

I'm around him, like Tye in his initiation, and expect Ares to pierce my skin. It would be safe to be nervous around him, but then, I always have been, and that never stopped me from trusting him before.

I enjoy the nerves.

Ares was always defiant, and a little unpredictable—like the way he left me on edge in the hidden cave pools. He'd made me feel vulnerable and worshipped at the same time, and it was bliss. Now I'd always be vulnerable in his presence.

Me. The Alpha of the Titanium pack; the strongest Alpha ever to live. But I am so, so fragile next to the immortal King of the Day Walkers.

The title sends my heart racing as I play it through my mind.

The King and the Alpha; the vampire and the hybrid. What a tragic pair.

How could we have ever considered him weak? He's been hiding his magic within him. He's been fighting himself—his purpose, his darkness—and we doubted his strength. In the earliest days, he'd told me he didn't want to mutate and lose himself to the monster inside; he'd known what he was capable of, the full extent of his power. I always thought he was charming, convincing, but what if he'd been able to sway me?

If the magic had been in his system from the first time he evolved, could he have used it without realizing? Is that how he'd broken down my walls, sucked secrets from me, and changed the way I viewed the world?

Had he been compelling me this entire time?

Had he compelled anyone else? White? Marshall? Solace?

I shiver against the warm duvet and decide to use the compulsion device once everyone wakes. It will flash red if I'm under compulsion.

But Ares died, and therefore, any compulsion will have ceased to exist, so the device won't work. It won't be able to tell me if I've been under vampire control in the past.

And that knowledge is surely an answer, because the compulsion will have broken when Ares died, and I don't feel any differently about him.

I'd still share all of my secrets with him and do anything he asks. I'd risk my life for him, and not because of his abilities, but because I'm in love.

He doesn't just have my mind, he has every beat of my heart; my soul. Every cell—human and animal—belongs to him.

He has me so entirely.

I'd be better off under compulsion, for love is far more dangerous. Because, more than hope or a responsibility or a distraction, love is a choice. And I'd choose him time and time again, no matter the circumstances.

Vampire or not, he is my freedom—even if he has the power to take it away from me—and I won't let him slip away again.

But what about the others?

What about Solace?

Chipper had poised the wolves to kill us in the forest. There was no logical way that Ares could have been able to tame her, but she'd listened to his every word; she followed him everywhere. And she hasn't returned now Ares is gone…

The Venos haven't returned either.

I hardly blame them.

The Farm isn't where I want to be right now either. It's in pieces.

White is in hiding. Wilson has taken over for the time being, but he's demanding answers about Flynn.

Hail and I returned the Night Walker King to -4 once the farmers retreated. Some of them had screamed; the farmers rarely come face to face with a vampire, never mind it being a human they once worked alongside. They couldn't bear to look at him, let alone talk to Flynn.

I'm becoming uncomfortably open to the idea, but not as trusting as Hail, who's currently with Donnah on -4. I search for him in the Alpha bond, feeling nothing but happiness and warmth when I find him. He's okay.

He's better than okay.

I just hope he's safe down there, with so many red eyes and teeth surrounding him.

REAP

The Titanium hybrids don't yet know about the vampires living hundreds of meters below. I was too exhausted to explain over dinner last night, or later as we got ready for bed, but I'll have to tell them today. I can only imagine how Jayleigh will take the news—if she can stand to be in my presence. She avoided me all evening, and I'm still waiting for an apology.

I should tell the pack that Ares is back from the dead, too. But I know how that news will go down. It will be just as difficult for them to process as the idea of Night Walkers living within our territory for the past eight years.

I wonder if the hybrids-turned-vampires still hold on to their hybrid genes after death, as Ares does.

There is still so much to learn.

So much to figure out.

How had we ever planned to finish this war with so little insight to what's going on around us?

How can we finish this war without killing Ares? Because that will never be an option for me.

And, with that in mind, I wonder which side of the war I'm now fighting for…

CHAPTER FORTY-ONE

HIM

The sun's rays hit my skin, yet I feel no warmth, no brush of Solace's fur through my fingers, only the movement of the salty breeze through my hair. It's been two weeks since I've felt anything physical at all.

That's the curse of the Day Walkers. We can walk in the sunlight, but we can't feel it. It's no wonder Gretta and Mother lost connection to the world and the people they shared it with. They were senseless, just as I am now.

I send Solace away and she returns after an insignificant amount of time. Through her eyes, I can see all that she has experienced on today's mission. Then I turn to Dickward and the eighty-something Venos that remain.

REAP

"They search for us," I tell the hybrids I've taken under my wing since stumbling across them. The poor creatures were never supposed to live this long, especially without Marshall. But Dickward now follows me with little care of our past, and I let him, figuring the Venos might come in useful when The Farm attacks. Safety in numbers.

I ask the Venos for nothing. They are free to do as they wish and I still don't fully understand why they stay.

I've always wondered what goes on in their minds, especially Dickward's. I recall the way he used to stare at me as he planned the most evil ways to kill me. But now, seeing into his mind, I realize they plan nothing at all. It's white noise.

They don't think, as Titaniums do; only feel. They act upon instinct because they're urged to move, not because of a single thought.

It's an interesting way to live.

Careless.

No opinions.

Maybe that's why they stay.

I offer them leadership and freedom, and it doesn't matter to them that I'm a Day Walker.

How strange to find this acceptance from Venos, but not from the Titaniums.

The Titaniums… They're looking for me.

I've seen their drones through the eyes of the wolves.

The Farm is planning.

Searching.

Scheming.

I'm building my defenses from the inside-out, striking matches and lighting torches; watching fire spark to life.

I'm a gentle flame.

How long will I flicker before the Titaniums figure it out, and everything explodes? And will Lora stand by my side when it does?

CHAPTER FORTY-TWO

LORA

Every night, I stare at the moon, counting phases. It's been a four weeks since the battle at The Farm's gates, which makes it an entire month since I last saw Ares. It feels like an eternity has passed, and with each day I grow more anxious of the person he's becoming.

He's been a Day Walker for a month, feeding on human blood, compelling minds, possibly even killing, but we've had no evidence to prove it—no evidence of him at all.

My distraction worked too well.

The farmers had been so shocked by Flynn's appearance that it provided Ares enough time to run. He avoided the drones around The Farm's perimeter with ease, as he'd been the one to station them, and slipped away undetected.

By the time The Farm recovered from the shock, it was already too late. I tracked him to the river, and that's where I lost him, his scent submerged by the water.

Once I returned to the Observatorium, I sent drones downriver and searched for signs of him along the riverbank, but we found no sign of him. I've found no more proof of his location since.

He won't have gone too far, though. He promised to come back for me—that we'd do this together. And unlike me, Ares has always stuck by his promises.

His silence must mean that he's planning something, and that makes me nervous. I no longer understand him enough to guess what's on his mind, but I'll be ready when he returns—day or night. I've been camping in the Observatorium for the past few weeks, not feeling comfortable in my bed, and watching the screens until I finally drift into a restless sleep.

Every morning, the council gathers. It's the only time that I encounter certain members of my pack. They've lost trust in me and my purpose, and I can understand why.

I've given it a lot of thought over the past weeks, everything that Flynn told me, and Ares' actions. Although I'm uncertain that we can trust the Night Walkers, I know for sure that killing them isn't the answer to our problems.

Ordering the Titaniums to let the Night Walkers live didn't

sit well. We've trained our whole lives to kill vampires, and now I'm convincing them to do the opposite.

It must sound mad. Maybe I *am* going mad.

Jayleigh and Diego are convinced that Ares will try to restart his bloodline—being the war hungry Day Walker that he is. They think I'm letting my emotions cloud my judgement. But besides my love for Ares, I don't imagine him wanting war when he has always stood for peace. He isn't causing havoc. There's no evidence of him setting the world alight, as he suggested he might. He's behaving like a *Night* Walker; keeping the peace, taking only what he needs. He's playing it safe—to such an extreme that he's become impossible to locate. I almost wish he'd act a little more Day Walker to give me a clue of his whereabouts.

"You're delusional, you know," Tye says as he lingers around at the end of today's council meeting. Jayleigh and Diego talk to Tim as they wait for Tye at the bottom of the ramp, not wanting to spend more time in my presence than they need to. Tye draws my attention away from them. "We can't live alongside the vampires."

"Can't, or you won't?" I give him a pointed look. As annoying as Tye can be, he has been there for me, attempting to make me see reason, which is more than I can say for Jayleigh and Diego.

Hail has all but moved in with the Night Walkers. He

continues to show his face, offer a shoulder for me to cry on, and—unbelievably—make me laugh. But once the sun fades, so does Hail, vanishing into the night to be with Donnah. He persuades me it's out of choice and not because the Night Walkers compel him to, but I'm not fully convinced. Maybe I'll use the compulsion device on him one of these days, just to be sure.

Unlike Hail, I've not been back to level -4. I should pay Flynn a visit and ask the questions that play on my mind. But I can't bring myself to do it—to follow that overgrown path in the woods, baring too many memories of a day I'd rather forget. I need to stay hopeful, and too much of my resentment lingers within those woods. I promise myself that on a good day, should one ever arise, I'll make the journey to the hut in the forest.

"You know what the vampires are capable of, Lora," Tye says. His eyes close slightly, and he offers a small smile. I imagine he's pitying me, but I'm past caring what the Titaniums think. "It's not safe for us to be around them."

I turn back to watch the screens, not wanting to miss a glimpse of Ares should he cross a camera outside the fence.

He's coming back for me. And when he does, I'm not sure what I'll do.

I can't leave the hybrids; they'll die if I travel too far from them. And I can't bring the Titaniums with me because they'll kill Ares at the first chance they get.

"It's not safe for us to be around bears, but we haven't wiped their entire species from the planet. What makes Night Walkers any different? Day Walkers were the problematic ones, and they were all wiped out when Ares died. We have no reason to believe he's created any more."

Tye turns with me, facing the wall of windows to the world above. "That's the thing, though, isn't it? He's able to create more. He can control us and turn us into one of them against our will. If a bear bites us, we die. If a vamp so much as looks at us then we lose control over our bodies."

"Only if they want to control you, and I can guarantee that they won't."

"How?" Tye loses his patience and his body jolts towards mine as I push him to the limits. "How can you guarantee that?"

I raise my eyebrows in response to his behavior. "Because Night Walkers have always lived alongside us. They didn't start the damn apocalypse, Tye. The humans did. Let that sink in, then tell me who we can and can't trust."

For a moment, I think he might consider it, but then he jerks his head, sending his hair backwards. "That boy has always been bad news, Lora. The best thing Nerd can do is surrender. And you need to pick a side." With that, Tye storms from the balcony.

Surrender? So they can lock him up like Gretta?

No. Not on my watch.

I sigh as I slump onto the white leather sofa at the back of the room, which has been doubling as my bed for the past few weeks, and wonder if the hybrids are right about me. Am I delusional?

Or am I right to trust in a world where we can all live in harmony? So long as Ares behaves, the war is over. The Day Walkers are dead and the Night Walkers rarely kill humans. The world has found balance.

Sure, the humans have the shitty end of the deal, but it could be a whole lot worse for them.

I scream into the pillow, likely drawing a few strange looks from the farmers working at their computers below.

Wilson stands at my feet when I lift my head.

"Coffee?" he asks as he holds out a mug.

I've never tried it—put off by the memory of Marshall's breath—but I feel rude declining when Wilson is the only farmer to show me any sense of comradery in weeks.

"Thank you." I take the cup from his hands and sniff the brown liquid inside. It smells pleasing in this state. I wonder how much of it I'll be able to drink before my breath turns as sour as Marshall's. "Why do you wear green, Wilson, when the other farmers wear gray?"

His eyebrows raise as he sips from his own mug. "I'm from the Northern Camp. Green was our color, just like gray is The

REAP

Farm's. I wear it as a reminder of who I am and where I come from. It's a symbol of respect for the people we lost when the vampires overran our borders."

Finally, somebody who thinks sentimental value is important. "Day Walkers or Night Walkers?" I ask.

Wilson shrugs and sips his coffee. "They attacked at night, but given the intelligence of Day Walkers, I think they most likely wanted us to believe that they were Night Walkers. As with the Farmers here, we didn't realize that there were two species of vampire."

I nod, respecting his decision to honor those he lost through what he wears. It reminds me of the invisible scars coating my skin, and I reach for my pocket and pull out my dagger. Wilson's eyes widen and he gulps down his coffee, as though expecting I might attack him. I spin the handle towards him and offer him the weapon.

He doesn't ask why. Instead, he studies the handle, the addition to the crossguard, and waits for me to explain.

"That stone." I nod to the sea glass in the center. "Ares found it on the beach. I've had it zipped away in my pocket for months, but I decided it was finally time to put it on display." I blink away the tears of the memory. Our moment—us and the sand and the sea. What I'd give to relive it; the way he'd looked at me, and the feeling of my heart exploding as he admitted he loved me for the first time.

"Fitting." Wilson smiles as he returns the dagger to me.

"How so?" I ask, resting the dagger on the arm of the sofa so I can study it as I sip at my coffee—it's like a warm hug, and suddenly I understand Marshall a little better.

"That piece of glass would likely have been from a bottle. It's been smashed, knocked against rocks, and swirled around the ocean. But each bruise and each setback has turned it into a stone beautiful enough to hold a place on your dagger."

He offers a small smile as he retrieves my empty mug and retreats from the balcony. I play his words over in my mind and turn my attention back to the screens.

The Titanium hybrids continue training as though there are still Day Walkers left to defeat. The farmers expect more. They're preparing for it.

But Wilson intrigues me, drawing my mind away from the mess. Why, when everyone else has discarded me, is he being so nice? Nobody brings me coffee. Nobody stops to chat, if not to tell me I'm wrong.

But Wilson? If I understand correctly, he's trying to reassure me that the best is yet to come.

CHAPTER FORTY-THREE

HAIL

The air feels fresher here. Crossing beneath the fence with Donnah always lifts a pressure from my chest. It's our little secret. Our get away. Nobody knows we leave—except the Night Walkers, of course.

It's best that the pack and the farmers don't find out, but I'm yet to tell Lora. She's not ready. She doesn't trust us enough, and it's too soon to change her mind. When the truth comes out, I need to be sure that she'll take our side.

Nobody else can know because they'll try to stop me, if not kill me.

Being a spy isn't as fun as it sounded when Flynn first offered the job. I have a lot of information in my head that I can't share, and I'm not a good liar. But I am good at playing dumb. Flynn says people expect it from me. I try not to read too much into it, but whenever I slip up, I take Flynn's advice and finish with "Oh wait, that was a dream," or "just kidding," and they laugh it off.

After three weeks of secret missions, I'm yet to be called up on anything.

We travel by night, not that we really have another other choice.

Flynn checks the screens to make sure Lora is asleep. Her Alpha powers will make her aware of my growing distance if she's awake, and we can't risk that. So once Flynn gives the signal, we leave through the tunnel that takes us outside The Farm's gates. Flynn always changes the footage on the Observatorium's screens, so the farmers don't see us go.

And we run.

It's the most exciting part of my week, evolving and racing Donnah through the trees towards the meeting point. She's fast, but I'm faster. I try to make her feel better by reminding her that my legs are longer.

"You might be faster, but I'm the better spy because I'm quieter. What good is a noisy spy?" she says.

I laugh, but it's true.

"We're not actually spying out here though," I defend myself. "I spy on The Farm, but out here I'm just a messenger.

REAP

And a faster messenger is a better messenger."

"Fine." She climbs onto a fallen tree so that she's almost as tall as me, grabs my hands, and kisses me on the cheek.

I stare at her, thinking she's most beautiful under the light of the moon. Her skin was made for the night. Her eyes sparkle, reflecting the energy that flows through mine, and I'm about to kiss her when a voice interrupts us.

"Hail, Donnah." It echoes through the trees. I smile, kissing Donnah quickly as it grows louder. "Hail… Hail… Hail…"

I've learned that the easiest way to tell the difference between a Night Walker and a Day Walker is how much they like to play with their powers. And, of course, whether they can walk in the sun.

I roll my eyes as his voice continues to whisper my name. "Give it up, Bro. We get it, you're a Day Walker."

A figure steps through the trees and my smile grows as he approaches, holding his hand out to welcome me in our usual handshake. "But annoying you is so much fun."

After our handshake, I pull him in for a hug. "Dude, I've got some super crazy gossip for you today."

CHAPTER FORTY-FOUR

LORA

I'm at a complete loss.

Three months, and still no sign of Ares.

Has he changed his mind? Does he still plan to come back for me? Did he ever plan to come back?

Some days, I question if Ares died on the battlefield and I've made all of this up as a coping mechanism.

There's no sign of him out there, although I don't watch the screens within the Observatorium as often as I used to. It no longer fills me with hope, just an overwhelming sense of absence. Disappointment. Anger.

I keep myself occupied around The Farm while I wait for news from Wilson, although I'm not sure what I'd do if I got the call. Too much time has passed. When Ares told me we'd be together again, I'd assumed he meant soon. Where is he, and why haven't I heard anything? He hasn't given me the slightest clue. Not even a whisper in the wind.

Thinking about it drives me further into the hole of self sabotage, so I find distractions. I train the Omegas and become familiar with their names and faces; help the outer communities within the fence; and swim to the middle of the lake once everybody else has retired to bed.

Tye is doing his best to make me smile, but the only time I do smile is when I out-strength him on the training matts. I imagine how Ares would have laughed, and it's good to let off steam.

Jayleigh and Diego don't join us in combat. I rarely see them around The Farm, and that's the way I like it. Once Jayleigh apologizes—if she ever does—I might consider forgiving her, but until that day, I'd prefer her to keep her distance. The animosity radiates from me whenever we're in the same room and I can't hide it.

Her friendship with Hail has taken a turn, too. Not surprising, really, considering Donnah is a Night Walker and Hail prefers to spend more time with her than his pack.

Hail's slowly becoming nocturnal. He wakes in the early afternoon and spends his evenings with me, before retiring to the underworld when darkness falls to be with Donnah.

I should visit the nest below The Farm. It would be an easy promise to keep, but like all others, I break it.

The Night Walker hybrids used to be my friends, but I can't bring myself to face them—to look into their red eyes—because they'll remind me of my mistakes. And they'll remind me of *him*.

The thought of Ares always sends a sharp charge of energy through me. It's growing stronger than usual, probably because I've lost my outlet, so today I detour towards the secret lab within the chemicals cupboard. I need to find a new way to offload it, instead of using the lake after-hours.

I haven't been back to the lab since Ares found it, too distraught by the memories to revisit. I had no need, anyway, once Ares died. The synthetic energy is useless to anybody else.

The cupboard door is locked, as always, and I scan my print to let myself in, but I'm taken aback to find the fluorescent light is already on. I pause and survey the room. The bookcase isn't in its usual spot, but somebody has dragged it forward.

Had we left it this way after I ran after Ares? Has nobody been back since?

Guilt sweeps over me as I think about the poor Titanium frogs inside the lab. They haven't crossed my mind until now, and I rush through the gap in the wall to see what has become of them.

The tanks appear clean—the frogs are still alive, glowing

brighter than ever.

White stands at the far side of the room, fully equipped with goggles and gloves. He holds a pipette in one hand and a test tube in the other.

He's aged considerably in the last twelve weeks, wrinkles visible through the plastic of his eye protectors and glasses. His hair is wild and unkempt, reaching well past his ears. He looks every part the crazy scientist as I intrude on his experiment.

"Goggles on please, Lora. What have I told you about safety in the lab?" is all he says as I stand, frozen, in the doorway.

After three months, that's the welcome I get?

No *hello,* or *it's good to see you.*

I blink away my surprise and reach for my goggles, still hanging on the wall where I'd left them.

"What are you doing?" I ask, studying the tube in his hand, then the cabinets and the whiteboard where we record our notes —it's still covered with equations for synthetic energy.

"You did it," he says as he finishes dropping some chemical into the test tube on the counter. "The experiment you were working on the day that Ares lost his humanity—it was an exact match. It would have worked."

I stare at the equipment on the table, wondering what to make of the information. It doesn't fill me with joy because the energy is no longer usable. Just a waste of the precious time I should have spent with Ares when I had the chance.

But, it's nice to know that I did something right. It's one of the few little wins I've had in recent days.

White turns to face me, and at this closer distance, I notice his face appears thinner, the skin at his cheeks drooping where it used to be round. Not surprising, considering nobody has seen the doctor in three months. I wonder if he's been eating properly.

"I'm sorry for dragging Flynn onto the battlefield to distract you from Ares. It was wrong. I'm sure the last thing you needed was to see your undead boyfriend's skin melting from his face. Especially considering you didn't know he was a Night Walker," I say, and White is quiet for some time as he thinks.

He's well practiced, pouring measurements without double checking the instructions. I track his actions. How much time has he spent under this blue light?

"Yes, it was quite horrible, Lora. You are right, but I accept your apology none the less, just as I have accepted what happened and come to terms with the news."

"Do you have questions? I'd be happy to answer them." I assume he must want to know the truth about Flynn, and Gretta, and Samantha. Did he ever meet Gretta? He doesn't even know that Samantha turned into a Day Walker.

He shakes his head with a small smile. "I think I've pieced it together, and accepted the story I've created. Hearing the true story might prove a little difficult for me. I'd rather live in my bubble of ignorance, thank you."

"Okay." My heart steadies in relief. My shirt is thick with sweat at the idea of retelling the events. "I tried to visit you."

He continues his work, and the liquid in the tube turns from blue to purple. "I remember, and I'm sorry I couldn't be there for you. I understand it was a difficult time for us both."

You're damn right.

"I got through it," I say as I sink onto a stool, tucking a leg underneath me.

He gently plucks the rack from the countertop and places it into the climate controlled cabinet I'd used for my experiments. It's full. He's certainly been busy.

He pulls out another rack of test tubes; the solution glowing inside.

"Are you going to tell me what all of this is?" I ask.

White gives me the side-eye over his experiment. "I'm creating an antidote." I brace my hands against the counter, knuckles turning white. That hadn't turned out well for the last group who'd tried to cure vampirism. "But don't worry, I've been speaking to Flynn, and I know the dangers. It's not what you think."

My eyebrows raise, and the surprise is clear in my voice. "You've seen Flynn?"

"Oh, no. I've not seen him. But we've been exchanging

messages. Baby steps."

My heart melts for him. "That's great news. But, I'm assuming he told you how he became a Night Walker? About the antidote he created?"

White waves away my doubt with a flick of the wrist. "Like I said, this is not what you think. I'm not meddling with venom of any kind—I can't be the only one to think that's a disaster waiting to happen. You know, I always considered Samantha smarter than me, but now I'm questioning it… no, not venom. I'm using your synthetic energy, Lora. In small repeated doses, it's proven effective to stop Night Walkers controlling humans."

"What? My energy?" I loosen my grip on the worktop and drag my fingers through my hair. "You're sure? There are no strange side effects? Who have you been testing?"

White adjusts his goggles on his nose, still slightly bent from where Ares broke it. "Hail was the first to sign up to my trial. He was an obvious choice, given that he already generates his own energy, and he spends a lot of time with the Night Walkers, wherever that may be."

"They're right underneath us," I say, to fill the silence as I process the information. "Level -4."

White looks momentarily puzzled by the information, but he says, "Flynn reported it a great success. Each Night Walker tried to compel Hail to raise his hand and none of the hundred-or-so succeeded. I used the compulsion detector on him and he passed. The antidote lasted for a full week, with no short-term side effects. It works, Lora. We've moved onto human trials. It works."

"That's incredible." I'm still in shock, turning the information over in my mind. "It's revolutionary. This could change everything."

I consider Tye's take on how vampires are different to bears. Would he change his mind, knowing that the Night Walkers could no longer control his mind?

"How am I only just hearing about this? It's been under trial for weeks, by the sound of it. Hail knew, the farmers knew, why is everyone hiding it from me? I thought you'd been in your room this entire time."

The doctor places his pipette onto the counter, guilt written across his tired face. "I wasn't sure of your mental state, Lora. I've been asking for daily updates, and from what I've heard, you've been out of sorts. I didn't want to draw you back to this room until you were comfortable, given its history."

The floor tiles hold my attention. "I needed you, Dr. White," I say, my voice losing stability. He's the only one who's been there from day one. "You know I've always had your back, but where were you?"

The words strike a chord within him and his eyebrows curl up. "Oh, Lora. You have the pack. I thought that was enough?"

I can't hold in the scoff. "Didn't Hail tell you?"

"I hardly see, Hail. Only to discuss the antidote."

Hail never discussed the antidote with me…

"The pack no longer accepts me as their Alpha. I've lost their respect after rumors spread that I risked their lives for Ares." Rumors that are true. "They talk to me, train with me, but I am no longer their leader, friend, or somebody they can trust. Jayleigh has made sure of that."

White surprises me with a hug. "I didn't realize. I am sorry, Lora."

I sigh and close my eyes as I accept his embrace. He is Ares' uncle, sharing Ares' blood. White is the only family I have left.

"Hail still thinks highly of you, you know." he reassures me. "He's waiting for you to find yourself again. I think we all are. Where's that Lora lightning gone?"

He's not referring to my energy, I realize. "My lightning? That died with Ares."

White shakes his head, tutting as he pulls away.

"What?" I ask. If he's judging me, I need to know why.

"You forget yourself. You've given up."

Rage sparks within my blood. "I have not!"

If I'd given up, I'd refuse to rise from my sofa every morning. I'd cry until my tears run dry. I'd run away from The Farm and all the responsibility it holds.

"Hmm," White considers. "Maybe you have a little fight

left in you, then."

"Fight?" The stool flings back as I stand. "I've been fighting every day for the past four years, and the Gods be damned if anyone thinks I've surrendered."

"That's more like it." White pours liquid into a syringe. "That's the Lora my nephew fell in love with."

I halt.

After three months of waiting, is that the reason Ares hasn't returned? Is he waiting for me to recover? Has my moping been the only thing holding us back?

Because for him to return would mean war, and he would know that I'm not up to the challenge in my current state. Not after the battle—holding his dead body in my arms. After everything, has he been giving me time to fix myself? Has he been waiting because he still cares?

"Well, I believe this is it," White says as he offers me the needle.

"This is it?" I ask, looking at the antidote in his hand and absently reaching for it. "This is what?"

White's smile reassures me in a way that only he can. "It's time we visit the dead."

CHAPTER FORTY-FIVE

HAIL

The dream world has been my happy place for too long, but even the best sleep can't compare with the sight I wake up to.

I'm no longer disappointed when I blink the sleep away. Even through the fuzziness, Donnah is the most perfect thing in the world. Blurry Donnah is still more beautiful than anyone I've ever met.

She doesn't sleep—because she is a Night Walker and vampires don't need to—but she rests, closing her eyes and laying so still beside me. Her chest rises and falls to make me feel more comfortable, I think. I'm not sure if she actually needs to breathe. I don't ask her because I don't want to break the silence. She doesn't know that I'm awake yet, so I take a moment to watch her. She looks just as I remember with her eyes closed. Maybe her skin is clearer now, brighter, and her lips are redder. She has always been pale, so I don't think avoiding the sun has made a difference, but the scattering of freckles on her nose seems more visible. I want to count every single one of them, and then the number of hairs on her head.

I run a hand through her wavy black hair and her eyes open. It surprises me for a second. It'll take years for me to get used to her eyes being red instead of gray, but her smile is as kind as ever.

"If you were a fruit, you'd be a strawberry," I say, kissing her on the nose.

She laughs quietly in response, such a peaceful sound. I could listen to it all day. My heart is happier in this moment than it has ever been.

"Have you even tried a strawberry?" she asks.

I shake my head. "Nope." I kiss her lips this time. Sweet. So beautiful. "But I imagine they're delicious."

"Just like you," she whispers and tickles my stomach.

We laugh until it hurts. My side begins to cramp and I beg her to stop, so I'm thankful when a quick knock on the door distracts Donnah long enough for me to catch my breath. But then Flynn pops his head around the door and I am no longer pleased by the interruption.

"Dude, I could be naked right now," I say, throwing a pillow in Flynn's direction. I'm not naked, but I could be.

He raises one eyebrow. "I didn't think hybrids were concerned about nudity."

He's right. I wouldn't care. I've got nothing to hide. "What's up?"

Flynn was happy to have a small storage room cleared out when Donnah suggested I stay on -4 with them. The Night Walkers have taken me under their wing, treating me as one of their own, but they never usually call for us. It must be important.

"Lora is on her way to see us with Danny. Get up. Get dressed."

I poke my finger in his direction, but climb out of bed as I tease. "Make me. You can't control me, Vampy."

Flynn rolls his eyes and leaves us.

I'm glad that whatever the doctor keeps giving me is still working, otherwise Flynn might actually have compelled me.

"He wouldn't compel you." Donnah smiles as she lifts the sheet and smooths it over the mattress I'd stolen from level -2. "He's not like that."

I nod in response. "Yeah, I know."

"Then why did you think it?" She laughs.

"Hey!" I pick her up, like a feather in my hands, and throw her onto the bed she just made. "Butt out of my head, please."

REAP

"Hail!" she complains, but pulls me down with her and messes the sheets even more. We roll, laughing, and I wish we could stay like this forever.

"Me too," she says as she climbs back to her feet and pulls on her leggings, ready for her training in the pod thing. She places neatly folded clothes on the crumpled bedsheets beside me.

I stand, pull the shirt on, and by the time I poke my head through, Donnah's already in front of me, on the tips of her toes. She reaches for my neck and reels me down to her level, kissing me with those prefect strawberry lips. My heart races.

I wrap my arms around her waist and lift her from the ground.

I've had her back for three months, but I'm still not used to it.

I grip her tighter just to make sure she's really here, wanting to bury my nose in her neck but deciding against it, and I pull back long enough to confirm it's really her.

She wraps her legs around me. "It's me, Hail. I'm here. And I'm never going away."

"You'd better not." I kiss her again. "I love you more than life."

Eventually, when I let her, she replies. "And I love you more than death."

Flynn knocks on the door again, and I groan. He's more

impatient than Jayleigh.

"We're coming!" I yell, but my mind stays here, within this moment, for several hours.

"What is she doing?" Lora asks as she watches Donnah move about in her pod.

"Training," I reply, thinking that it's obvious.

Lora doesn't seem to think the same, her face screwing in as she says, "Training for what?"

Lora's sure been struggling since Ares turned into a Day Walker, but I didn't realize it has affected her mind. "The war," I say. Surely she hasn't forgotten why we're on this stupid farm?

She looks between me and Donnah, and then towards Flynn and the doctor as they speak quietly together by the screens. Flynn seems more nervous than usual. He stands straighter, shoulders tensed.

As I notice it, his eyes quickly look in my direction, and he relaxes. He's always rummaging through my mind.

"The war?" Lora repeats my words. "I don't understand… Are they planning to attack humans?"

"Why would they attack humans?" I shrink into the chair and enjoy a loaf of bread Lora brought from -2, since I overslept and missed lunch.

"I don't know." Lora's really out of it. She's scanning the room, picking out every detail between every wall.

REAP

"Chill, Lora. They won't hurt you. They fed three days ago, so they'll be good for another day or two." Her eyebrows raise and I sigh. She has no faith. "I went with them. Don't worry, it's actually not as bad as I thought it would be. Nobody died. The humans seemed pretty happy when we left, but that could be because Flynn ordered them to forget about it." I stop talking when she looks at my neck. "And no, I wasn't part of their meal —if that's what you're thinking. The doctor gave me the jab-thing, so I'd remember if someone tried to eat me."

Lora stares at me and says nothing. I can see her mind ticking with information, but she avoids the subject of Night Walker meal time and asks about the war instead. "So why are they training, if not to fight humans?"

"You know they don't want to wipe out every human on the planet, Lora."

She lets out a heavy sigh. "Just answer the question, Hail. *Please.*"

I hate to see her so defeated.

"They're training for Ares," I say. I don't know if I should give this information away. Flynn trusted me enough to tell me, and he told me not to tell the others… but Lora isn't the others. She's my Alpha, my friend, and she's on our side. She's on Ares' team, whether or not she knows it yet. "To help him."

"Ares?" His name sounds painful in her throat. I barely hear her words. "Do you know where he is?"

Yes.

Her eyes fill with tears and I wish I could take it all back. This is a bad idea. I shouldn't be speaking to her about this.

I feel Flynn's eyes on me. He's listening to my thoughts, and when I look at him for reassurance, he gives a small nod. The doctor doesn't even notice it as he dabs at his eyes with a tissue.

"This was all a part of his plan, Lora."

She gulps and quickly sits down next to me, her fingers playing with the hem of her sleeve. "His plan? So, he planned to die? He knew he'd turn into a Day Walker?"

I look from her fingers back to her face, which gives nothing away. "What?" I try to follow her line of thought, wondering how she jumped from training to Ares' death. "Oh! No, that wasn't part of the plan. He didn't mean to die on the battlefield and turn into a Day Walker. He was just trying to stop us all from killing each other."

Typical Ares.

Lora shakes her head and presses her lips together in a tight line. "If not that, then what? What was his plan?"

I look to Flynn for more guidance, but he's no longer watching us, his focus solely on the doctor. So, it's up to me to decide how much I can share with Lora.

I point towards the Night Walkers in their pods. "Come with me. It'll be easier to show you." Over the past few weeks,

REAP

I've learned enough about their training to understand the basics and know I can explain what they're doing—even if I don't understand how. I walk towards Donnah's pod. Only Lora isn't following. She stands in front of Shyla's pod, reaching forward and touching the glass.

Shyla's eyes open, sensing a disturbance on the other side, and she watches Lora with her usual judgemental scowl. "Hi?" Shyla says, pressing the button of her mask.

"Hi." I watch Lora's throat tense as she forces a swallow.

Shyla doesn't make small talk. She's always been too self-obsessed to care about others, so asking questions doesn't come naturally to her. Instead, she waits, gaze lingering Lora as the Alpha's mouth opens, but she makes no sound.

"Can I help you?" Shyla urges.

Lora clears her throat. "What did Marshall do to you, Shyla? After he dragged you from the barn? Was it over quickly?"

We'd lost so many hybrids in Phase One that I don't remember how Shyla died, but memories of that night return as Lora speaks.

"Marshall took me straight to the Veno Alpha—told me I was *sure leaving The Farm alright, but not through the gates.* Thankfully, Flynn's people got to us before we arrived back at the barn that day."

"Flynn knew Marshall would kill you for damaging the

fence."

"Yeah. He compelled a farmer to inject me with venom after training, so the venom was already in my system when Marshall dropped me into the pit with the Veno. Marshall left us there, knowing the Veno would finish me if I didn't evolve, and he was right. I didn't stand a chance."

Lora's bottom lip trembles just a little. "Oh, God. Shyla… I'm so sorry. You shouldn't have gone through that. I should have stopped Marshall, kept a better eye on what you guys were doing—I never should have let that happen to you. I failed you, and I'm so sorry." One tear rolls down her cheek as she steps back and studies the hundred pods before her. "I failed you all."

I reach out and rest my hand on her shoulder to comfort her in any way possible, but Shyla's words do better than I ever could. "It wasn't your fault, Lora," she says, red eyes squinting in disbelief. "We are all responsible for our actions. We died because of our own mistakes, not because of anything you did. You surely can't believe that it was your fault?"

Lora opens her mouth, most likely to defend herself and tell Shyla exactly why she feels responsible, but there are no words. Instead, she stands there with her mouth open for a long while. "You… you don't blame me?" she asks finally.

Shyla laughs through the mask over her mouth, throwing her head back to reveal the mess of wires attached to it. "Of course not," she says once she's calmed herself enough to talk.

REAP

"Damn, no wonder you always seemed so uptight. You honestly believe it's your fault." Shyla laughs again and Lora whispers a reply, but it's too quiet to hear over the speaker of Shyla's pod.

Lora's head is shaking back and forwards and I want to hold it still. She'll make herself dizzy if she carries on. But, out of respect, I don't hold Lora's head and she doesn't stop repeating that same line, even though nobody can hear her. It's only once Shyla calms herself that I'm able to make out Lora's words. "Why are you laughing?"

Shyla retreats in her pod, away from the glass, to continue training. "Lora, you really are something else. But, for what it's worth, I forgive you." She closes her eyes and tunes us out once more.

Lora is still speechless.

"They don't blame me," she whispers, her focus on something near, but her mind far away. "They don't blame me for their deaths. Shyla forgives me."

I don't think she's talking to me, but it feels rude to ignore her.

"They don't blame you, Lora," I say. "And there is nothing to forgive."

She falls into my arms as though she's shattering, but in reality, I think she's finally gluing herself back together. I hold the broken pieces of her tighter, hoping it helps.

CHAPTER FORTY-SIX

LORA

White once told me that hybrids heal at exceptional rates. I've both seen and experienced it, but I realize now that the injuries he spoke of were physical.

Mental damage isn't something that heals overnight. And it's only now, as an immense weight lifts from my soul, that I realize the extent of the damage I've been living with for the past four years.

The farmers had taught me that the responsibility of keeping the pack alive fell to the Alpha, and the hybrids' blood would stain my hands if I failed them. I would wear their deaths on my skin.

But everyone has a choice. Just as Ares should have had the choice to let his alter-egos merge if that's what he wanted, each of the hybrids floating before me also had a choice.

I have a choice.

The revelation leaves me shaking.

The room spins.

My only true responsibility is to myself. I can't control everyone. I can't make their decisions for them.

But I can choose a path to a peaceful future—it should have been my goal all along.

I sob into Hail's chest, a release of all the pressure and responsibilities I've been holding on to. He holds me tighter and strokes my hair, never rushing me.

When I pull away, everybody stares at us.

I truly don't care.

They can see me cry. They can watch me break in front of them, because I am human—mostly—and when humans break, they come back stronger. It is a metamorphosis. It is a part of life, and I am no longer afraid.

I smile through the tears.

"Thank you, Hail," I say.

The hybrid's silver eyes narrow with concern, but he returns my smile. "You never need to thank me, Lora. You are my Alpha, and my friend, and Ares once said you're also like my mother—which I still don't understand—but that makes us family. I'll always stand by you, even when the others don't."

It doesn't send me into a mental spiral to hear these words, as it might have earlier today.

Yes, I've lost the respect of Jayleigh, Tye, Diego, and the other hybrids. But their focus is violence and destruction—a choice I can't hold myself responsible for.

I can try to help them understand my line of thought, but first I need to know Ares' plan. I need to know what Flynn's Night Walker hybrids are doing here, so that I can make an informed decision on my next move.

I reply to Hail, "I'm not your mother, but we can clear that up later. Why don't you show me whatever it was you had planned?"

"Oh, right! Yeah, follow me." It seems he might have forgotten where he was taking me for a moment, but he knocks on Donnah's incubator and she rises to the surface. She unlocks the lid, removes her clear mask, and climbs out to meet us.

"Donnah," I greet her with the usual Titanium welcome. She smells of chemicals and musk, a far cry from her original cherry blossom scent.

She pulls away quickly. "Lora. It's good to see you." She's just as timid as ever. Her touch is fragile despite her vampire strength and when she steps back, she refuses to meet my eyes. Hail wraps an arm around her and she giggles, letting her wet hair fall in front of her face.

"We'll explain the pods later." Hail runs Donnah's hair back and kisses her forehead. This time, he speaks to her.

REAP

"Come on. It's time to show Lora what you can do."

They lead me down the tunnel that ends in the woods outside of the fence, and Donnah yells at him as I imagine a mouse would. "Hail!"

"What? Oh! No, not that. Definitely not that… but I like where your mind is at."

She laughs for a moment, seeming to forget my presence, and she shoves him.

Hail flies into the paneled white cladding, splitting the large tile in half upon impact.

I try to hide my amusement as he peels himself from the wall. "Ouch."

After a few more minutes of walking, we reach our destination—an empty room that splits off from the corridor.

"We use this room to practice," Hail says. "They're getting pretty good now."

"I'm intrigued," I reply, having no clue of what he's referring to.

They ask me to close the door, so I do, and I take in the empty room. It's coated in the same white walls as the rest of -4, and is the length of the barn. It appears to be a training room.

They both walk to opposite ends while I linger near the doorway, and Hail focuses on Donnah, his eyes lighting up as he evolves. Donnah copies, much to my amazement.

"What's happening?" I ask. "Are you evolving? Can Night

Walker hybrids evolve?"

"Bro, just chill for a sec and watch," Hail says and holds a hand to calm me.

I straighten up and pin my hair behind my ears. "I'm good." But I'm far more than good. I'm excited, sensing Hail's eagerness. Whatever he's about to show me is big, and it's all a part of Ares' plan. "I'm ready when you are," I say and lean against the wall, hoping it makes me look as care free as Diego.

"Ready?" Hail questions, but he's talking to Donnah, and her eyes are a gleaming scarlet red.

"Ready." She nods.

Hail projects his energy into a ball within his hands. It's easier than the last time I saw him do it in training, so he's been practicing down here with the Night Walker hybrids.

To my amazement, Donnah copies. My hands fly back against the wall, using it to center myself as I watch the Night Walker form a ball of swirling, inky shadows.

I can't believe my eyes, recognizing the shadows as the same darkness that clouded Ares' aura. My heart races, unprepared for the visual reminder of him.

Donnah moves her hands in an outward motion and the shadows expand, stretching, growing, swallowing her whole. I can only see her simmering red eyes through the stormy bubble that she's created.

Hail repeats, "Ready?"

REAP

"Ready!" Her voice no longer sounds mouse-like, but full of power.

My heart drops to my stomach as Hail throws his energy in her direction. Time seems to slow down.

No. No. No...

What is he doing?

It's too dangerous for a Night Walker to be struck by Titanium energy. It will paralyze her for hours.

I need to do something, to divert the energy somehow, to send it off-course. But it's not my responsibility.

I need to trust them; they know what they're doing. Hail would never hurt Donnah.

So I fight my instincts and watch as the Titanium energy hits Donnah's protective shield of shadows with a zap of red. The energy changes color upon impact, flashing over the clouds of darkness, and vanishes completely.

Donnah regathers her ball of shadows and her eyes stop glowing. She smiles at me as though she hasn't just revealed a trick that could change the dynamics of the war.

"Cool, right?" Hail beams, his hair wafting as he nods his head in encouragement.

"Cool?" I repeat, not knowing if it's the word I would choose to describe what I just witnessed. "Yeah, it's pretty cool." I try to keep myself from exploding. "So, um, can you all do this?" I ask Donnah. My fingers fiddle with my hair, my chin, my sleeve.

"Yes. Some are better than others. And if we all do it, we can expand and join our shields to protect everybody within," she says, not meeting my eyes again.

"That's amazing…" my words die out. I'm thinking about Ares' aura again, wondering why it absorbed my energy instead of protecting him against it—like Donnah's energy does. Wondering how it's different. Wondering if he can also do this, despite never being able to evolve like the other hybrids could. But as the awe wears off, nerves creep in. The Titanium energy is our greatest weapon against vampires. Without it, we have no advantage. It will level the playing field—should the Night Walker hybrids expand their shield to protect everyone within. "You said it was all a part of Ares' plan? How does he plan to use this?"

Donnah looks at me. Really looks. Diving into my mind and uncovering all of my worries.

"Ares wasn't coming to the battlefield to kill anyone the day he died," she says. I pick harder at my sleeve. I'd known it—that Ares was there for a reason, but hearing that reason doesn't ease the nerves. Killing has never been Ares' style, but it's a relief to hear that losing his humanity hadn't altered his morals.

Hail meets Donnah in the middle of the room, and he puts an arm around her, reeling her closer. She responds by wrapping her arm around his waist. They're inseparable and my heart aches.

Donnah continues, "When he lost his humanity, he could recall everything from his past, including turning Gretta. He knew he was their rightful leader, and they would listen to him. Vampires must swear their loyalty to their King or Queen. They kill and feast on those who prove to be disloyal."

I flinch, revolted, but Hail barely blinks at the news. He's heard all of this before, but he's mentioned none of it to me. I wonder if sweet, shy Donnah has ever eaten one of her friends; and then a more worrying thought… I wonder if Ares ever wanted to eat me for lying to him.

"Ares came to the battlefield to call for a peace treaty," Donnah says, and I let out the breath I'm holding. "He was going to call a meeting between you and Gretta. He got you from the tower and into the woods by attracting Hail's attention, and he knew Gretta would wait for the Alpha to make herself vulnerable. She would have followed, and Ares would have ordered her not to attack. The plan would have worked if Jayleigh hadn't killed off Ares' entire bloodline… Gretta died as soon as Jayleigh… you know."

A peace treaty…

Although on separate paths, it seems the Ares and I are still on the same page.

I nod. "But what is his plan for you?" I try to piece together what Ares might have been thinking.

"We're Plan B," she says, bowing her head slightly, it as though it's an honor to represent the Day Walker King.

"Of course he has a back-up plan." I laugh lightly.

"Ares didn't know if he would be successful in his mission, and he didn't know if he would come back if he died. But once Flynn revealed we can still evolve, Ares gave Flynn instructions to explore our abilities—and a solution to end the war. To do what his father never could; stop attacking and defend."

"But he came back, so what is his plan now?"

"His mission failed, Lora. There is no peace treaty because he died. The Day Walkers might be gone, but the threat remains."

"So he wants you to train… to defend. But why? What need do we have for a peace treaty now that the Day Walkers are gone?"

Donnah offers a sympathetic smile, and I feel small. "The hybrids. We still need a peace treaty with the hybrids."

I pause. "The Titaniums?"

"You can't trust your pack, Lora. They know Ares is still out there, and you've given them free rein as you mourn." She leaves Hail's side to rest her hand on my cheek, as a mother would to a child. I no longer have the Alpha bond with Donnah or the other Night Walker hybrids, and it changes the dynamics between us.

I swallow.

Why would Ares need a peace treaty with my Titaniums?

What have the hybrids been planning in my absence?

Terror seizes me. I retreat from Donnah's touch, needing space to breathe.

The Titaniums had continued their training. I'd assumed it was under the farmers' orders, but what if, while I've been soul searching, the hybrids have also been searching? What if they've been planning an uprising, right beneath my nose?

All the signs were there. Tye had warned me to side carefully, but I hadn't realized what he'd really been trying to say.

"They're planning to kill him, aren't they?" I ask as I back against the wall, dizzy, sinking to the ground as the world spins off its axis. "They're going to kill Ares."

CHAPTER FORTY-SEVEN

HIM

I force the darkness to bend to my will. I've seen hybrids control their energy a number of times, so I know how to do it, yet the shadows merely seep through my fingers and then die out. Donnah has tried to help me. She's given me clear direction, but the shadows belong inside me and refuse to leave my body.

Donnah and Hail's most recent visit brought alarming news. I need to get a grip over my energy, but it's impossible, as I'm unable to evolve, and our time is running out.

What good is a powerless King?

It's a relief that I have a powerful army under my wing.

I turn only the dying into Day Walkers, offering them a life of immortality in return for their help in the war.

Once the Titaniums accept the terms of my peace treaty, I

will offer my Day Walkers freedom—on the one condition they take only what they need. But for now, I keep my bloodline close. If the hybrids suspect I am building an army, they'll attack sooner.

And if they discover I've turned the Venos into Day Walkers, it would be chaos on Earth.

It wasn't a part of my plan to change the Venos, but they volunteered themselves once my Day Walker army started to grow. They felt threatened, knowing they were vampire food. I wasn't sure if they fully understood what they were asking, and I wasn't sure of what they would become. But one by one, I turned them—starting with the Gen. 2s. They're now forever in their mutated state. They're monstrous, if I'm honest—large werewolves with arched spines and raging red snake eyes. The Venos listen well—just as loyal as they'd been before—and like all Day Walkers; they follow their King.

A powerless King.

I can't shift the ever nagging reminder that, just as I'd been the only Titanium without energy, I'm now the only vampire hybrid without energy.

I yell as I tense my fingers once more, pushing, forcing the shadows to form into a ball within my shaking hands, but apart from a small wisp, there is nothing. I can't evolve, and I can't create energy.

The Titanium army will be here in a matter of weeks, and I

am completely defenseless against them.

But I will not run from them.

I will not hide.

I may be powerless, but I am not weak. I am a warrior, and this is my war.

My family aided the apocalypse, and I will fix their mistakes. I will restore peace to the world.

I will fight until the bitter end.

CHAPTER FORTY-EIGHT

LORA

The blue lights of -4 flash by as I run through the corridor, toward Flynn and White. Has the Night Walker King told the doctor about the Titanium's uprising yet? I doubt that White already knows. He wouldn't sit by and let it happen. Even though he refused to help when Ares lay dying, I'm sure he'd intervene if he knew the Titaniums were planning to kill him.

I growl through my anger. I should have questioned why the hybrids continued training.

Hail and Donnah are hot on my heels and we storm through the underground world while I determine how best to handle the situation. Has it already gone too far?

Will the Titaniums ever listen to me again?

White and Flynn turn abruptly as we burst into the room. They'd been deep in conversation and our interruption comes as a surprise, upsetting the quiet hum of the machines.

"Is everything alright, Lora?" White's concern is clear in his voice, his tone apprehensive.

"You didn't think to tell me about this?" I yell at Flynn, pointing toward the unguided monitors. "The Titaniums are planning to kill Ares, and you kept it from me."

Flynn's eyebrows raise. "Why don't you take a seat, Lora, and we'll talk about it like rational human beings."

"Neither of us are human anymore. And you can shove that chair up your ass," I reply as I push the chair across the floor and start for the exit.

"Lora, listen," he says. I halt, but I don't turn around. "We weren't sure we could trust you. It was difficult to know whether you trusted us, and we couldn't risk you siding with your Titaniums once you learned of their plans."

"I don't trust you," I agree, turning slowly to face him, "but keeping Ares alive will always be my priority. Hasn't that always been clear? From now on, I want you to consider me a member of the A.P.P. Pass me a badge, I'll sign a contract—whatever you need me to do." I take a deep breath and try to contain my rage. "Now, I think you owe me a little help in clearing up the mess going on above our heads, before it's... too... late." I look at the screens above Flynn and my words fade as I process the images.

The Observatorium is empty. In all my time underground, I've never seen the room without at least twenty people at their desks.

My stomach knots.

Flynn stops talking as he notices the horror on my face and whips around to look at the screens. White falls into line beside us, and Donnah and Hail stand not far behind.

I gulp, my mouth turning dry.

None of us speak.

I want to yell at Flynn again.

I should accuse him of abandoning his post to talk to White, but I can't—I'm just as guilty of letting love distract me. I would be a hypocrite to blame Flynn for this.

It's too late.

The Farm lays abandoned.

The hybrid camp is empty, tents left open and belongings littered along the ground. It's as though the Titaniums had received an order and instantly dropped everything.

The training rooms look the same.

Level -3 is void of farmers.

They have raided the Weaponry.

And the gates…

An army of Titaniums—700 strong—and just as many farmers stand at the entrance of The Farm, watching as Jayleigh readies them for war.

It's too late… it's too late…

The gates open, and the army pushes forwards.

We watch as they run across the road, through the battlefield, and disappear into the woods below.

I charge for the corridor, the one that will lead me outside the gates, but I don't get far.

"You can't follow!"

Too many arms hold me back as I attempt to run after my hybrids. They were waiting for this. How could they attack when I'd always been with them or within the Observatorium? They were waiting for me to return to -4, and there will be no talking sense into them now.

No turning back. But I need to try.

I can't stand by and watch them launch an attack on Ares.

"The more distance between you and the Titaniums, the better," White tries to talk sense into me as I continue to fight against their restrictions. "The distance will weaken them considerably. They're expecting that you'll follow."

The Alpha bond.

They knew I'd never go with them voluntarily, but I'd follow to stop them. They're counting on it because they need me. The Alpha bond won't allow them to go far.

I hate that White is right.

I fight against Hail, Donnah, and Flynn for a while longer in frustration, rather than wanting to leave. We need a plan.

"You will not follow them, Lora," Flynn demands.

My stomach twists. "Fine! But we need to warn Ares." I

shrug everybody off, pulling myself free and holding my hands out in surrender. "He needs to know that he's in danger."

"Ares will know," Flynn says. "The wolves will tell him."

I spin to face the Night Walker King. "The wolves? You mean Solace and her pack? They're with him?" So he's not been alone all these months.

"They're with him, and so are the Venos. Although, they're not much in terms of company since he turned them into Day Walkers."

"He did what?" Hail backs away from us in shock.

"How do you know all of this?" I ask, and then it occurs that Flynn has followed Ares from The Farm before, using the A.P.P.'s supply of drones to watch our progress last year as we rescued Hail from the vampires.

He knows where Ares is. He knows exactly how to find him, and maybe if I'd pulled myself together and visited Flynn sooner, he might have told me. If I'd only asked for help, I could have found Ares long before the Titaniums turned their back on me and planned a revolution right beneath my nose.

Flynn is reading my mind, so he doesn't reply.

"Ares has a plan," I say. "Do you know what it is?"

Flynn backs away from the group, whispering to the Night Walkers in control of the incubators. The machines stop their gentle humming.

The incubators' blue lights turn off, and the Night Walker

hybrids rise to the top of the cylinder chambers. They pull themselves free of the slime and descend the ladders.

Dead hybrids stand before me, family I've loved and lost, with recognition in their red eyes. They're an army of ghosts—faces I thought I'd never see again.

And they bow.

It takes a moment for me to realize it's not to me they're offering this symbol of respect, but to the Night Walker King at my side. Surprisingly, it fills me with an immense relief.

"The time has come," Flynn says. "Prepare yourselves for sundown."

The army rises, pumping a fist to their chests in one quick beat, and the sound echoes through my bones. The unity is chilling as the Night Walkers march-step away from their incubators and through the corridors of -4.

Sundown.

It's early summer—the first week of May, I believe—and the sun won't set until 8pm. They can't do anything until night falls. They can't do anything for another five hours.

That gives the Titanium army a massive advance.

"What will Ares do whilst he waits for your army?" I question. "How will he hold the Titaniums back for that long?"

Flynn offers me a small smile. "You lack faith, Lora. Trust that Ares knows what he is doing. He is capable of everything you've ever doubted in him."

REAP

"I haven't doubted—"

"Trust him, Lora," Flynn says.

I sigh.

I have always trusted Ares, even when others couldn't. But I know that is not what Flynn means. He's referring to the part of me that has always tried to change Ares. The part of me which questions Ares' place within the world.

Because Ares' place, I realize, has always been at the top.

He is the highest point on any food chain.

He generates magic.

He was *made* for this world.

I've been the one to convince him otherwise.

"I trust him," I confirm and, in that statement, admit the brutal truth that I had been wrong... wrong about so many things.

"And trust in yourself," Flynn says. "You have a large part to play in this war, and you must believe you are stronger than you've ever imagined."

"But I'll be on The Farm when they attack. How will I impact—"

Oh.

Now I sink into the chair—the one I'd earlier told Flynn to shove up his ass.

He isn't talking about physical strength, but mental and spiritual strength.

This is war. Titaniums will die. And, as their Alpha, I'm going to feel every single bond break.

CHAPTER FORTY-NINE

LORA

The Titaniums can't use their hybrid speed thanks to the several hundred humans in their army.

With the farmers at the Titaniums' side, I'm sure my days searching the screens in the Observatorium have been a waste. How long have they been working together, hiding their plans from me? Was the footage I saw in the Observatorium even a live feed?

Flynn told me to rest, but my brain won't allow it. I'll need to be at full strength to make it through the battle, and sleeping now would be the best thing I can do to prepare. But I'm furious. I can't sleep.

That could also be because Flynn advised I eat my weight in sugar. Hail helped me with that, raiding the shelves of the pantry on level -2, before he returned to the Night Walkers. He will fight alongside them tomorrow. I'm envious, wishing I could leave The Farm too. But the more I think about it, the more I realize I could never fight against my hybrids. I could never hurt them.

I'd be stuck in the middle of the battlefield, calling for peace. I'd be just like Ares on the day that Gretta's Day Walkers attacked The Farm and killed The Sanctuary. Caught between two sides. That hadn't ended well for Ares.

I'm certain Jayleigh's behind this—certain it was her idea to turn the farmers and Titaniums against me. I'd seen her talking to Tim and Wilson in corners of the room, and watched her train the hybrids to evolve. Jayleigh started the rumors. She'd built the rebellion.

She started a war.

I storm across the barn. She must have planned this at night, whilst I slept in the Observatorium, watching over fake footage, hoping to catch sight of Ares. He might have come back for me after all. He might have sent signs, but I never could have received them. Wilson wouldn't have told me as he'd been working alongside with Jayleigh to keep this secret.

Only somebody as precise as Jayleigh could pull this off. Her stall door slams into the wall as I push it open and proceed to upturn everything within her room in a silent rage..

I don't know what I'm looking for. Proof. A sign. Anything to justify my anger. I find it as I fling her mattress and it lands upside down on the floor; the fabric inked in black marker.

Her handwriting is meticulous. As is the detail of the map—the podiums within the forest, the sea, the wonky wooden steps leading from the cliff to the beach, and the caves. I recognize the location instantly.

The Sanctuary.

My heart drops.

It's too far.

They're so sure I'll follow that they're risking everything. And if I don't follow? The hybrids will likely die before they reach the beach. Ares would be safe.

I'm frozen as I think over my options, uncomfortable with the power I've been granted.

And then my eyes catch on one minor detail of the map, just four lines sitting above the cave mouth where Ares first confessed his love.

Jayleigh has labeled the box as *The Cottage*.

The pain starts as a tightness in my chest, growing and pulsing with every beat of my heart.

The cottage wasn't there last year, and it wasn't shown on the screens of the Observatorium any time we scouted. The farmers *have* been hiding footage from me, and they know where to find Ares. They've told Jayleigh, though.

This is where Ares has been hiding. Preparing. Building.

A cottage by the sea.

My cottage.

I can barely breathe, my mind recalling the last words he spoke to me before he died.

"I'll meet you there," I whisper as the memory returns, and in my fury, I throw the mattress through the door and into the bench on the other side of the barn.

The Sanctuary is the only beach we're familiar with, so of course, that's where Ares would go. He'd told me exactly where to find him. If only the farmers had been honest with me and shown me real-time footage when I'd asked for it.

I'm a fool.

They've been playing me for months.

I call Flynn. He likely knows where Ares has been hiding, but I tell him to zoom in on the cameras within the barn. To study Jayleigh's battle plans.

"You should rest, Lora," is all he says.

"How can I rest?" I hiss. "Did you know they're heading for The Sanctuary? You know that they'll die, stretching the Alpha bond that far, right?"

"We're aware, Lora."

"The hybrids are making a mistake, but they don't need to die. There must be another way. I won't sit back and let this happen."

"I'm afraid you have no choice. I compelled you not to follow. Your body will not leave The Farm's gates."

REAP

My spine tingles, and my inner animal stirs in response. "You did *what?*"

It doesn't matter that he compelled me because I've taken the antidote that White had prepared. But Flynn doesn't seem to know this. How ironic that he abused my trust before lecturing me about trusting in Ares.

"It's better for everyone this way," he says. "If they do, by some miracle, reach The Sanctuary alive, Ares' army will be ready. It's a two-day walk for the humans. The Night walkers can run the distance in one night thanks to the shortcuts we've been creating over the past few months. You just have to accept that this is the right thing to do. You told me you want to be a part of the A.P.P. and this is your best chance of protecting Ares. Everything will go according to plan, and Ares will be back in your arms by the end of the week. Just let us take control."

Ares, back in my arms. It's all I want. But to do nothing? To sit back and watch seven-hundred of my hybrids die?

That sounds far from peaceful to me.

"Marshall had a line, something about knowing when sacrifices need to be made," Flynn says, interrupting my thoughts.

"For the greater good," I mutter, barely listening to him as I continue my own line of thought.

"Oh, no. That was Samantha's—"

"I don't care, Flynn. You should know that didn't like either of them."

The Night Walker King goes quiet on the other end of the line, and I'm thankful he's not able to read my thoughts via my tablet.

"Fine," I say finally, a plan forming in my mind. "I'll stay here with White. Just promise you'll keep Ares safe."

"That has been my only aim for the past twenty-four years, Lora."

I grit my teeth. "That doesn't fill me with confidence, Flynn. You've already let Ares die once. And if he dies again, he won't be coming back."

CHAPTER FIFTY

HIM

The Titaniums have reached the town weeks earlier than expected. They're taking the path best known to them—familiar thanks to Hail's rescue mission, and the army settles within the old buildings.

But why didn't they bring the vehicles?

Lora.

They'd been expecting her to follow, and they need her to catch them.

The wolves show me that she remains on The Farm, which is a good thing, but the part of me that craves her company can't help but sow seed of disappointment within my mind. I hoped to see her just once before the battle—to tuck her silver hair behind her ear and kiss those enticing lips once more. Because things might go horribly wrong, and I may never get the chance again.

But at least she is safe within The Farm's fence, and her safety is all that matters.

I laugh, the noise echoing through the cave, as I realize that her being on The Farm means that she has sided with the Night Walkers. She doesn't lead her pack.

She has sided with me.

I only doubted it for a second, but that was long enough. She hasn't responded to the messages I've sent—the wolves, the small fire in the woods. Maybe they've been too subtle, but I feared from her lack of response that she'd sided with the Titaniums.

That's not the case. She is letting the Alpha bond stretch.

The Titanium army will be here tomorrow night, but Flynn and his Night Walkers will be here within the next five hours. I will have a small amount of time to steal Donnah away and practice drawing the shadows from within me.

Time.

It should feel so careless to an immortal, but I value it now more than I ever did as a human.

It's running out.

The fire is spreading.

Come this time tomorrow, the world will be in flames.

CHAPTER FIFTY-ONE

HAIL

I've never felt nervous to leave The Farm with Donnah, but I do today. We stand at the exit of -4—the exit that leads into the village—and wait for the others.

Night is fast approaching. We watch the sunset through the branches of trees, and I wonder how it'll look tomorrow. Will I see it through new eyes? Will I still be here to see the sunset tomorrow?

"Is everything okay?" Donnah asks as she reaches for me. "You don't have to fight with us, you know. We understand if you feel out of place. The hybrids are your family. They're your pack. We don't expect you to fight against them. You can stay here with Lora if that's what you want."

I shake my head, holding my hand over hers. I've been thinking about where I stand with the pack a lot recently.

Jayleigh, my closest friend—the friend I would have trusted with my life before she'd killed Ares. I'd been there for her when she needed me, but she pushed me away. She replaced me with Diego.

She cast me aside for not killing Donnah.

She'd asked me what my plans were after she found out about the Night Walker hybrids. She thought I was going to use my connection with Donnah to my advantage, gaining their trust so that I could take them out from the inside. Jayleigh wanted to help. She wanted to kill them all.

Even Donnah.

She called me a hypocrite for siding with the enemy.

I tried to make her see that it didn't have to be that way, but she told me I was just like Lora and the two of us could rot in hell with the vampires.

I should have seen it then.

I should have realized that she wouldn't let Ares or any other vampire walk free.

It doesn't matter to her that I'm stuck in the middle. In her eyes, I am no longer family. I am one of them. I am the enemy.

Soon, I really will be.

"I want to fight alongside you, Donnah. It's not about the pack," I kiss her quickly, aware of the setting sun and the Night Walkers who will soon join us. "I just… I want to ask you a question whilst we're alone."

REAP

I squeeze her hand and wonder if she's reading my mind, already aware of what I'm about to ask. Her gentle eyes give nothing away.

"You know where I stand in the war. My being here proves that. But I need you to know that I'm not fighting for the Night Walkers. And, as much as I love Ares, it's not for him, either." I tilt her head back with my fingers on her chin. I need her to see what I'm saying—the question I'm really trying to ask. "I'm fighting for you. For our future together. So if I'm going to do this, I need to know we're forever."

I hold my breath, wondering if I'll still need to breathe tomorrow.

Donnah giggles as she reads my mind, "Forever and ever, Silly."

"So, is that a yes?"

"One-hundred yeses." She kisses me with one-hundred more. "In life and in death. I love you, Hail, and nothing will ever change that."

"In life and in death," I nod. "I like that. And in that case, I think I'm ready."

CHAPTER FIFTY-TWO

LORA

Hail left me several hours ago, joining Donnah and the Night Walker Hybrids.

The Alpha bond stopped me from sleeping, and now I sit in the Observatorium with White, playing over our options—and we don't have many.

The first is to join the battle, pick a side, and likely die in our fight for peace.

Or, White suggests we can drive to a safe area close to The Sanctuary so that the Titaniums won't die. We can stay clear of the war and give the Titaniums the power to fight without the restrictions of the Alpha bond. Let it all play out. But I'll never forgive myself for being so close to the battle and not trying to help.

Our third option is to sit here and let my hybrids suffer. As much as I want to give Ares that advantage, I can't justify it.

I'm leaning more towards one particular option.

"You don't have to come with me," I say. "There's no reason for you to fight. You shouldn't put yourself at risk."

White gives me a complacent smile. "You will need me to drive the truck, Lora, so I must come with you. Vehicles are programmed for farmers. And, might I point out, you don't know how to drive."

"Really?" I stare at him. "Ares spent all that time leading The Farm and didn't think to change our access?"

"I'll point out again that hybrids do not know how to drive. There was little reason for him to alter your access."

"Oh, come on!" My words echo around the empty room. It's uncomfortable to see it abandoned, and it strikes me that this might be the new normal. If we don't intervene, the hybrids and farmers may never return. My skin crawls at the idea. "I can pull electricity through my own fingers. Driving can't be that difficult."

"I failed my driving test eight times," he confesses. "My reflexes are extremely poor."

"Did you tip the examiner on your ninth test?" I joke. Me —making a joke. Ares will be proud.

White chuckles gently to himself. "There never was a ninth test. The apocalypse made sure of that."

"Well, you got lucky there then, didn't you?" It's a relief to forget the stress of our situation for just a moment. My shoulders relax as I appreciate White's laughter, and I sip the coffee he prepared ten minutes ago.

He'd found me here after I decided that sleeping in the barn wasn't an option. It's been months since I last slept there. And now, knowing that the senior hybrids have been using my absence to talk strategy and plan their attack? Staying in the barn was impossible.

I returned to my sofa in front of the screens, and White, also struggling to sleep, wanted the company.

"I can't believe they're gone," I whisper, the sound haunting the empty space between the glossy walls. "I can't believe they betrayed us."

White places a hand over my knee. "If there's one lesson to be taken away from this battle, it's that passion often leads us astray."

I study the wary look in his eye.

"I convinced myself of something similar after the Alpha Arena." My doubt is obvious in my tone.

White was there. He knows my past, but despite it all, he shakes his head. "There's a difference between passion and love. Often, we can love things but lose passion for them, just as we can care for things but fall out of love. I'm passionate about my job, although I lost my love for it when Samantha died. I care for Flynn, although I'm not sure I still love him."

"What are you trying to say?"

"You're here because of your love for both sides, and I… I'm only passionate about making the right decision." He's lost me completely—I'm too tired for his riddles. "I've lost all ties and connection to everyone I've loved. I am a man with no passion, yet you have too much. That gives us a great deal of power. We are the fortunate two with perspective, Lora, sitting at opposite ends of the spectrum. We need to use our advantage wisely to make the right decision."

He sips his coffee as though we're still joking about his driving and not discussing the future of our people.

I watch the screens, wondering how many decisions have been made on this balcony—decisions that impacted life as we know it.

How many of those decisions brought us here today? And how many mistakes could have been avoided if only for a little more perspective?

White's right.

Though I feel at a complete loss, we have a great deal of power in our hands. I can sense it in the room, tugging at my skin and pulling me forward with urgency. It's begging me to decide now, before it's too late. To decide selflessly.

"Lora." White stops abruptly, turning and resting a hand on my shoulder. "Whatever happens tonight, I want you to know that I'm unbelievably proud of you. We might have gone about the synthetic energy situation a little insensitively, but despite our mistakes, your devotion and passion must be praised. You have always protected your pack to the best of your ability. And in situations where Alphas have broken in the past, you have prevailed."

My body twitches. I've never received compliments, and I don't know how to react to White's kind words. I'm not worthy of them. All of my actions have been to rectify past mistakes. "That devotion you speak of is only a series of broken promises."

Promises I've made to myself, and those I care about. I've never kept a single one.

"Did you, or did you not, lead your pack to victory against the Venos in Phase Two?"

"We lost Teri along the way."

"Because of The Farm." He tuts. "You saved numerous hybrids from their initiation trials, dangerous challenges, and talked many down from leaving The Farm."

"But I lost so many, too. I promised to keep them safe, and I failed them."

"You've failed nobody. Your promises were never the problem, Lora. The Farm was."

"But I killed everyone in the Alpha Arena, Dr. White. I turned them all to ash, because I couldn't cope with the betrayal. I killed farmers that day, too."

REAP

"The Farm created your issues, and The Farm created your power, so you can't blame yourself for what happened in the Alpha Arena. We thrusted you into a high pressure environment with no knowledge of your power. Your emotions were justified, but you didn't have the skills to manage everything you experienced. You did exactly what The Farm asked of you. Don't you see? The blood is not on your hands, but The Farm's; Marshall's, and my own. I'm sorry for everything we put you through, and I feel it's time I repay my dues. I will aid you in this battle, Lora. It's the least I can do."

I stare at the wall—not the one with the screens, but the blank one to my left—and let the words sink in.

He's sorry.

I'm just a product of The Farm.

I'd thought something similar when trying to process Jayleigh killing Ares. *She's The Farm's yield.*

So, why had I never considered myself the same?

We are all a product of The Farm. We've followed its rules, swayed to its influence.

Without The Farm, I could have lived a life free of violence. I could have learned to paint and watched the ocean roll beneath my feet. I could have kept my promises.

I wouldn't have lied to the people I care about most or tried to change them into something they're not. I'd have been a reasonable person. A likeable person. A human.

The Farm has toyed with my humanity my entire life, and in its name, I've sacrificed myself.

It's time to take back control. To forgive myself for not having the knowledge to control my energy. To forgive myself for thinking it is my responsibility to save everyone.

The Farm has done me wrong, and today, I'm breaking free. I'll fight for the lives we should be living. All of us. Titaniums, humans, and vampires.

I think about everything I've learned over the past four years. My regrets, my knowledge, my training, spending time with White, creating synthetic energy, and a plan clicks into place.

My heart races.

My tablet reads 06:18. It's still early enough to make a difference.

It's Ares. The answer to all of my questions has always been Ares.

The reason he can't evolve. Our connection, and why he can steal my energy.

My Beta—it's in his genetic code.

"We need to get to the lab," I say.

White stands faster than I've ever seen him move. "You have a plan?"

"Just how bad is your driving, old man?"

CHAPTER FIFTY-THREE

LORA

The door to the chemical cupboard hangs ajar. White rushes to examine the security system, and his shoulders sag.

"I thought only authorized personnel could open this door," I say, glancing around him to look at the screen. "It's a fingerprint system. Who else could get in here?"

White shakes his head. "There is nobody else, Lora. The scientists have only ever entered when I've been with them, and the system is saying that you opened the door…"

"Me?" I step forward to make sure he's reading it correctly and the lack of sleep hasn't affected his eyesight. But there it is, my name clearly displayed at the top of the screen. "That's impossible. We closed the door behind us earlier."

White waves it off, letting himself inside and kicking through the mess of the upturned cupboard. "It doesn't matter now. No matter how we try to make sense of it, it won't change the fact that somebody got in and destroyed the place."

I ignore his attempt to drop the conversation. "Who else knew about the lab?" I ask.

White sighs and props the chair back into place along the back wall. "Tim, Sally, Wilson, and the scientists who helped us—"

"Wilson." His name leaves a bitter taste in my mouth. "That little shit."

White turns back with a quirk of his eyebrows.

"He came to talk to me a couple of months ago, completely out of the blue. He made me coffee and chatted to me when nobody else would. I thought he was being nice." I try to recall our conversation, but memories from that time have fogged over, my mind eager to forget. "He told me the vampires destroyed his camp," I recall, realizing that this is the perfect opportunity to avenge his family. "I reckon he's taken your antidote so that he can fight without the vampires controlling his mind."

White nods. "He was Marshall's only friend, as far as I'm aware. I wouldn't be surprising if he used your grief and lack of awareness to his advantage. He likely took your prints from that mug, knowing what you were doing in the lab. If not to use the energy to his own advantage, then to destroy it so that Ares could never use it."

REAP

"I should be used to betrayal by now." I kick through the rubbish on the ground.

"People do…" White's voice trails off as he studies the state of the lab, and I hold my breath as I follow him through the hole in the wall, scared of whatever he's seeing. His voice breaks. "It's all gone."

We stand motionless at the edge of the room, trying to take it all in. The cabinets are bare; the computers smashed, and all notes wiped from the board. Countertops look as though Wilson swept his arm across them, pushing everything they once held to the ground. There are dents in the chemical units from where he's tried to break in, but at least some cabinets were stable enough to hold their lock.

The antidotes are gone.

White wipes the tears from under his glasses, and then moves on, studying what little we have left.

"What do we do now?" I ask, heading for the cabinet that once held my experiments. Wilson got into this one. The door hangs on only one hinge.

"We salvage what we have left and rebuild."

I swallow. "But your equations, your supplies… they're gone."

White gives me an odd look—one that suggests I should know him better. "No, my dear, they're not. I prefer to work the old-fashioned way." He lifts a countertop, and I'm surprised to find a stack of folders and equipment inside.

The furniture opens?

"I copied everything you've ever noted into a folder and stored spare equipment in case of an emergency. Now, let's see if we've still got everything we need."

"You're a hero," I blurt, relief and lack of sleep making me giddy. There's still a chance we can do this.

"I've never been called that before, but I could get used to it."

I'd told White my plan as we journeyed from the Observatorium to the lab, and he suggested I rest while I can, needing the energy.

So he gets to work, and I end up napping with my head resting on the countertop. He doesn't wake me, but when I regain consciousness, he's humming quietly to himself in the corner of the room, a test tube of glowing liquid between his gloved fingers.

"You did it," I mumble, the sleep not yet cleared. I rub my tired eyes, feeling the grit of fatigue, before I squint at the time on my tablet.

15:02.

The stool flies back as I scatter to my feet, crashing into something behind me. "Three in the afternoon? Why didn't you wake me? We need to go. The hybrids will be there soon!"

"Calm down, Lora." White's voice is focused. "Our plan

will not work without this."

The room spins.

My heart hurts with a familiar sensation—as though it's being ripped in two. "They're too far, White." I gasp, my hands prying at my chest, hoping to relieve the pressure. "The Titaniums are too far. We need to go now, or they'll die."

White's eyes lift from the equipment just long enough to study me. "I cannot rush this, but we're almost there. Ten minutes. That's all I need."

Ten minutes?

I try not to yell out as the Alpha bond stretches to its limit. I'm not sure we have ten minutes.

"Distract yourself," White suggests. "Grab us food for the journey and meet me in the bunker. The hybrids may stop. They may pause to rethink their plan."

"And if they don't?" I say through gritted teeth, clinging onto the table for stability.

White purses his lips. "Ten minutes," he repeats.

I nod, stumbling across the room and through the hole in the wall. Once in the corridor, I evolve, hoping it will ease the pain. It works, but the feeling is still there, like a trapped nerve shooting spasms through my body. At least I'm able to move through the hallways without losing balance. I pick up the pace and opt for the stairs instead of the lift, knowing they'll take me directly to the canteen on -2, and I fill my arms and pockets with whatever I can carry.

I've barely eaten in the last twenty-four hours, despite Flynn's recommendation. I raided the cupboards for sugary items with Hail last night, but all I've filled my stomach with today is coffee.

Hail.

I try not to panic—not to think of where he is now as I eat through half a loaf of bread and two bruised, slightly sour, green apples. The farmers took a lot of the food with them to feed their army, so we're left with scraps, but it's better than nothing at all.

I'm on my way out when I notice an empty sack on the shelf, so I unload the food into it and throw it over my shoulder. Then I return to the staircase and wait for the doctor to arrive with his creation.

"Eleven minutes," I say as he comes into view.

He hurries across the empty bunker with a polystyrene box in his hands. I wonder how old the crumbly container is and where he found it. "Many apologies, Lora. I didn't account for the journey from the lab to the bunker."

"I'll forgive you. Here." I pass him an apple and follow him through the wide corridor which leads to the vehicles and the ramp towards the gates.

We climb into the truck, and I place the sack of food at my feet. White hands me the box as he starts the engine and I cling

REAP

to it for dear life.

"Hold on, Lora. You're in for a bumpy ride." White laughs. The heavy thrum of rock music blares through the speakers and the doctor sings along as we tear off, through the underground garage, up the ramp, and through the gates that'll lead us to war.

CHAPTER FIFTY-FOUR

HIM

My army appears small as we gather on the field above The Sanctuary in the light of the setting sun.

Fifty Day Walkers await further instruction in a triangle formation, and eighty Day Walker Venos take up the back row, towering over us with haste.

I'm glad they are fighting my war. I'd hate to battle against them.

I hope the Titaniums know little about my army. The Venos will most likely come as a horrifying surprise, and I relish in it.

And I assume the Titaniums will expect Flynn's Night Walkers to be far behind them. The hybrids won't know of the old train tunnel that allowed the Night Walkers to arrive early this morning, just before sunrise.

REAP

Flynn's Night Walkers are not the only ones who have come to my aid. Last month, I located a nest I'd heard of through the whispers of small human communities, and I reached out to Queen Matilda, who has walked Earth for an entire century. She offers her support, should we need it, but her mature nest is located fifty miles from us.

She might not make it in time to join Flynn and his people, but we could use their experience. In vampire society, Flynn and I are both Omegas. Night Walkers have graced Earth since the dawn of man. They're connected to it in a way I am just beginning to understand, and we have a lot to learn from our elders.

Flynn's nest hides in the forest behind the Venos, a little way up the hill, but not so far as Lora's cottage. My uncle will hold his nest in the woods until he thinks it necessary for them to attack.

Hail is here too.

Our meetings in the woods over the past weeks were surprising enough. But to learn that he's committed so fully to the Night Walker army was enough to leave me speechless.

He's here to support Donnah, but that he has turned against the Titaniums to support the undead is… warming. He accepts Donnah for what she is, and he accepts me.

He is one of the greatest gifts I could have asked for in life, always having my back; I will forever have his.

We have a lot to talk about once this is over.

The Titaniums will be in for a surprise.

The sound of paws in the brush of the woods perks my attention, and I stop gazing at the sunset to find Solace weaving through the grass at the far side of the field. She trails the parameter of the battle zone, which will soon be covered in blood.

I crouch, running my hand through the amber fur of her neck, and witness all that she has seen through the windows of her eyes.

Hybrids and humans—their numbers far greater than ours.

I sigh, although I'm not worried. The humans are a minor threat to us; we can compel their minds if they get too close.

But the Titaniums are here, which can only mean that Lora has left The Farm. I glance towards Flynn, wondering why his compulsion hasn't worked.

"It's time," I say, letting the wind carry my voice to my army and the Night Walkers within the woods beyond. The wolves make up the empty space on my front line, turning the triangle into a rectangle, and we wait in silence.

We listen for them.

Still, my mind is with Lora. My heart beats, and it speeds with the realization that she is not following our plan. She isn't safe.

I've tried to prepare myself for the worst. I will not kill her if we are to fight, but surrender myself and my army out of respect for her decision. And, in doing so, I will have her kill me.

I cannot live an eternity without her. It is a punishment far worse than death and I'm afraid of what I will become in the absence of her love.

The only reason I've been able to keep myself grounded—controlled—all these weeks is the hope of ending the war so that we can be together, as we've always planned. But if she cannot love a monster, then I see no point in feeding on humans to keep myself alive. My Day Walker army will die alongside me.

They stand prepared now, copying as I call out to the glowing Titaniums. The hybrids march through the trees on the other side of the field like avenging stars.

"Jayleigh." I lay eyes on her as she leads the hybrids forward and stops to let her army gather. Her eyes are ethereal, brighter than I recall, my body warning me of the danger her light could bring.

Tye and Diego take either side, and Diego rests his hand on her shoulder in reassurance.

"Cute," I say, waiting for my words to hit them. I want them to know just how bitter I feel that they have each other, when Jayleigh ended my relationship at the same time she ended my life. She has found happiness after ripping mine from me. "My friend, Jayleigh…" I smile. It is not pleasant and I know it.

I should have let her choke on that carrot.

I try to ignore the memories of a friendship I once cherished. Memories of a different life, where we were both oblivious to my vampirism, and united in our differences. A fickle friendship.

Her body tenses as my words reach her and Diego moves closer to her body, but she doesn't need his protection. Fighting vampires is what she enjoys. She moves around him.

How many times has she dreamed of this moment? Of throwing her dagger through my heart for a second time?

I won't let it happen. If I die today, it will be at Lora's hand. There is no other option.

"It's not too late to back down, Jayleigh," I say. "We are only here today because you are forcing our hand. You can turn around now and walk away. We'll let you go. We don't need to fight."

But I see the doubt in her eyes; the lack of trust. She was raised to believe the worst in vampires and cannot walk away. None of them can. She has deluded them.

Jayleigh steps forwards, five, six paces, and she is close enough that I can focus on her eyes and see into her mind. I'm able to piece together how she made this possible; getting hybrids and farmers to distract Lora whilst she placed notes into the hands of her allies. She'd used Hail to get updates on the Night Walkers. Taking advantage of their friendship, she tricked him into giving her information without him realizing what he had done. She'd bribed the techs in the Observatorium, spread news of Lora's abandonment, and claimed the Alpha has sided with the enemy.

My anger rises.

Jayleigh seems to sense it, with a familiar, dangerous smile playing on her lips.

She turns her attention to my army, its numbers weak compared to the united hybrids and humans behind her. She doesn't seem at all phased by the Venos. No reaction. I seethe.

"Is that all you've got, dead boy?" she mocks, her voice loud and patronizing. Her army laughs.

It's not the first time she's underestimated me.

They've *all* underestimated me.

"It's all I need." This time my words fully form, no longer a whisper that scratches at her skin.

"Aw…" She pouts and draws her daggers, standing with one hip cocked to the side. "In that case, it looks like this might be over by the time the sun sets."

Fifteen minutes—that's how long it'll take for the sun to set. Such a shame to ruin the peace of a beautiful night, but it'll be worth it for an eternity without The Farm.

Fifteen minutes.

Then they'll be in for a *real* surprise.

CHAPTER FIFTY-FIVE

HIM

My army is motionless behind me. Solace gazes up, waiting for my command, while a couple of wolves shuffle further along the line.

"Well?" I ask, rolling my neck in preparation. "What the fuck are you waiting for?" And I smile, because they'll recognize Marshall's line; my brother, whom they hated as though he were a vampire himself.

Anything to ruffle their feathers.

Tye steps forwards, and I pinch my lips together, suppressing the laugh bubbling inside. Tye once warned that he'd squash me like a bug; this is his chance to make an ant out of me and he knows it. He spits to the ground. "Nerd," he whispers.

Jayleigh's smile drops, nose flaring and eyes scowling. She's never looked so fierce.

Gone is my friend.

Gone is the girl who'd first made me feel accepted.

In her place stands a raging, death fueled monster. She crosses her daggers above her head, a symbol to her people, and they draw their weapons.

The hybrids project their energy into blinding orbs within their hands. Pure Titanium.

Jayleigh yells, and her battle cry destroys the peaceful summer twilight, filling it with hatred and disgust. Her army copy.

"Shh," I whisper, but the people of The Farm do not listen.

We remain still. Silent. We are one with the grass we stand on and as fluid as the breeze that urges us to end this—to bring balance and restore peace.

"It doesn't have to end this way." I let the wind carry my warnings to the opposing army, but they don't listen.

They run.

I urge them to stop, to turn back—I command it—but most of the humans resist my control. They ignore my attempts to save them.

Tim grins at me from across the field, mocking. He's taken an antidote of some kind.

Wilson's mind gives it away. He's stolen whatever Dr. White

has been creating over the past few months. They've shared the antidote between humans so that the vampires can't control them for the next few hours.

Idiots.

So be it.

I've done all I can to dissuade them. I've tried to prevent this battle and all the deaths that will come. The Farm has brought it upon themselves.

My army plants its feet, as ordered, and we wait.

Titaniums from the far sides of the line expand their energy, race forwards, and the line curves to form a protective circle around Jayleigh and those who join her in the center.

They take aim… and fall into the camouflaged pit I'd prepared in the middle of the battlefield.

Two-hundred drop—unable to avoid the push of the bloodthirsty beings behind them—to the bottom of the pit where thousands of wooden pikes line the base.

I doubt anyone will survive.

Loopholes. Jayleigh should have suspected it.

A quarter of Titaniums defeated, and my people are yet to move.

Jayleigh, Diego, and Tye slow to a halt at the edge of the pit, looking down to their fallen people. I try not to think of the loss, of how many of them I knew. My mind is only with Lora as I pray the break in the Alpha bond won't damage her completely.

"I warned you to stop," I say. I'm not gloating, because loss of life isn't something to be celebrated.

Jayleigh glares from the other side of the pit and her eyes are beyond recognition. I don't know them, and I don't know her. Her mind does the math, configuring the length of the pit—effortless for Titaniums to clear, but not so easy for humans. They'll have to take the woods.

What Jayleigh doesn't know is that Flynn and his nest loiter in the shadows, awaiting the humans' diversion. The humans can't be compelled, but they still won't stand a chance. The Night Walkers don't need mind control to overpower a human.

Jayleigh gives her orders, her voice lost to the fervent screaming around her, but enough of her army hear and act accordingly. Everybody else follows suit.

I watch Tim and Wilson run for the trees and wonder if I'll ever see them again.

The Titaniums retreat, building up speed as they leap over the pit and onto my side of the battlefield. Just five more minutes, that's all we need. Five minutes until the sun sets.

The humans can't see in the dark. They will be completely useless.

"Now," I say. I don't turn, but I hear the Venos thunder down the bank behind me. With a single leap, they cover the expanse of my forces, and the earth trembles as they touch down. Solace and her wolves howl in celebration.

The Venos intercept the Titaniums' path; eighty werewolf vampires standing at eight feet tall. Their snake scales have turned as red as their eyes and shield their bodies from any Titanium energy thrown their way—like reflective armor. I hide a small smile as I watch the energy bounce back. The Titaniums are not powerful enough to paralyze the Venos. Only an Alpha can hold that amount of energy.

They tilt their heads sideways in a birdlike motion, listening for my instruction, as well as watching for attacks through their beady eyes. They are no longer bound spiritually to Dickward as they were before they turned. Still, they work as one large, barely thinking unit.

One more minute…

The humans who fled to the woods shriek in horror as they come face to face with Night Walkers. I see the closest of them drop, smell their blood as it spills onto the leaves and roots below.

I've been practicing composure; I've exposed myself to human blood over the past months and learned to ignore the cravings. It's always been within me—the fascination with blood, although each state reacted differently to it. Now I only feel an immense hunger.

Thankfully, my Phase One training taught me how to cope with starvation and I can withstand temptation.

REAP

Ignoring the tingling beneath my tongue, I breathe in deeply through my nose. I inhale the scent, become accustomed to it, and then cast it from my mind completely.

My attention turns back to the Venos and Titaniums, who seem momentarily distracted by the Night Walkers' interruption in the woods.

Some Venos have already fallen, multiple Titaniums working together to bring one down, but the Venos use the Night Walkers' distraction to their advantage, pushing the Titaniums into the pit.

The once peaceful Sanctuary has become a war zone. If I focus, I can just hear the waves crashing against the rocks and sand below us through the sound of slaughter.

I close my eyes and sigh.

When I reopen them, we are in dusk—dark enough for the Night Walkers to leave their shadows, but they don't reveal themselves yet. They're waiting for the perfect moment.

Jayleigh and Diego break through the wall of Venos, covered in black blood, and their eyes light up the night as they locate me.

"So much for ending this by nightfall." I push my words towards them and they echo as Jayleigh lets out another battle cry.

Half of the Venos are down and the other half continue to fight the glowing crowd.

I call on the support of the remaining Day Walkers behind me and the wolves. They charge into the army before us and I pray it will be the sign my uncle is waiting for.

I'm still not able to shield myself like the Night Walker hybrids, no matter how much I've tried, so my teeth are my only weapon. And I can't run, not this time. This is my battle, and I must see it out.

Jayleigh places her daggers into the holsters over her cargos, lighting the night with the white energy in her hands. She stands thirty feet away and I tense my jaw.

"How has it come to this?" I ask.

Jayleigh studies me, her face blank. "There is no other way, Ares. It's us or you. That's the way it has to be."

All Jayleigh has to do is push that small orb of lightning towards me and this might all be over. Paralyzing me would be costly. If she kills me, all the Day Walkers will die. Only Flynn's nest and the wolves will remain.

My heart yearns for Lora.

I hope that she's okay, and that she will forgive me. What I'd do to see her face just one last time…

"There is always another way!" The Night Walker's voice cuts through the noise and I try to cover my sigh of relief.

But Jayleigh isn't watching me. Her focus is on the lanky silhouette within the woods, and upon recognizing it, her energy stutters and flickers out.

REAP

"Hail?" Her eyes widen as she makes sense of the situation, and he steps from the shadows, red eyes glowing in the darkness of the night. "What have you done, Ares?" she spits. "How could you—"

"I'm not a Day Walker, Jayleigh." Hail approaches from the treeline, his Night Walker energy binding him within a ball of shadows. "Ares had no part in this. It was my decision, and my decision alone."

Jayleigh stares at him, trying to process why he appears hazy, why his eyes glow red like warning beacons.

"We can still work this out. This planet is big enough for all of us." I try one last time to persuade her to do the right thing.

But I see enough of the plan that builds in her mind before she reacts.

"No!" She pushes her energy back through fingers, into her hands, and towards me.

Time slows as the energy brightens the area around us, the glowing orb of electricity hurling in my direction. Hail charges forward to throw himself in front of it, knowing he can shield both of us from its attack, but he's not fast enough. I know he won't make it in time.

I'm in danger.

I should move.

I should do what I've always done best and run, but something tells me to hold my ground—like the hybrid that still lives within me wants to share a long held secret.

Run, the human inside screams.

But I remain as calm as the summer ocean as I wait, reaching my arms forward, acting upon instinct alone, and I catch the ball of energy within my hands.

Instantly, the light turns from white into electric red; the shadows sweep out and wrap around my arms as though I'm wearing them as armor. They snake around my shoulders, down to my chest, and then bleed through my skin. I absorb the energy as I would Lora's aura.

Jayleigh says nothing, but stares as Hail dives through the air in front of me, blocking her view of what has happened to me.

I fall to the ground as the impact of the energy takes over my body, and I close my eyes. I can feel it—the energy—as I never have before, circulating through my veins.

Power.

This is what I've been missing, the reason I've never been able to evolve. I cannot create my own energy, but I can absorb it.

I try to make sense of the unfamiliar sensation as I lay there. Jayleigh quickly approaches. I can hear her eager footsteps through the grass as she rushes in to finish the Day Walker bloodline once and for all.

My bones hum.

REAP

I have practiced the movements, building muscle memory, but I've been lacking one crucial element. The energy. I've never had it before, but I have it now.

I open my eyes, charged with new life, and Jayleigh flinches backwards, taken by surprise as I hold my hand out. My steady gaze settles on Jayleigh as I rise from the ground, and I light her up like a target within my mind.

Hail watches as he gets to his feet. I wonder if he will try to stop me, or if, like me, he's come to realize that they will not listen.

They will not learn.

I raise my hands, willing the energy to leak through my fingertips. Unlike Donnah's shadow shield, my hands harbor a raging ball of scarlet storms. This is Day Walker energy. Mutated magic, fierce and unforgiving.

I'm not sure how it will affect a Titanium upon impact, and whether targeting Jayleigh will kill her. She has quickly shielded herself with her own white energy—as Lora once did to protect the pack from Dickward—but I can see the doubt in her eyes.

Her mind whirs with a thousand escape routes. She searches for a distraction, panicking, but I sense no ounce of regret.

Not for starting this battle, or killing me, or winding up in this position.

Her only regret is that she hadn't killed me sooner, for if

she had, she'd have wiped out the Day Walker bloodline before Samantha and the Night Walkers kidnapped Hail. She wishes she had killed me in training. She wishes that we'd never been friends at all.

It's easier to disconnect myself from my emotions now, but reading her thoughts hurts. I've done nothing to deserve her hatred. How can one individual possess enough unjustified rage to start a war? Enough rage to want to kill me—twice.

The red energy glows brighter.

I never expected I might one day feel the same for Jayleigh as I'd once felt for Marshall.

So much unnecessary violence. So many avoidable deaths. I've never wanted to cause her pain, not like I do now. She caused this.

The girl who values organization and perfection; craves control above all else. From her lifestyle to the tightly pulled braid of her hair, but some strands have pulled loose, her control slipping.

I wonder how she will fare to lose as I have lost. To have everything she cares about ripped away. To have it all within arm's reach—but watch, helpless, as I tear all of it to shreds.

My hands expand, the red lightning and wisps of inky darkness swirling faster and faster as I turn.

I know the location of my target thanks to Jayleigh's mind, and I release the sparking red ball, projecting it into the only other thing Jayleigh cares about besides this war.

The energy crashes into Diego with such a force that it pushes him flying backwards, and he falls to the ground. The Titanium energy in his eyes dims, flickers, and dies out.

His body is limp, but his heart still beats. We watch his chest rise and fall, and after a moment, he stands, turning to face us. Jayleigh breaks into a run towards him, but Hail holds her enclosed within his shield. Donnah appears by Hail's side to help bubble Jayleigh into a force-field of their shadows.

Her Titanium energy can't break through it and she is stuck, left only to watch. She is well and truly out of control.

I stalk towards Diego, mildly aware of Jayleigh's hysterical screaming, and block it out as the diffused Titanium stands before me.

"Diego," I greet him.

"Ares," he says, making no move against me. His mind is silent as I try to read it, hollow, as though my energy has emptied him of all that he is, but I don't think it will stay that way. Just as a vampire eventually overcomes the paralysis caused by Titanium energy, Diego will regain control of his mind. But for now, it's mine.

"Do you love her, Diego?" I ask, directing his eyes towards the cage of shadows which keep Jayleigh contained.

"Yes."

I almost feel guilty.

"And does she love you, as Lora once loved me?" I say.

"Yes."

My gaze goes back to Jayleigh so she might understand exactly what I'm about to do and my reasons behind it. My eyes meet hers and she pounds her fists into the cage of shadows, screams, threatens to kill me once more.

She calls me a monster.

I smile in response.

A man or a monster? I realize now, staring at her, that they are one and the same.

There is a fine line between evil and necessary. When I inherited The Farm from Marshall, I promised to lead with fairness, whereas my brother bordered on wicked. It's not in me to kill for sport and claim it's for the good of the people, so on that basis, Marshall was more of a monster than I'll ever be. Jayleigh, too. Even now, as my eyes glow red and my teeth ache to delve into flesh.

The question I should have been asking myself all these months is not if I am a man or a monster, but whether I want peace or destruction.

And today, just as every day, I choose peace.

"A heart for a heart," I whisper, the sea breeze carrying my message through the screams of the battlefield to Jayleigh.

I plunge my teeth into Diego's neck with just enough venom to kill. My words haunt Jayleigh as I place Diego down

REAP

to the bloody grass and his eyes and nose begin to bleed. He splutters pink foam from his mouth, skin sizzling, and chokes as his lungs burn.

Then, as painful as the war around us, he is gone.

CHAPTER FIFTY-SIX

LORA

My knuckles turn white as I grip onto the handle above the passenger window for dear life. The truck dips and jumps through the holes of the abandoned roads as the tarmac crumbles away and grows over with greenery.

White speeds along the coastline, the road too near the edge of the cliff for my liking. Especially considering that the doctor, who has always shown so much care in his profession, is such a reckless driver.

He yells abuse at two rabbits blocking the road as the first tear in the Alpha bond hits me. I pull the handle above the window clean off as I cry out.

White does his best to calm me and promises we're almost there, but it's not soon enough.

The tablet interrupts my screams, instructing him to turn

left.

"What did she say?" he asks, his human hearing unable to pick up the tablet's directions through the noise I'm making.

"Turn left!" I yell, grabbing at the leather of the chair and sinking my nails into it.

I'm sweating.

Panting.

Wishing I'd eaten more today.

And this is only the beginning.

I'm certain I have lost six in the last minute, though I could be wrong. The intervals are too close. It's difficult to decipher one from the next.

"Pull over!" I order, my stomach churning with shock, grief, and car sickness.

We should have left sooner. We should have got to Ares before all of this started. And we would have, if not for Wilson.

I jump from the car before it's stopped moving, and I roll, spewing onto the grass near the edge of the cliff on all fours.

Luckily, I'm still in my evolved state. The pain is not as extreme and my balance is steadier than my human state, but I'm certain it's using too much energy.

How will I ever make it through the entire battle?

How many more will I lose before we reach Ares?

I heave again, but this time nothing but clear bile leaves my mouth.

The salty air stings my tastebuds as the sea crashes beneath me, and I wish I could only jump in, craving the cold water on my skin.

Tears blur my vision and I'm faint, yet we have to reach the battle. We can't waste any more time.

I suck in a breath and hoist myself to my feet. Reluctantly, I climb back into the car. White witnesses the state of me, the sweat beading on my skin, and he cranks up the air. The truck hisses as an icy breeze sweeps over me, just in time for another three hybrids to separate from the Alpha bond in quick succession.

"Not long now, Lora. You're doing a fantastic job."

I barely hear him through my screams.

My head spins. I hope we're not crashing.

But White drives on, and continues to comfort me in the only way that he can.

I'm fading.

Through the ringing in my ears, I hear the tablet instructing us to turn right in eight-hundred yards, and then we'll reach our destination. But the pain is too much for me to process and my body shuts down.

White hovers over me as I wake, shining a light in my eyes as he mouths my name—he's probably *saying* my name, but I hear nothing but noise. It's almost as though I can hear the Titaniums' screams as their souls disconnect from mine.

White puts the light away, and when he does, I'm able to see the stars.

He's pulled me from the car, dragged my body to the grass, and now he runs back to the vehicle to grab whatever he's left behind.

I'm unable to move.

My inner animal is blocking out the pain, shielding me from whatever I'm truly feeling, but the reality of the situation is that I'm completely senseless.

Is this what it feels like to die?

White returns from the truck and fiddles with the item in his shaking hands, leaning over me with concern in his eyes.

I'm able to blink, but the world is still hazy.

"Come on, Lora. Atta girl! You've got this." White's encouragement is sinking in. I can hear it now, accompanied by the distant sounds of yelling. "We'll get you through this."

My fingers twitch, and I can wiggle my toes if I try hard enough.

White watches me, looking for a sign that whatever he's done has worked. "Blink twice if you can hear me, Lora," he says, and I comply. He nods, glad with the progress. "Good… good."

He hoists me into his frail arms.

The doctor isn't strong like the other farmers. The scientists have always worked in the labs, giving them no reason to train. White's lack of physical strength shows as he carries my limp body through the woods, the battle cries of warriors growing louder as we near the war zone.

I want to yell. I want to tell him to put me down and return to the safety of the truck. This was never part of the plan. White was never supposed to enter the battlefield.

I'd made him agree to stay in the vehicle whilst I got the synthetic energy to Ares. The energy which we predicted he'd be able to use since he couldn't generate his own. We planned to give him a lifeline, a way to shield himself like the Night Walker hybrids, by injecting the replica of my energy into him.

The energy in the polystyrene box.

The energy that White isn't carrying as he hefts me closer to the fight.

"White," I mumble, but the name mushes between my tongue and my lips.

The trees are thin. We're too close.

He's carrying me onto the battlefield.

"Stop," I say, my voice stronger this time, but it's nothing more than a whisper.

"I can't stop, I'm afraid," he says as he circles the outside of the field. I'm guessing he's found Ares. "You lost too much energy, Lora. You would have died, so I injected you with the synthetic energy instead."

The synthetic energy?

No.

No… That's for Ares. He needs it more than I do.

"I know you will be mad, but I've come up with another idea… a better idea." He stops talking to catch his breath as we walk and White shifts me in his arms. "The synthetic energy is making its way through your system as we speak, recharging you whilst your body regenerates at its usual rate. You'll eventually end up with too much energy in your system."

White stumbles and we jolt forwards, but he catches himself before we tumble.

"When I gave the Alpha hormones to Ares and his mutant absorbed them, they were your Alpha hormones, Lora, so that he could take over your pack in your absence. You were bound on a spiritual level, and I suspect that you still are. He should be able to absorb the synthetic energy from you."

Well, at least that explains how he's been able to mind jump without evolving.

"What if he can't?" I ask. He is a Day Walker. I could paralyze him by throwing the energy at him.

"Well, then he might die."

I can't go through with this. I can't take that risk.

"Either way, Lora, you're going to have to release the extra energy somewhere, and soon."

"Then take me to the sea." At least that way I won't hurt anybody.

White pauses, his chest rising and falling, as he studies the ocean on the other side of the battlefield. He'd have to cross through the war of Day Walkers, Titaniums, Night Walkers, Venos, wolves and humans to get me to the water.

It's a lot to ask of him.

"I've changed my mind," I say. "Leave me here and return to the truck. You'll be safe there. I can get myself to the ocean once I'm strong enough." I feel the steady, familiar spark of energy within my veins. "You've done more than enough as it is, Dr. White. I'll never be able to repay you."

White huffs. "For Pete's sake, Lora. How many times have I told you and Ares to call me by my first name?"

My eyes are glowing again. They light up White's pale skin, and I know that it's now or never. I need to decide.

White places me down, almost dropping me. I struggle to find balance as my feet take my weight, and then I turn.

The field is a scene of nightmares. Bodies cover the grass, lifeless eyes peering at the sky. Wilson's body lays nearby, his eyes streaming, and skin bubbled away where the vampire venom has touched it. His green uniform is now red with blood and brown of mud.

Anger ignites me, and I search for Ares.

My heart stops as I witness the boy I love for the first time in months.

I can't breathe.

My skin tingles.

My body calls for him, longing to hear his voice and feel his skin on mine.

He is covered in blood—not his blood as it's red—and bodies lay at his feet. He doesn't see me, not yet, and I watch as he catches a ball of Titanium energy thrown in his direction. At his touch, the lightning turns a luminous scarlet, and he throws it back at the hybrid who'd provided him with the energy.

My body twitches as my limited energy begs to be shared.

He can't produce his own energy, but he can steal it. Just as he'd absorbed the light of my aura.

He is capable of everything you've ever doubted. Trust him.

I don't have time to fully think through the idea that springs to my mind. I just pray that White is right.

"Daniel," I say, turning back to the doctor, agreeing that we've been through too much to still use formalities. "Thank you for everything. Now get your ass back to safety before the light show begins."

Daniel smiles as I agree to go through with our original plan. "That's my girl."

He doesn't waste any time in following my orders, turning away as I catch sight of an enormous figure bounding through the night. I'm all too familiar with the odd proportions and the caw-like screech, but not the way the sound carries through the air and wraps itself over my skin. The sound of a Day Walker Veno chills me to my bones. Steven's red eyes scorch over mine as he leaps, and I have no time to push White out of the way.

Steven crushes down on top of us, rolling over us and holding us between his claws, his teeth biting for my neck. I yell out.

My dagger is in the pocket of my cargos, but I'm unable to reach it, and my energy is not yet strong enough to use.

"We're on the same team, Steven!" I'm yelling, my fingers stretching to grab my weapon. "We're here to help Ares."

He's larger than I remember, and stronger, too. The Venos have always been slower in their animal state, but the vampirism has eliminated that weakness. Steven is a killing machine, and if he's worked out how to compel humans, then White is in big danger.

"Ares!" I yell, scrambling my brain for a plan to get us free, but coming up with nothing.

White is motionless beside me. If not for his panicked breaths against my ear, I'd worry that he's unconscious.

I push against Steven's arms.

The energy is growing. I'm getting stronger, but not fast enough.

Steven's red eyes focus on mine as he fights back.

Just a little more. If not enough to push him off

completely, then at least for White to escape and get Ares' attention.

I grit my teeth and yell; the Veno responding similarly, but the sound he makes is significantly different. My arms shake as I pry his claws from White.

"Go, Daniel!" I scream. "Get help."

But the doctor doesn't leave me trapped underneath the Veno Day Walker. Instead, he rushes to his feet and straightens his glasses as I grunt against Steven's weight.

"For the greater good," White says shakily under his breath, and then, instead of running, he lunges forward.

My heart pauses.

White grips the pen he always carries in his coat pocket as he moves to save me, burrowing it through the Veno's eye.

"Run!" I yell, hoping he'll listen this time.

Steven retaliates, the rage obvious in his pain filled wail. He throws his head back as his crying ends, the pen still firmly lodged within his eye-socket. And then, in one swift, vampire-fast movement, he bite's White's head clean from his shoulders, spitting it to ground beside me.

White's body lands at the same time.

I scream.

It's a nightmare. An awful, heart wrenching nightmare. Is it a vision? Has the Veno planted the scene in my mind?

I want to believe it, but Steven loses balance as he regains posture and I throw him away, freeing myself from the ground and grabbing my dagger.

I jump onto his back as he tries to steady himself, pushing the blade into the fur of his neck and sweeping it up in one swift motion, underneath his scales. Black blood seeps through his reptile skin and down the blade of my weapon. It's not enough to kill a Day Walker, but once he's distracted, lifting his claws to his neck, I'm able to drop to the ground and crouch beneath him. It gives me a clear entrance to his heart.

I plunge the blade up. I don't hesitate in killing my rival Alpha.

Blood gushes across my face as the dagger hits its mark, and I retract the weapon before his body can squash me. I roll and the ground shakes as Steven collapses beside me.

"For the greater good," I repeat Whites' words in response, unable to look at his body. If not for the energy building within, I might cry.

But the battlefield is no place for a scientist, and White knew it. Still, he risked everything to get me here, refusing to turn back.

Maybe this had been his plan all along and a moment like this had been exactly how he wanted to leave the world; making a difference.

He'd enjoyed it too much when I called him a hero.

I take a deep breath and pat his leg, still unable to look at

REAP

his body. I will never forget his sacrifice; it will not be for nothing.

I still have to hold up on my end of the bargain and end this war once and for all.

CHAPTER FIFTY-SEVEN

HIM

She screams. No matter how large a crowd is, I would always recognize her voice.

It's her. She's here. And she's in danger.

"Lora!"

Hail and Donnah still have Jayleigh contained, but the Titaniums fight to free her. I thought killing Diego would be enough—that Jayleigh would admit her mistakes and surrender. But she still hurls abuse in my direction and encourages the hybrids to continue.

I tune out of Jayleigh's insults and search for Lora's screams amongst the others, but hear nothing. I wipe my bloody palms on my clothes and reel in my nerves.

She's here somewhere—in the middle of the chaos.

Beams of white light collide with shields of darkness.

REAP

Bodies fall as daggers fly. The people appear tired and scared as the war continues without end.

What has become of our world?

Then I see the blinding energy, far stronger than any other on the battlefield, and Lora's eyes lock with mine. Black blood stains her face and Dickward lays limp beside her. She killed him. She killed one of mine.

I push my way through the thinning crowd, ducking and jumping through intimate battles. It doesn't matter if Lora has sided with the Titaniums and I'm about to meet my end. With all this death surrounding me, I just need to see her, to hold her, to feel something besides this hopelessness.

Time refuses to move any faster.

I am aware of everything going on around me, but I see nothing—nothing but the only thing that matters.

The only one who ever mattered.

Bodies fly past me, wolves tackling humans to the ground. White lights flash in the corners of my eyes; shadows haunt the dark of the night, belonging to glowing red eyes.

A ball of Titanium energy hurls towards me, and I sweep a hand out to catch it before pushing the energy in the direction it came from. Not once do I take my eyes from Lora's. She is radiant. She is more beautiful than the sun, the moon, and the planet we live on.

She is here.

"Lora."

We meet in the middle of the storm. My arm reaches around her waist, scooping her closer so that our bodies press together. It is still not close enough.

She drops her dagger to the ground and reaches for my neck. A sigh escapes me as she runs her fingers through the curls of my hair and pulls my face down to meet hers.

Our lips touch, and finally, *finally,* all is right in the world once again. Her skin smells exactly as I remember—fresh lilies and clean cotton—and I breathe her in.

Her mouth is devouring. Eager.

I'm senseless. Although I touch her, I don't feel her, but to know it is happening is enough. It is all I have wanted.

She's just as oblivious to the battle surrounding us as I am.

"I'm going to spend every day for the rest of your life showing you how much I've missed you," I say, and her heart explodes.

Literally. I feel *that*. Just as I'm able to catch a Titanium's ball of energy, I feel her light leak into my skin like she's feeding me with magic. Her body is humming and I pull away from the kiss to make sense of it all, to read what's going on in her mind. Is this what it looked like to her when I stole the light of her aura?

Do I even have an aura now?

I don't know what's happening.

"Do you trust me?" she asks, her whole body aglow as though

REAP

she's swallowed starlight. The energy floods over me, turning red where it transfers to my skin.

Her eyes…

Such sorrow and relief and loss and passion. She looks different since the last time I saw her, as though she's aged more than the three months we've been apart, matured, and she has never looked so beautiful.

Even as she supplies me with the very energy that could paralyze me.

I think of everything we've been through, every reason she's given me not to trust her. She's just killed Dickward—killed one of my Day Walkers. But I read the story in her mind and it doesn't matter.

Despite how it looks from where I'm standing, she only had one intent in coming here today, and that is to help me. It's all she's ever wanted.

She's on my side. She's fighting against her own hybrids for me and my people. And I trust her with all of our lives.

She glows brighter as I think it.

"You can hear my thoughts?"

"In the same way that you're able to speak to my mind, Ares," she replies through the bond that connects us.

Not the Alpha bond. No… this is something else entirely.

"I trust you," I say against her lips. I can feel her—our souls connected once again as the energy transfers between the two of us.

I'm not stealing it as I used to absorb the light of her aura. The light flows into darkness as it reaches me, but I'm able to return it just as freely. We're an ecosystem.

But the energy still grows within Lora. I sense it building and see the panic in her eyes. There is only one way to get rid of it. A catastrophic, deadly end to the war.

"You can offload the extra energy onto me," I assure her. *"I'll be careful with it."*

Small flames are much more my angle. I'm not looking for an explosion.

"Trust me when I say that an explosion is exactly what the world needs," she says, and for a moment, I don't follow. I search her mind for an answer and step away as the light of her eyes becomes too bright.

We can't.

To release the energy will be fatal. The Titaniums... the humans... we would risk their lives based on a theory.

"They're already killing themselves, Ares," she says. *"It's our responsibility to offer them another way out. We can offer them peace."*

Peace.

The wind picks up, pushing the Alpha's hair back as though the world is agreeing with her, urging me to trust her. And Lora seems certain as she studies the energy I feed back to her. It feels different, she thinks. Weaker. Diffused. Malleable.

REAP

"I love you, Ares," she whispers, catching me off guard.

Through the fog of my worry and anger and frustration, her words cut in, swarming me in a bubble of relief and acceptance. She has seen everything I have done through the windows of my eyes. She knows what I am—*who* I am—and still, she loves me.

My body reacts like she has flicked a switch, and I grasp at the power within me. I feel it racing through my veins, igniting me. I can control it, and gather it wherever I see fit. The energy swirls through us, so loud I can hear it growing, reverberating, warming my ever-cold skin.

I have evolved, and I understand now that the energy is looking for an out.

It's looking for a match to set it alight.

And Lora? She has finally found her freedom.

"We can do it, Ares. Alpha and Beta verses the apocalypse," she says, and her kiss is all the encouragement I need. *"Let's set the world on fire."*

This is the one order I don't object.

Together.

Shared energy. Shared destruction. Shared responsibility.

The electricity we've been building within us explodes in a rush of white and red lightning and I squint my eyes closed.

As I breathe immortal life into her, I take the death from her power. I feel the heat, the silence. I feel the story her lips tell as they brush against mine. For the first time since I died, I feel everything.

We are the sun and the moon. The world awaits our command, but my eyes remain shut long after the kiss ends and the dust settles. The light fades.

I hear the waves. The screams have stopped and the field is quiet. Silent, but not dead.

Lora clings onto me as though she couldn't stand without my support.

"Are you okay?" I ask, more than aware that she's not. Her eyes and hair no longer glow, but somewhat match her ghostly complexion. I try to feed the energy back through our connection, but it appears the explosion has rid me of my evolved state, too.

I grip onto her, her body weak in my arms. I've seen her this way before, when Titanium hybrids die. She's still experiencing breaks in the Alpha bond, but she's exerted all of her energy to stop the war.

"It was my idea," she says. *"It was the only way to get them to listen."*

She's right, but at what cost? The battle would have continued until they tore each other apart. But she is so weak. I think she might be dying.

I sweep Lora off her feet and into my arms, not taking my eyes from hers as she rests her head on my chest. She needs to rest.

"Where are we going?" Lora asks, too fragile to turn her head. I'm on the brink of tears. *"Careful, Ares. They might mistake you for a human if you cry."*

I chuckle, the sad kind, as I kick open the gate and maneuver Lora through the gap in the picket fence.

I am a Day Walker hybrid. I doubt anyone will mistake me for a human, but they are not my worry right now.

They can wait.

Our energy was enough to stop it all. I have disabled the Titaniums thanks to my shadows, and the humans are under my compulsion just like the wolves. Lora's energy has paralyzed every vampire within the area.

They'll be stuck that way whether or not we're there to watch.

"Home, Alpha," I reply aloud so she can hear my voice against the waves of the ocean. "I'm taking you home."

CHAPTER FIFTY-EIGHT

HAIL

I stroke Donnah's tiny hand with my thumb as we wait for Ares and Lora to return.

We have no idea what just happened, but I'm glad it did. Jayleigh has stopped shouting now, finally. She can be mean when she wants to be.

We kept her in a shield of shadows as Ares and Lora started to glow.

I recognized the sound of Lora's energy from the day that Ares died. She'd buzzed like that when she forced Flynn into the woods. She'd scared me then, just as she scared me now.

That's why I kept my eye on them whilst Donnah focused on Jayleigh. And that's also why, when Lora and Ares' energy projected into a bubble of white and red around them, I separated my energy from Donnah's and freed Jayleigh.

REAP

Instead, I pulled Donnah close, wrapping my energy around us in a shield of shadows as the ground shifted. We watched everyone around us fly backwards from the power. The grass around our ankles whipped back, the ground rippling, dust floating up as the silence settled.

Everybody stopped moving.

They're still alive, at least. I know Lora has turned Night Walkers to dust before, but thankfully, that hasn't happened today. Maybe Ares' energy weakened her somehow, balanced her? Or maybe she didn't want to kill today? She might have been able to control how her energy affected people all along.

I don't care. We're alive, they're alive, and the battle is done.

"What are they doing up there?" I crouch to speak into Donnah's ear.

She spins to kiss me, catching me off guard, and she giggles in response. I stick my tongue in her ear to one-up her.

"Ew, Hail!"

I win.

I tap my foot and make a noise with my lips to fill the silence. What's taking them so long?

Everybody else is quiet. They look towards the cottage up the hill, and I wonder if they can hear us.

Jayleigh is expressionless as I squint at her. I focus on her eyes, trying to read her mind, but I get nothing. I see nothing in her head, so I'm probably doing this Night Walker trick wrong.

She doesn't even blink when I poke her.

"Stay silent if you're an idiot," I say in her ear and then laugh. Donnah tries to hide her giggle with a cough. "Stare at the cottage if you're sorry for starting this battle and killing our friends."

This time my laugh isn't quiet. It ripples through the field and I hope that the frozen people won't remember this when they're able to move again. I don't want them to think I'm being disrespectful, but I can't help my good mood.

Donnah said yes.

"So, is now a good time to start the wedding planning?" I ask my future wife.

She gives me the side eye. "Now's not a good time to plan the wedding, but it is a good time to think about a ring," she says.

A ring? Where am I supposed to find a ring in the middle of the apocalypse?

"How about this?" I crouch, picking a trodden, blood covered daisy from the grass and wrapping it around her finger.

She laughs through her nose.

"No?" I tut, throwing the daisy over my shoulder. It lands in Tye's afro and I leave it there. I spy a ring on the finger of a dead Day Walker nearby, shuffling slowly towards it so I don't further disrupt the peace. "What about this one?" I pop it over Donnah's finger, but it's too big.

REAP

"Ew. That's a dead woman's ring, Hail. And it's too big. And it's on the wrong hand."

I frown at her. "Fussy, are we? I hope this isn't an insight into married life."

I shuffle back to the body and place it back on. It's best not to disturb the dead, anyway.

"How about this?" I wrap my pinky finger over her ring finger, guessing that this time I have the right hand because she doesn't complain.

I'll find her a ring soon enough—once Ares and Lora finally come back to free us.

Donnah beams. "Perfect."

CHAPTER FIFTY-NINE

HIM

I place Lora on the bed I'd sourced from a nearby town, facing the window and overlooking the calm, rolling sea. I left the windows open on purpose, light curtains blowing in the salty breeze, and Lora breathes in gently, filling her senses with our new bedroom.

"You built me a cottage," she says, voice barely audible. As though there aren't one-hundred other things we should talk about right now.

Like the fact we've just compelled an entire battlefield of warriors into our control. Or how I can feel her heart scarcely beating next to mine. And her energy isn't regenerating as it usually does. And I can sense her hybrids as though they are my own.

"I'll build you ten more cottages if you give me a smile like that every time," I reply, trying to hide my panic. I'll give her the moon, just so long as she stays with me—I can't lose her now. Not after we've finally made it to our cottage by the sea.

But she can read my thoughts just by looking into my eyes. Whatever this shared connection is, it leaves no room for secrets.

"I'll be fine, Ares," she tries, and fails, to reassure me. "I just need to rest."

I squeeze her leg in understanding as I unlace her boots, hoping she's right. It's logical that, given the number of Titaniums she has lost today, her exhaustion is slowing down the regeneration process.

Or maybe it's me.

I quickly remove my hand from her ankle.

"It's not you," she says. "You're not stealing the energy from me like you used to, because now you can give it back. I'm just tired." She fights back as her eyelids threaten to close.

"Sleep, Lora." I nod. "It's okay. It's over. We won."

"Alpha and Beta verses the apocalypse." She laughs lazily and gives in to the exhaustion.

My heart warms. I feel it, just as I felt everything else when I evolved. The energy might have faded, but my senses have not. I experience the cool leather of her boots under my fingertips, and the burn of the lace as I move too quickly to untie it. I'm no longer numb.

"I'm sorry for the way I've behaved," Lora whispers when I'm certain she's drifting off to sleep.

"Shh…" I hush her as I slide the boots over her ankles, then drag the blood stained cargos from her legs. "We don't need to talk about this now."

"But I've been waiting twelve weeks to apologize. I've been dying to tell you how wrong I was."

"I don't need to hear it, Lora." I smile. *"I've already seen it in your mind."*

"But that's cheating. I had a speech planned out."

I know. I've already searched through it, and all the things she planned to say but discarded. Wrong of me, I know, but it was so present in her mind that it was the first thing I found when I looked at her.

"You can share your speech once you've slept."

She huffs. "Then let me show you now."

I pause in folding her cargos, absorbing the words with a shortness of breath.

"You're too-"

"Let me show you," she replies, "before I sleep."

Her pulse races, the veins in her arms and neck swelling slightly. Strange, how she is no longer scared of sharing with me now, when others would find me my most threatening.

Throwing her clothes into a crumpled pile on the floor, I kick off my boots and bloody clothes and roll over her on the bed. My lips crash against hers with a thirst so strong I'm unable to think of anything else. She breathes into me. I've missed the feel of her skin against mine, especially the soft strokes of her fingers against my spine. We are a reunion of hands in hair and entwined limbs.

She gasps against my ear as I trail kisses down her jawline, stopping at the base of her neck, just below the vein, and her breath hitches.

"I'm in control, Lora," I reassure her. "I know who I am and what I'm capable of."

I trace my fingers over the bare skin there as I talk, transfixed in the way she reacts to my touch, and I sigh. Saying the words aloud is solidifying.

"I am both a man and a monster. I will never fit into one community because I'm a being beyond labels, and that is okay. I am okay."

This was nature's plan for me all along.

"You will not fit into one community," she says, taking my hand and kissing each finger in turn. "You will fit into all of them."

Lora studies my face as I process. Her gray eyes are soft, willing me to understand what she's implying.

"What if I don't want to be a leader? I never asked for any of this. All I've ever wanted is a simple life."

"The decision is yours, Ares. It's a lot of responsibility, but should you chose this path, you can finally settle your peace treaty." She shuffles beneath me so that she can look me directly in the eye. "It *will* be simple once everybody adapts, but all good things take time and effort. We can do it together, like we always planned. Today marks the start of a new era. A peaceful future."

"A peaceful future sounds nice," I say, "but does it have to be me? You've always been the better leader."

Lora smiles, and I want to kiss her again. She speaks before I'm able to. "You're the only one all parties will accept. Or, we can wait for the paralysis to end, and let them fight it out for themselves. We don't have to be a part of it."

To stand by and let them suffer? Or to finally fulfil my life ambition.

No more war. No unnecessary killing.

The only one all parties will accept.

They'll listen. This is my chance.

"Together?" I ask. *"Promise you'll stay with me."*

But I feel that she's done making promises she can't keep.

"As soon as I'm able to join you." Lora squeezes my arm in response. "But it's you they're waiting for, not me. You know what to do."

Her confidence is assuring.

A scrap of a plan forms in my mind, but will it be enough to end the war?

Even though they're under our control, I won't coerce the

beings on the battlefield to obey me. Instead, I will use this moment of silence to share my plans, to call for the peace treaty that I should have settled before I died.

They can decide for themselves whether to follow, but I can be pretty damn convincing.

I'm not made for war. Going to battle has never been high on my agenda, but I was born to test the boundaries of normal —to offer an alternative way of life. I'm not a loophole, but a lifeline.

"They're still waiting for you," Lora reminds me, and I groan.

The wind picks up as I let the air from my lungs, swaying the curtains I stole from an abandoned factory. Does it count as stealing, if I am to be the supposed ruler of the people?

"See, you're already getting used to it." Lora pushes me out of bed. She's stronger than she'd been ten minutes ago and it catches me by surprise.

I flash my teeth and nod. "I guess I am."

My gaze lands on something beneath her pile of clothes on the floor, and I kick the fabric away to reveal Lora's titanium dagger.

I back away, as though it has the power to kill from its place within the clothes, and Lora laughs as I stumble into the dresser. My head cocks to the side, studying the stone on the handle of the dagger. "Is that…"

"The sea glass you found on the beach," she finishes my sentence for me.

"You kept it."

I thought she might have thrown it back into the sea when I wasn't looking. I certainly hadn't expected her to forge it into her dagger.

"Of course I kept it. On the bad days, that memory was the only thing to pull me through. It was a beacon of hope."

"And now I'm about to leave you again."

"The beacon of hope will become a beacon of death if you leave me waiting another three months."

I quickly reach for my shoes. The sooner I accept my responsibilities, the sooner I can return and make up for lost time—and this time, I *will* come back for her.

Lowering myself onto the edge of the bed, I close my eyes and focus in on the bond between us. Lora's heartbeat is stronger. She is gaining stability, but her energy remains weak.

"This feels like a bad idea," I say as I pull on my boots, double knot the laces, and then turn towards her.

Lora rolls slowly onto her elbow, cropped silver hair tickling her shoulder as the moonlight lights up her face.

She is so beautiful.

"Want to know a secret?" Her eyes glow with life for the first time since the battle. "The bad ideas have always been my favorite."

CHAPTER SIXTY

LORA

Hail and Donnah wed on the beach beside The Sanctuary one month after the battle.

The ceremony is stunning—if I say so myself—with chairs on the sand, facing out to sea, and an old carpet rolled through the middle. Vampires, and hybrids, and humans sit comfortably among each other as the moon's light dances with the waves. Torches are piked into the sand so that the humans can see, and we've bunched more flowers than I've ever seen—tying them to the backs of chairs and laying them at either side of the carpet.

Hail waits impatiently at the temporary altar, with a nervous smile playing on his face. I have to give it to him—he scrubs up well. He's had a haircut, too.

I squeeze Ares' hand as Donnah descends the wooden steps to the beach. My mouth hangs open as I witness her pale skin contrasting against her red flowing dress—the same shade as her eyes.

My fingers twitch, resisting the urge to cover Ares' eyes with my hands.

I click the play button on the stereo Ares found on level -2 of The Farm, and music fills the summer air with magic.

Contrary to common belief, vampires can cry.

Hail sobs as he watches Donnah walk bare-footed through the sand, and Ares wipes a tear too, so I hold out the piece of fabric I brought especially for this occasion.

"Thanks," he says, so only I can hear.

"You can thank me later," I reply, trying to keep the smile from my face as Donnah walks past us.

"Again? Come on, Alpha. Give me a break. You won't get any sleep."

I squeeze his hand. *"The heart wants what it wants."*

He rolls his eyes—I can sense it. I can feel his playful smile.

I've thought long and hard over the past month on what White did when he gave Ares the temporary Alpha hormones—my hormones—in order to keep the pack alive. Our spiritual connection has changed ever since Ares became my Beta, but I'd never paid it too much thought until the battle, assuming it was the Alpha bond.

Only, it's so much more. Whatever White had done that day, knowing or not, it had saved us. All of us. I only wish he was here now to see it.

The connection makes things easier in council meetings. The chairs seat humans, Night Walkers, Titaniums, and Day Walkers, but our conversations are private so long as I don't look into another vampire's eyes.

Ares' peace treaty worked. Everyone accepted him and his vision; his promise to keep the planet from war; his plans to unite us all. They likely worry about what might have happened if they'd disagreed.

The hybrids were the most reluctant, as predicted, but Ares made them a deal they couldn't resist. Security and freedom. Even Jayleigh accepted the conditions.

She's the only one vacant from tonight's celebrations. Unlike the rest, she keeps to herself, secluding herself in the quiet of the woods.

I fear she'll never forgive Ares for what he did to Diego, but although Ares might have dealt the final blow, she'd provided the weapon. Jayleigh brought them to battle, and she pushed forwards when Ares gave them multiple chances to retreat.

They'd brought it upon themselves.

Now Jayleigh has to live with the consequences and adapt to the changes surrounding her—two things she's sure to struggle with.

Everything is changing.

Hail smiles through his tears as Donnah meets him at the altar. "You're the most beautiful strawberry I've ever seen."

"Aw, Hail!" She wraps her thin arms around him. "Stop it, or you'll make me cry. Shyla's just finished making me look pretty, and you know she'll kill you."

Shyla shakes her head from the front row, pointing her finger at Hail with attitude.

The ceremony isn't a religious affair, but it's led by the Night Walker Queen, Matilda. She binds the couple's hands together in fabric, the way her people did hundreds of years ago, and she chants in time to the waves.

Matilda never joined Ares on the battlefield. She claimed her nest would only fight if needed, and from where she was standing, it looked like we had everything under control.

We've met with Matilda and her nest twice since the battle, and she's welcomed us into her world. She's allowed us to study her people and their abilities for the sake of the peace treaty between all communities.

Being attentive individuals, the Night Walkers have a deep connection with Earth. They're able to sense the rain before it hits, predict how long the daylight remains, and knowing hollow ground when they walk on it.

They're ritualistic beings.

It's something I already knew from my short time spent in The House of Nightmares with Benji's pack. I guess there was a peace treaty there, too, and they planned to expand on it by welcoming my pack into their nest. When she'd asked me to join her, she hadn't wanted to turn me, only band our forces. Ironically, for the greater good.

Saying White's words every morning when I wake has become something of my own ritual. I feel his absence like a void in the Alpha bond, and although I don't wear his scars, he was every part of a hybrid within my pack.

It didn't seem right to bury White's body beside Samantha, Marshall, Katie, Indigo, and Gretta on the cliff. White never knew what became of Samantha, or that she was the one to turn Marshall. But it made sense to lay White to rest alongside his twin sister, for the person she'd been before The Farm. It's what he would have wanted.

When we visit his grave, often, we only need to follow the tunnels in The Sanctuary, beneath our cottage.

Ares didn't take the news of White's death well. The last time he spoke to his uncle was the argument before Ares' humanity merged into his other states, but I could show Ares everything that had happened since. Memories of White creating an antidote against vampire mind control, and his reunion with Flynn. I recalled his terrible driving, his concern, his pride, and his sacrifice. He'd known exactly what he was doing by carrying me onto the battlefield, but he'd done it for us—for Ares and me, and for the future he knew we'd create.

I showed Ares the memory of White's speech in the Observatorium.

It seemed to help, to see White through my eyes, but as I've learned, there is no instant cure for loss. There is no vaccination. No method or right way. Just time.

Thankfully, Ares has plenty of that. He has an eternity.

In contrast, the wedding ceremony is short and sweet. And once the couple is done with their vows, they share a shy kiss before the spectating crowd. Then we push the chairs to one side to eat and dance and learn how it feels to be merry for the first time in our lives.

I kick the water up as I dance with Ares, our feet sinking into the sand. He is an awkward mover—his movements fall behind each beat, but he clearly enjoys it. Maybe it's not the dancing, but the freedom it makes him feel.

"Maybe you're wrong on both accounts," he says. I swear I'm absorbing his happiness. *"And I'm not that bad a dancer, am I?"*

"Maybe," I say, *"it's dancing with me that makes you feel so alive."* He doesn't deny it or counteract my *maybe* with another of his own as we swap places, link arms and turn clockwise. *"You're a fantastic dancer, my King. Don't let anybody tell you otherwise."*

He scowls playfully and my heart stops. Danger lurks there —the kind that suggests I'll pay for my sarcasm later.

"On that note, I think I'm ready for you to return that favor," I announce as the song comes to an end.

REAP

The humans have mostly retired home by now, and the hybrids linger against the rock, waiting for my approval. I give a quick nod.

Only three-hundred Titaniums remain, and each has apologized for their part in the battle. I've forgiven them, as there can be no peace without forgiveness, and the hybrids have claimed an abandoned town less than a mile from here as their own. They spend their days renovating the crumbling buildings into homes.

Several hybrids beat us to the steps, eager to leave.

Solace meets us at the top of the cliff and lingers as we wave to the nearby groups. And, placing my hand in Ares', we climb the hill to our cottage.

The wolf has warmed to me over the past few weeks. I think she can sense Ares' energy within me, and mine within him, ever circulating every time we touch. She realizes now that we are one, and she has no other option but to like me.

I open the gate to let her in and she runs between our legs, through the garden, and towards the house.

"You should have made her door a little larger," I say as she squeezes through the dog-flap at the bottom. It's not big enough for a wolf.

Ares sighs. "I become the King of my species and you suggest I become King of all species. I build you a cottage and you ask for a bigger door. When will I ever be enough?" The sarcasm is palpable.

I suck in a breath, mocking offense.

"But of course, the next time I build a house, I will make Solace a door big enough to fit through without squeezing."

"No." I shake my head as I drop onto the bench overlooking the sea. "You're not building any more houses. This is it. This is the cottage I've always dreamed of, and sitting here with you is all I'll ever need."

My heart is full.

"*All* you'll ever need?" Ares smirks, reminding me once again of my latest obsession.

"You, the cottage… and coffee." I tick them off with my fingers. "And Solace might be creeping onto the list too."

"Well, I guess that's my queue to repay you for the tissue." He kisses my hand before letting it go and retreating into the house.

I watch as the party rages on far below us, the Night Walkers' numbers growing now that the mortals have left. They chant to the stars; the torches burning shadows of the vampires' bodies into the sand as they move in time with the ocean.

It's mesmerizing.

The Night Walkers have centuries of culture unseen by the human eye and I feel honored to witness it, but haunted by the realization that it could have so easily been lost.

We did it, White, I think, wishing he'd only have died in a slower manner, so Flynn might have been able to turn him. I wonder if that's what he'd have wanted if given the choice.

I look out to sea, the rich aroma of hot coffee drifting by in the breeze, and I close my eyes and inhale. For a few moments, I allow myself to simply be. The summer night is warm and heavy, clinging to my skin. The sounds of chanting have vanished, and instead, Donnah sings a gentle melody.

I'm still holding my breath when I open my eyes. Ares is standing there, holding the coffee out for me to take. I flinch. It's rare that he can sneak up on me, but I was so lost to the moment.

"Thank you." I take the coffee from him and sip it as I wait for him to sit, but instead, he pulls me to my feet. I quickly pop the mug onto the bench, just in time for him to twirl me out of time to Donnah's song.

He spins me until I'm giddy, laughter spilling from me in waves of happiness. The energy between us is static, igniting us in an abundance of white rays, red lightning, and shadows that blend into the night.

Ares catches me. His eyes are two gleaming rubies that bare into my soul. His mouth takes mine and I collapse into him, one hand on his shoulders to keep me balanced, the other on the slightly cool skin at the back of his neck—my fingers fiddling their way into his hair.

He stops with a smile, slow-dancing with his arms around

my waist as he joins in with Donnah. He sways us through the garden.

"How do you know the lyrics?" I ask. He's getting it right, word for word.

He stops singing long enough to reply, "I've heard Hail sing it so often over the last year, I guess I've just picked it up." He kisses me quickly. "Your coffee's going cold."

It is. And I'm enjoying this moment too much to care.

"That coffee is like gold dust. It's a day's journey to The Farm to get more." He scowls and suggests, "Drink and sway."

A small laugh escapes me. "Alright, Beta, but only if you keep singing."

"You have yourself a deal."

I grab for the coffee and Ares stands behind me, draping an arm over my shoulder and resting his chin on my head as I sip. Solace has joined us, sitting at our feet and copying as we admire the view.

The vampires on the beach watch Donnah sing to Hail, waves lapping onto the sand, as the sky turns orange with light. It promises hope for a new dawn, although it's still early enough to be night.

The newlyweds still have an hour or two before they're forced into the underground world of The Sanctuary.

Hail joins in on the final chorus. His voice is wildly out of tune and Ares snickers into the back of my head as I gulp my coffee, fearing it'll end up spraying through my nose.

"Classic Hail," Ares mumbles through my hair.

"It was such a perfect moment until he spoiled it," I agree through my laughter.

"He didn't spoil it. He made it better."

We chuckle.

And I decide then, as optimism and love swells in my chest, that it's time to start believing. A new age. A new start. We can put the horrors of our past behind us and trust in our future—to build a life worth living. We're free to be who we are, and not what The Farm turned us into.

"From here on out," I say, my voice hitching, "every night is going to end like this."

Ares turns me around to face him, his nose scrunching as he smiles. "Is that an order, Alpha?"

"No." I tilt my head back to kiss him lightly. "It's a promise."

EPILOGUE

HIM

The world was left to me in my brother's will, alongside The Farm, the hidden levels that lie beneath it, and the burden it once carried.

He died 150 years ago, and since then, I've continued as he wished, making more than a few changes here and there.

The world I've created may not be the one Marshall had planned, but his vision for a free world, where humankind is safe to roam the lands, is very much alive.

As are the dead things he loved to hate.

Within the first few years, a lot of time went into discovering how the different species acted around each other.

REAP

Under Flynn's expertise, we conducted many scientific studies. I divided my time between The Farm and the hundred other places I was required, while Lora spent most of her days with the Titaniums. She couldn't travel far from them, being their Alpha, and they worked hard to restore villages and towns to their former glory—without the unnecessary extras.

The world had started to fix itself in the forty-five years since the war began, so when the new law was passed, created by members of a council built of all different species, we deemed it important to keep to the basics.

No peace comes without sacrifice, but most of us had never lived with cars, computers, or central heating anyway. Instead, we opted to find sustainable solutions to ensure future generations still have a world to live in.

We fixed train lines between villages and towns, making it easier to connect with other communities and trade goods—grown and made. And we built one very important line to The Farm from all areas of the land.

It became the only scientific hub in the country, its utilities altered and adjusted to fit the needs of the people.

Level -1 is now a donation center for humans. Every two months, they're required to give one pint of blood to the vampire banks.

In the early days, this was a topic of great dispute, but it ultimately encouraged humans' safety, and most agreed to the proposition. As time passed, giving blood became routine and not something to worry about. Future generations grew alongside the vampires and now we consider it normal.

After the donation, humans are welcome to use the underground hot pools and gym. I've read that some look forward to donation day, although I try to stay out of human minds as much as possible.

Level -2 continues to store goods: electronics, outdoor equipment, human food, and now vampire food transported from the higher level.

-3 is used to house vampires during their donation year.

In response to the humans' blood donations, we found it only fair that the Night Walkers and Day Walkers give back to the human community. And, given that the vampires are so deeply connected with the planet, it made sense for us to take over the farming duties.

Above ground is 185 square miles of open space, and we operate most of it for agricultural and livestock use. Vampires can predict the rainfall, so we know the perfect time to plant and harvest. We can sense life, not to mention we're far stronger than humans, too.

Once the year is over, we pass over our titaniumless tools to the following nest in rotation, and then we're free for the next twenty-five years.

I did, in fact, end up building a second cottage for Lora,

but this time I up-cycled the Titanium barn. We need it for my years donating to The Farm; a place for us to stay in the evenings once Lora and the wolves return from restoring the villages. The Titanium barn is our home for that year only.

Returning to our cottage by the sea feels sweeter each time.

Level -4 continues to nest Flynn's Night Walker hybrids, no longer the A.P.P. but they like to travel between The Farm and The Sanctuary at their own command.

Hail and Donnah are happily married. How Donnah has put up with Hail for so long, I'll never know. I see Hail a couple of days per week and that's plenty enough for me, but I've noticed Donnah's *Ew, Hail*'s are becoming more frequent. I've even managed to teach Hail to read the time, although I'm sure it's easier now that he's a Night Walker and can sense the position of the sun.

My Day Walkers have integrated with Flynn's group. We felt it was only appropriate to stick together as we are family. We take yearly trips to the cliff above the theme park to visit the graves of Uncle Danny, Marshall, Mom, Gretta, Indigo, and Katie.

Flynn is dating again, finally. It took some convincing from Lora and myself. "Dr. White wouldn't want you to mope around like Jayleigh for an eternity," I'd told him, and that comparison was enough to kick his butt into gear.

Nobody likes to be compared to Jayleigh.

She's miserable.

I know it's my fault, but no matter how hard I try, I can't bring myself to feel guilty for what I did to Diego. I've often wondered if I should apologize. Would it make a difference?

But I'm still waiting for an apology from her. She hasn't yet spoken to me about the day she killed me, and I doubt she ever will. We're both too stubborn.

The only time she talks to me or Hail is when she has to, at council meetings or full moon gatherings, and even then the interaction is awkward and forced. She will always hate us for what we have become.

I dread each full moon gathering for knowing I'll see Jayleigh there, and Tye. He has fallen in love with a human but continues to pine over Lora and still calls me Nerd.

Lora does good to remind me of my place. It is my job to lead the ceremony, not fight with Gen. 2s. I am to bring the people of the world together, where we can celebrate each other and our differences; to give thanks for all that the other communities do in our favor.

It is a symbol of respect.

The night is full of dancing, sharing stories, creating music, and celebrating all that is good in life.

We adapt.

We learn from past mistakes.

We evolve.

REAP

We rebuild all that was lost, from the cities to the wind turbines.

Flynn and I modify Uncle Danny's idea for using Lora's energy, turning it into usable electricity. Soon, the trains run on Titanium power, cutting the journey time from The Farm to The Sanctuary in half.

We have nothing but time, yet we just can't wait to return to our cottage by the sea.

Decades pass. Our names become myth and our story becomes legend.

The average life expectancy for a Titanium hybrid is 200 years, so we find out, yet Lora doesn't age like the rest.

Our connection works both ways.

I am able to share the burden of the Alpha bond breaking, muting her pain when a hybrid dies, and she can draw from my immortality. She barely ages.

Jayleigh is the last Gen. 2 to pass, and we rush to her side when Lora first feels the connection fade.

We've tried to make amends, but the dust has never settled. Yet we can't forget the history we share. It unites us, strangely, once there are no other Titaniums left to turn to.

Jayleigh asks us to take care of her kitten, and I feel it is her chance to get the last laugh. She knows we are wolf people, raising sixteen generations of Solace's bloodline, so asking us to welcome a cat into the family is like cursing us for the next... however long cats live.

But it is her dying wish, so we comply.

The cat is ginger, just like Jayleigh, and she has named it Carrots.

Definitely a joke on my behalf, I figure.

Carrots, unsurprisingly, doesn't get along with the wolves, so once we're sure Jayleigh's soul has parted, we pass her on to Hail and Donnah. They love the cat like a child, and Hail changes her name to Kebab after the two things he loves most in the world—his wife, and human food.

The wolves aren't enough to keep Lora's mind from the hybrids once they're gone. The Alpha bond is a tree with roots, but no branches, and she feels as though she's lost her sense of purpose, so I propose we do all the things she couldn't do before. We live a thousand lives, traveling to far reaches, exploring sea and land. Ours is the only country to survive the apocalypse; every other is vacant of humans and vampires, leading us to ponder how it all went so wrong. The animals have reclaimed these lands, and we choose to keep it that way.

We return to our cottage by the sea.

Using the abandoned equipment and yellowing paper from Marshall's room, we paint.

We continue to work alongside Flynn to develop new

sustainable technologies to better the world and its lifeforms.

We garden.

We Farm.

Picking the coffee beans in the Biome, I suggest we refurbish Jiggle's Coffee Shop and name it Marshall's.

We display my brother's paintings and postcards on the walls for all to see. Lora's paintings sit above the counter, but only one of mine makes the cut. Art isn't my strong suit.

Marshall's Coffee Shop keeps us busy for many years, but eventually we hand it over to Shyla and Zaync to oversee.

We return to our cottage by the sea.

Watersports, learning to play instruments (I try, at least), tracking the stars, and hiking. Partying with our family and meeting new friends; traveling to new cities and nests. We attempt everything our hearts desire.

But an eternity is a long time to live.

Eventually, we rediscover the incubators we'd once used on The Farm and make adjustments, transporting them to The Sanctuary and up the hill. Piece by piece, we carry them through the door of our home and set them up in the bedroom, next to the bed and facing the window. I fuse the two incubators into one, adding new technology to replace the old.

And for one hundred years at a time, we hibernate. We wake to rediscover what has become of our planet.

Each time it grows stronger and greener.

Hail and Donnah never change, although Flynn's fashion transforms from one extreme to the next each time we wake. His partners change too, although he tells me none of them will ever compare to Uncle Danny.

We stay awake for a few years at a time—celebrating, traveling, loving, refurbishing, revisiting—before going back into hibernation. Our arms and legs intertwined, skin touching. My cheek pressed against Lora's. We become one with the ocean below us, suspended in time.

Our loved ones know where to find us, should the world ever need us. They know how to wake us. But for now, all is perfect.

Together—as we always dreamed.

We live out an eternity…

…within our cottage by the sea.

THE END

Sign up for the
Kirsty Bright
Newsletter

Sign up to the author newsletter for first chapter reads, release dates and more!

For more details, visit
www.kirstybrightauthor.com

Love this book?
Leave a review!

With special thanks,

Kirsty

ABOUT THE AUTHOR

Kirsty is a British small-town girl with a big love for coffee and mexican food. She spent her childhood on the border of England and Wales, surrounded by vast countryside where she enjoyed horse riding and time outdoors with her family and friends.

She found herself drawn to the creative arts in her early teens, especially music, drama, and writing; and she still continues to sing locally from time to time. But reading or writing, with a candle lit and a mug of coffee in her hand, is where she feels most at home.

#		Title	Album	Date	Length
1		**Let It Begin** Saysh	Let It Begin	Jan 31, 2023	2:23
2		**Halfway Gone** Lifehouse	Smoke & Mirrors (Interna...	Apr 30, 2023	3:15
3		**Ghosts & Monsters** Saint Chaos	Ghosts & Monsters	Apr 30, 2023	2:44
4		**Kick** Saint Chaos	Seeing Red	Jan 31, 2023	3:17
5		**Monster** Fight The Fade	APOPHYSITIS	Apr 30, 2023	3:24
6		**Sirens** Saint Asonia, Sharon Den Adel	Flawed Design	Apr 30, 2023	3:50
7		**Rise Up** 2WEI, Edda Hayes	Rise Up	Jan 31, 2023	2:52
8		**White Flag** Daughtry	Cage To Rattle	Apr 30, 2023	4:54
9		**Warriors** League of Legends, 2WEI, Ed...	Warriors	May 1, 2023	3:25
10		**Living Legend** Club Danger	Living Legend	Apr 30, 2023	2:34
11		**Chosen Ones** Mountains vs. Machines	Emerge	Apr 30, 2023	3:13
12		**By the Sea** Gone Gone Beyond, The Hu...	Things Are Changing	Apr 30, 2023	4:02

Search

Reap: The Titanium Trilogy-inspiration playlist

0:24   2:56